The Lost Sacrifice

Book One- The Tavern's End Trilogy

Stacie Crenshaw

TrustRock

TrustRock Publishing

Cover Art Photography by Edward Crenshaw

Cover Design by Stacie Crenshaw

Map Artwork Design by Edward Crenshaw

ISBN: 978-1-7373893-0-9

To Josiah,

Thanks for challenging me to write a book you'd enjoy.

I hope it brings you joy the way you bring me joy.

Table of Contents

CHAPTER ONE

It couldn't be true. It just couldn't. Her dad was the fiercest warrior known to Crestavia. It just was not possible that he and his men had been overtaken by simple bandits. A surprise ambush would barely have made them break a sweat. There was no way they were all dead. She refused to believe it.

Kendry lay exhausted in the bottom bunk of one of the beds in the loft above the tavern where she had run after hearing the news. Her long strawberry blonde braids had flopped on the pillow as her teenage body had collapsed in torment from the words she had read. The note had simply stated that General Walbrek, his instructors, and the men they'd been training, had been attacked by bandits while traveling. Kendry had known they were on their way to an undisclosed location for their special mission training. Being attacked by bandits would not have been unusual. But it was the last line, that caused the sharp pain deep in her gut. The note ended with a statement she would never forget. *"Unfortunately, there were no survivors. General Walbrek and all his men have been killed."*

The message had been official and came from King Gadden, himself. All the residents of the tavern were in shock. But to Kendry, the news was more than shocking. It was devastating. Her whole life was over.

Kendry had been raised at the Academy with the military men training to be spies. She'd witnessed the 'General' train the cream-of-the-crop from the army into elite spies for the king. The prestigious General Walbrek, also called the 'Warrior,' was the same man that she simply called 'Dad'.

Kendry hadn't been allowed to venture with them on their training mission, so she had been sent to the tavern to stay, instead. This was normal protocol. When she was a young girl, she had been allowed to play amongst their feet as they trained and stay the nights at the Academy. But as she got older and gained the attention of the young men, her father purposely had her spend more and more time sleeping at the tavern. Still, most of her daylight hours were spent alongside her father at the Academy.

It had been hours since Kendry had collapsed onto the bed shocked by the dreadful note. Time had ticked by as tears soaked her pillow in intermittent silent bursts. She chewed on the words in the note, unable to sleep. The thought arose that it must already be near dawn. The night had stretched on and on, never seeming to end. She glanced around the room. Shalia and Tarah were both sound asleep. She should be, too. Customers wouldn't stop arriving at the tavern the next morning just because her heart was exploding from pain.

All was silent and the room completely still. Kendry dazed out, numb from wrenching thoughts. She envisioned the fighting, the training, and the martial arts that the mighty men would practice, daily. They were experts. She loved watching them spar in their tournaments and even fight with all force that usually resulted in much bloodshed and bruises. She wasn't bothered by blood like other young women seemed to be. She considered herself much tougher than her friends.

Kendry fought against her thoughts, coaxing herself to try to sleep. But she was again dragged away by her memories. She visualized the men practicing archery, sword fighting, and boxing. She could hear the swooshing of the arrows through the air and the swords slicing the calm humid afternoon stillness. She could imagine the sounds of pounding fists and harmless taunting as the men sparred. She could even hear her father's voice warning them to always be aware of their surroundings and to never underestimate an opponent. The thought of his voice made her gasp in pain. She would never hear it again.

2

Angry at the thoughts that robbed her of sleep and caused so much pain, she shook her head and rolled over. Seconds after resettling, she found herself picturing papers that she would help grade in Professor Tredeau's multi-language classes. She found herself smirking with how impressed she had been with this latest classes' oral exams. Her mind wandered to the classroom next door where the men were instructed about different cultures and beliefs from all the neighboring kingdoms. Her eyes squeezed tight as she heard the echoes of her father's voice drilling the men on their knowledge of various customs. Her lips pressed shut, struggling to help hold in the tears. It hurt to think about him.

Across the room, Shalia rolled over in her bunk causing Kendry to release a breath she didn't know she had been holding. She relaxed a little. Her lips smirked as she reminisced over all the trainings to become 'invisible'. The spy trainees had to be able to stalk without being discovered. They had to be able to journey without leaving tracks. So many of them had been absolutely horrible at this skill when they first arrived at the Academy. It was to the point of being humorous. But, after her father's relentless training, they would leave the Academy as skilled trackers who couldn't be tracked! Kendry smiled a little. She loved that her father always allowed her to try to find them when they were practicing how to hide their footprints. She would listen as they learned how to not break branches or rustle leaves. It was like the best game of hide-and-seek, ever!

Her smile faded. There would never be another game of hide-and-seek like that. They were all gone.

Restless, Kendry rolled over, again. She coaxed herself to stop thinking about the Academy. She tried to force herself to sleep. But as the shallowed breathing of either Tarah or Shalia became rhythmic, she became more stir-crazy.

Kendry could picture what the men must've looked like, traveling on their horses to an unknown destination, and then tried to imagine them being ambushed by bandits. There was no way a thief, robber, or bandit could have stopped them. And she had trouble believing that any soldier, or even an army of soldiers, could've taken them down. These were the kingdom's special forces' warriors. They were the best of the best. Her father alone was such a skilled fighter that he could take out ten men without help. She'd heard many stories about him with a sword. Tales that had grown out of proportion over time, but usually focused on the way he had single-handedly taken down armies. He had laughed as the stories had been rehashed to him. But he never denied the fact that he was something special on the battlefield.

As she once again pictured their training exercises and remembered story after story about her father's brave antics and unbelievable defeats, she concluded that there was absolutely no way they were dead. Accepting the realization that the note was wrong, which she'd known deep-down since she read it, calmed her for the first time since she'd heard the news. She took a deep breath and relaxed. They'd be home soon. She was sure of it. It had all been a terrible mistake. Maybe it was part of a secret plan and they needed everyone to believe they were dead for some reason. She took another deep breath and closed her eyes. The tiredness and exhaustion of the past few hours rose to the surface and she realized she was going to be able to fall asleep after all. But just before she completely dozed off, she was jarred awake by a loud scream followed by a crash.

CHAPTER TWO

K endry jumped up in bed. Since the loft above the tavern was the only upstairs room, she knew the sound was coming from downstairs. She heard the scream again. This wasn't any scream. Somebody hadn't just been startled or scared. This was the scream of a desperate person crying for help. And she recognized the scream. It was Tarah's mother, the innkeeper. Madame Lansing would not scream like that unless something was seriously wrong. Kendry looked over at Shalia and Tarah. They were both sitting upright in their beds, eyes wide opened, faces looking frightened.

Without hesitation Kendry wrapped her hands around the outside of her bunk and pulled her body upward. Sweeping her legs up and over, she landed with a quiet thud on the vacant top mattress. Kendry scurried quietly along it until she was closest to the rafter that ran across the ridge of the tall cabin ceiling above. She pushed off the top post and pulled herself quickly, but carefully, up onto the rafter. Balancing and scaling heights were second nature to her. She had done this every single day of her life at the Academy. She'd even raced obstacle courses across small balance beams 30 feet above the ground.

When she got to the corner where the rafter dead-ended against the room's frame below, Kendry crawled down onto her tummy and pulled herself slowly forward to peek over the edge.

She couldn't have been prepared for what she saw.

Three men dressed in dark clothes were dragging an unconscious man across the floor. Kendry knew immediately who it was. It was Tarah's father, Mister Lansing, who ran the tavern downstairs. She couldn't tell if he was alive, but something told her he was. The men didn't seem to care that his body thudded and bumped as they scraped it across the room.

 Next, she noticed Tarah's mother. Madame Lansing was now gagged and her hands were tied behind her back. They had thrown her in a corner, where she struggled to her feet behind a broad shouldered gruff looking man in dark clothes. Then began the screams of Shalia and Tarah. Kendry's heart jumped. The sound scared her so much she almost fell off the rafter. She was forced to watch helplessly as two of the men dragged her friends down the stairs and into the main room. They were kicking and screaming but completely impotent against the men's strength.

She had to help them. Everything in her said so. But she knew she would die if she fell from this height, and was positive she wouldn't get to them in time if she tried to scurry backwards across the rafter on her belly without being heard.

Heart racing, Kendry followed them with her eyes and gasped as the two men began binding them with rope. One man, who appeared to be in charge, rambled off commands in another language. Kendry had studied many languages at the Academy. As a two-year-old she had played with dolls on the floor of Professor Treudeu's classroom as he taught language after language to the spies in training. She was fairly sure this language was called Regarian. But the name of the language was unimportant. Deciphering what he was saying was all that mattered. She caught enough familiar words to realize he was asking the men if they had found the one that they were searching for.

 The other men responded that they had searched but, pointing at Shalia and Tarah, indicated that these were the only two upstairs and they couldn't find anyone else downstairs. The frustrated leader rambled words off that Kendry couldn't understand but assumed were cussing. He blurted that they didn't risk traveling here to go home empty-handed.

Kendry listened intently, trying to steady her breathing. Her hands were getting clammy but she kept her arms wrapped around the rafter the best she could and lay motionless. She caught enough other words to realize at one point they were referring to her father. She heard the word she was almost certain meant 'warrior'.

Her brain raced as she wondered if they were searching for her dad there. Maybe he had escaped the rampage. Maybe these were the same men who attacked him and his men as they traveled. She didn't know but she did know she needed to help her friends. Would these men leave now that they didn't find her father? It didn't appear so, since they had just bound her friends.

Balancing silently on her stomach, she listened carefully and looked around for clues or things that could help her. The downstairs tavern looked like it always did. It was a restaurant of sorts with a large bar where visitors stopped for drinks between villages.

Taverns End, as they called their little village, wasn't much of a village, at all. It was actually just a rest stop. Glenville, to their west, and Galvenland, to the east, were small towns in themselves and not too far apart. But travelers venturing from one place to the other would stop at Tavern's End along the main road between them for a quick rest or a drink. Their small 'town' boasted of an excellent blacksmith and stable crew to allow horses rest and the best care while their riders quenched their thirst or filled their bellies. The inviting little tavern occasionally hosted customers who desired a break before getting to their next destination, but was rarely busy.

The tavern was also an inn, in the sense that they did have a few rooms with beds available. But most travelers would continue on to the next village to find a place to sleep for the night. The only time the tavern really ever got used as an inn for customers, was when someone got too drunk to leave and passed out. Occasionally, when there was a huge festival or something in a nearby town, finding accommodations in Glenville or Galvenland could become difficult. In those cases, a bed or two might be used at the tavern. But that was definitely rare. Kendry knew that there were no customers down there on this night.

The upstairs loft was where those working at the tavern slept. Kendry spent most of her time at the Academy, but also slept upstairs at the tavern, often. Tarah always stayed there as it was where she lived. Shalia stayed on busy nights or when she just needed a break from her six younger brothers and sisters. There were a few other people in town who would stay there occasionally when they helped at the tavern.

Their whole town, if you could even call it a town, had less than twenty people in it. It didn't look like a town to those passing by. It was simply a nice rest stop. But the residents of Tavern's End had a secret. They knew that if you'd lift the latch under the carpet behind the kitchen of the tavern, you would find a secret passageway.

The hidden passageway led down to the opening of an earthen tunnel that took the traveler out to a spot in the forest. The traveler would exit out of an inconspicuous crevice on the side of a cave and follow a few simple signposts, such as a hollow tree and a strange vine, to the entrance for the Academy. The Academy was hidden in the back of the Forgotten Forest. The Academy was huge and spacious, walled in, and invisible behind a thick barrier of trees. No one would ever know it was there unless they were looking for it.

Inside the Academy walls was another world. There were classrooms and barracks and training grounds. There were obstacle courses and courtyards, mazes and stables, kitchens and dining halls. The expansive compound was incredible to see for the first time. But, to Kendry, it had been home. A home that was hidden at the end of the Forgotten Forest and not known to exist by many.

The Forgotten Forest was thought to be haunted. The residents of Tavern's End did everything they could to encourage those rumors. They told stories to those who traveled of ghosts and dark magic. When they heard adventurers claim they would be exploring it, they would go through the tunnel passageway and come up from behind and hide throughout the forest to purposely play tricks on the brave pioneers. Some of Kendry's favorite memories were hiding high up in trees making scary sounds and dropping large branches. She also loved to steal explorerers' supplies when they weren't around and leave dead animals in their place. Anything she and her friends could do to keep the rumors flowing and keep people away from the Forgotten Forest, was encouraged.

The further away visitors were from the forest, the further away anyone was from discovering the Academy. The Academy had to be kept secret. It had been built decades earlier by King Gadden's great-grandfather. No one seemed to even know it existed as it was never mentioned in history books. King Gadden of Crestavia would accept recommendations from the army of soldiers that were extremely gifted and talented in fighting, swordsmanship, language, hunting, and other specified skills. He would personally recommend the best of the men to Kendry's father, General Walbrek, to be enrolled at the Academy.

These chosen soldiers were given a password. They would arrive at the tavern just like any other customer. They would eat, drink, and make conversation. When they started discussing how good Jerculberries were for overall heath, the residents of the tavern took notice. Jerculberries did not exist. This was always a signal that the person had been sent from the palace. Sometimes the person would simply be a messenger. Once the guests cleared out from the tavern, the messenger would hand his message to Tarah's father, Mister Lansing, to be given directly to General Walbrek. But sometimes the person would be the next candidate for the Academy. And if they wanted to become a trainee at the Academy and eventually become a spy for Crestavia, they would have to survive boot camp.

Surviving was one thing, but being successful was another. General Walbrek was not going to let just anyone pass his Academy. When spies didn't succeed, they were sent back to the army. Though disappointed, they had usually gained a huge repertoire of new skills that could help them on the battlefield.

The ones who did pass were given assignments in countries nearby such as Tegola, Lumera, Vestacia, or Sedania. The best of the spies would be sent to Shadenberg, a nearby nation that was always threatening Crestavia. Other talented spies would be assigned Breckenride, a country known for helping Shadenberg with their slave trading and exploiting of children. The spies would have to completely emerge themselves into those cultures. They needed to be experts in language, customs, and current events. They also needed to be prepared to spend many years discovering the secrets of these other countries. Their goal would be to eventually get information back to General Walbrek who, himself, would personally take a journey to the King in Crestavia-Capitalia to relay the information.

Lieutenant Trent was Tavern End's go-between man. He lived up at the Academy, but also spent much time pretending to be a worker at the tavern. It allowed him to hear the local gossip, scan for suspicious travelers, and keep both the officers at the Academy and the townspeople of Tavern's End on the same page. He had been at the Tavern mopping a table down when the king's messenger arrived with the note. There were no customers so the messenger delivered the note straight to Mister Lansing who then handed it over to Lieutenant Trent. He read it and the shocked look on his face told Kendry it was not good news.

Kendry had been busy teasing Tarah about a customer who had been there earlier in the day. The girls liked to try to guess the backgrounds and 'stories' of their customers. It was a little game they played to pass the time. They would make bets based simply on their first impressions and then spend the rest of their time serving the customer trying to get answers about their life story. The man they had been debating about, that afternoon, had arrived dirty and sighed loudly as he sat down.

Tarah immediately turned to Kendry and whispered, "His horse is sick. Or hurt. Or has a broken leg or something. He had to walk it all the way here from Glenville." She smiled, satisfied with her prediction. Tarah always tried to guess the customer's scenario before Kendry did. So, if she could get a prediction out of her mouth before Kendry even began, she was content, even if her hypothesis wasn't stellar.

"Nope," Kendry rebounded. "His shoes are too clean." Tarah's mocha-colored eyes looked down and she wanted to kick herself for missing that obvious detail.

"Ugh, your right! I'll try again...I bet he's bored with his job and wishing for adventure. I'm going to guess he's some sort of salesman or something," Tarah concluded.

"I'm going to say he's lost his job. No, I got it! He just left visiting a sick friend or relative. Or is on his way to visit someone sick. He looks tired and sad," Kendry rebutted.

The man slouched on the bar stool he had collapsed on. His somewhat clean shoes propped up on the bar's bottom ledge. He sighed again and then looked around for service. Kendry gave Tarah a wink and glided past her to the bar.

"Hello, Sir," she smiled as she greeted him. He only gave her a half grin back. She took a pitcher of water and asked if he would like a drink.

"Ale," he mumbled grumpily. Kendry hurried to fill a stein for him. She brought it over and set it in front of him.

"Nice day, isn't it? I've heard the blierbells are swarming?" she said cheerfully, referring to the beautiful bird-like insects that flew around Crestavia that time of year.

"I wouldn't know," he began slowly. "I've spent the last hour fighting with your stable boy about my horse's lack of appetite. A man would know if his horse was sick, wouldn't he? Maybe she just isn't thirsty or hungry! But, no, they insist she needs to rest. The last thing I need today is to be wasting time sitting at a tavern. I've got too much to do!"

Tarah's cheeks erupted in a huge smile. Sick horse! She was taking that as a win! She strolled into the kitchen, picked up a piece of chalk, and marked a tally point under her name indicating her victory. She arrived back at the bar just in time to hear Kendry's follow-up response.

"I'm so sorry to hear about your horse. That must be so frustrating," she leaned on the bar toward the man with a genuine look of concern. Her golden ringlets, highlighted with streaks of red leftover from when she was young, framed her beautiful face, but it was her stunning dark green eyes that drew the most attention to her. She continued, "And it sounds like you are so busy! Is the horse keeping you from your job?"

The man resituated himself on the stool. He was too grumpy to even look at Kendry. She continued to stare at him, smiling, waiting for a response.

Gruffly, he said, "No, I'm supposed to be visiting my aunt. She's sick. They'll be expecting me to help care for her, I suppose. But now I have to worry about my horse! Just figures!" He continued on grumbling to himself, but Kendry had already turned the corner for the kitchen and grabbed the chalk to tally her own win- a sick aunt!

Giggling and playful arguing resulted between the girls about who really won their game. Madame Lansing hushed them and walked past to see to their guest. An hour later, the traveler was gone and the girls were rehashing the score tallied on the chalkboard as Lieutenant Trent unraveled the note.

Tarah, with her chocolate-colored braid and rich eyes, insisted that her initial sick horse prediction trumped any other information they gained, even though she knew she would be arguing otherwise if she had made Kendry's prediction. She was laughing through her argument when Kendry's gaze caught the look on Lieutenant Trent's face. She froze out of concern. Her heart started pounding fast and she stared at him. Tarah stopped mid-sentence. Lieutenant Trent looked up slowly, making eye contact with Kendry, where his eyes froze. He knew her well. He knew how close she was with her father. He walked over and handed her the note, then hurried to the back of the kitchen to use the secret entrance to the Academy.

The mysterious trip General Walbrek, his instructors, and the men they'd been training, had been on this time, was simply a three-month excursion for special forces instruction. They had just left a few days earlier. Kendry didn't know where they were going but she knew when to expect them back. And getting a note instead from the king saying they were all dead was unacceptable to her. And now, here she was looking down at her friends, who were more like family to her than friends, being gagged, bound, and dragged across the tavern by dangerous strangers. And what was more upsetting was knowing that this was most likely happening because these people were searching for her father or the Academy.

Very slowly, Kendry slid on her belly back toward the way she had come. Drops of sweat trickled down her freckled nose. She gripped the beam tightly as dizziness from the disgust of what was going on below waved over her. She carefully used her upper body strength to push herself slowly upward onto her knees. She crawled backward, one knee at a time. Just as she was coming out of sight from being in the window of space where she was able to see her friends down below, she scraped her leg across the beam. It hurt a little and began to bleed, but that wasn't going to delay her. Until she noticed a drop of blood fall in what seemed like slow motion down to the floor beneath her. Terrified someone would notice it, she slowly pulled herself up to stand on the balls of her feet, while still crouching down low as to not hit her head. She stepped back a few paces, surprising herself when she whacked her elbow on the side of the beam of the upper loft. It hit hard and she gasped from the shocking pain of her funny bone vibrating. Responding to it caused her to wobble and shift forward. Her balance was thrown off. Fear choked her as she realized she was going to fall. She caught herself just in time. But the distinct noise from the bang of her elbow and her unplanned gasp had already done its damage. One of the men downstairs was running up the staircase toward her.

CHAPTER THREE

Thankfully, all her training with balance and obstacle courses paid off. Kendry was able to quickly crawl back forward, out of sight from the loft's view. The man in the dark clothes searched the upstairs loft, haphazardly throwing aside clutter gathered in the room's corner. He knew he had heard something and refused to leave after his cursory surface search. He tipped over mattresses and pushed the one small dresser that was up against the window. Frustrated, he grunted. Then, he strolled slowly toward the window and shoved it open, peeking his sun-kissed head out to look around. Still not satisfied, he looked up toward the roof and then feeling a bit defeated, pulled his head back inside. Anger showed on his face as he gritted his teeth. He knew there was something in this place they were missing. He began feeling the walls checking for anything that could explain the sound he was sure he had heard.

Kendry held her breath. From where she was balanced, there was a chance he'd be able to see her, if he leaned back against the wall at just the right angle and looked upward. She tried her best to be completely still but her heart was pounding so loud she was sure he'd be able to hear it. When he finally gave up and went back down the stairs, she released her breath not even realizing she'd been holding it for so long. Relief flooded her body like a cold shower. She stayed put for an extra few minutes, until she was positive the men had left. Then, she crawled back out on the rafter to look down again and be sure it was safe to come out from hiding.

Nobody was there. The room was empty. She dropped her forehead down to the beam and tried not to cry. This could not be happening! They just told her that her dad was gone. Now her friends were gone. She shook her head in disbelief. Then, a thought occurred to her. She was acting like any other common victim. Her father had taught her better than this.

Kendry had been raised her whole life to be prepared to improvise in emergency situations. She quickly got back to her knees and crawled backwards. This time she easily swung her body back down onto the top bunk and climbed off. Her feet hit the ground of the upper loft with determination. She ran across to the window that been left open by the intruder. With little effort she stepped up on the corner of the dresser which had been pushed to the side and propped herself through the window. She used her upper body strength again to pull herself up to the ledge and then she scaled the side of the wall using bricks that peeked out a little further than they should, to get to the roof.

Kendry had climbed up on this roof many times before. She loved to climb and had climbed most every building in Tavern's End at some point in her sixteen years. When she easily reached the roof, she looked out toward the horizon. The night breeze blew a few strands of her strawberry gold hair into her face, but her ringlets remained intact behind her. Her eyes were quickly drawn to the men carrying her friends off, against their will. There were only three of them, all dressed in dark clothes and looking unsoldier-like to Kendry. They definitely didn't appear to be forces from Shadenberg, Crestavia's biggest enemy. What she saw next made her sick. Up ahead a few hundred yards or so were more men in dark clothes. And, it appeared they had captured the rest of Tavern's End. She could see Shalia's parents and younger brothers and sisters. She could see Mister Carter, their local blacksmith and carpenter. There was Mrs. Jamison and Farmer Tinminn from down the road. Seeing Mrs. Jamsion caught her attention. Mrs. Jamison's son, Marvin filled her thoughts. He wasn't there and she knew why.

Kendry had been up at the Academy that morning. She liked when it was empty and most the men were gone. She had freedom to roam, ride horses, practice obstacle courses, and do as she pleased.

16

Lieutenant Trent and Officer Lew were on duty guarding the front gate, but things were very informal when everyone else was gone. The staff had been given leave, having a few months off from their duties. The cooks, servants, yard workers, and repairmen would not be seen until the fall. She smiled at the men as she passed. They teased her over her inability to stay away. She knew her father would be displeased at her presence there. He was very overprotective of her being near any of the men unless he or Malark were in her presence. But Kendry figured the two men weren't leaving their posts and there was no one else there.

Malark was like an uncle to Kendry. He was older than her father with grey thick uncontrolled hair. His burly beard matched his coarse face. But his eyes were kind and his heart was generous.

Malark and Kendry's father had fought together in many battles and had always been very close. Malark had helped care for her when she was young and her mother had died in childbirth. Apparently when her father had finally accepted the King's promotion to retire from daily battles and begin leading and teaching at the Academy, Kendry had been sent to the tavern to stay with Tarah's mother, Madame Lansing. Madame Lansing raised her for her first three years of life, with her father visiting as often as he could in evenings and such. It had worked out well until Kendry was three years old.

It had been a busy season as the New Moon festival was going on and many guests traveled through town. Tarah's mother was overwhelmed with mischievous toddlers and a tavern full of guests. Malark had stopped in for a drink and saw Madame Lansing's exhaustion. Possibly due to his lack of contentment and boredom being away from battle, Malark had offered to take Kendry for a day in order to give Tarah's mother a much-needed break. He said later that he needed a little adventure in his life and what was more adventurous than a day with a spunky three-year-old?

Having a toddler at the Academy was interesting. Malark brought her down to watch some of the men training in martial arts. She was a complete distraction to them. But Kendry's father, General Walbrek, was amazed at how distracting it actually was. He kept yelling at his men that when you are fighting in real battles and fights there would be distractions and you must learn how to fight anyway. From that point on he kept asking Madame

17

Lansing if Malark could come get Kendry during the day to bring her up as a distraction during fighting practices. As time went on, she ended up just spending the days there with the men. As she grew, she spent more and more time amongst the drills, teachings, and trainings. She hated it back at the tavern, where life seemed slow and nothing exciting ever seemed to happen. She loved being amongst the action. Kendry would play and keep herself busy in the dirt while the men trained and practiced. She sat at the back in classrooms during lectures and doodled and drew pictures. The trainees adored her and her father and Malark loved having her around.

As she got older, she started distracting the men in other ways. Her beauty was undeniable so her father made the rule that she wasn't allowed to be alone with any of the men. He also punished greatly anybody he caught gazing at her. And on the one occasion where a young man tried to flirt with her, he was immediately sent away from the Academy. Yet her father loved that she was still a distraction. He thought it was the best way to teach these men to be real spies.

In Kendry's free time she would practice the obstacle courses and balance training. She got really good at martial arts and archery and even excelled at sword fighting. She got better and better as each year went on. Her physical strength and overall athletic build made her a real challenge for some of the kingdom's best fighting men. She rarely beat them at anything, but she loved the challenge. The men all got a kick out of her and most of them made it their goal to try to defeat the general's daughter at the balance beam obstacle course. Nobody could beat her at that. She climbed faster than any of them. She practically ran across the beams. Her flexibility outdid any of the soldiers that entered the Academy. Lieutenant Trent would tease her that she should join the circus and be a trapeze artist.

After she said goodbye to Lieutenant Trent and Officer Lew at the front of the Academy, she scaled back through the forest. It was a lovely day and she had no intention of traveling back to the cave in the secret passage to the tavern. The sun was shining hot and the blierbells had been swarming. She hoped to chase them, but only saw some in the very distance. The trees and shade in the forest felt refreshing after the sweat she had built up at the Academy.

She glanced up at the angle of the sun and realized it was almost midday. Kendry and her friends, the few other teenagers in Tavern's End, made it their habit to meet at the coolest place at the hottest time of day. In fact, it had kind of become a motto. As one of them left the other, they'd say, "See you at the coolest place at the hottest time!"

Midday would be hottest and the coolest place was always down by the creek hidden deep in the forest. She rushed through the woods barefoot enjoying the feel of the ground on her feet. She smiled at the insects and lizards. She felt so at home in the forest. She loved climbing trees, swinging from branches. She even enjoyed hanging upside down on limbs from her knees. There was something magical about feeling her hair sweep back and forth in the wind as she hung with the ground below her head.

Kendry whistled to herself, taking her time heading to the creek. When she finally arrived, she noticed her friends had all beaten her there. Shalia was not amongst them as she rarely came down to the creek. She was kept too busy between her work at home and her job at the tavern. But her younger brother Frederick was there, as always, goofing off with the Tinminn twins. Hendrick was there. He was an orphan who was being raised by the blacksmith, Mister Carter. Both his parents had died from a disease when he was young. Marvin was also there. His widowed mother, Mrs. Jamison, raised him the best she could but was so relieved that he'd be joining the Army soon, off to wherever the orders he'd receive would send him.

As soon as she arrived, Hendrick jumped to his feet and headed toward the tree. He'd obviously been waiting for her to show. She released a short sigh. A tradition of sorts had formed. One that she could not get out of. Every time they met at the creek, she and Hendrick would race to the top of the large brandy tree. It was a big thick tree along the creek which had great branches for climbing on both sides. The goal was to reach a specific branch near the top. Kendry couldn't even remember how this challenge had started. But she did remember that she'd never lost to him. And yet, each and every day they met there, Hendrick would compete against her again. She had to give him some credit for trying. For a long time, their friends had cheered them on and encouraged Hendrick, hoping he'd beat Kendry. But as of lately, they didn't even bother to look up to watch the competition.

19

Kendry shrugged pointing at the tree to give the signal that he could choose which side he wanted. He went to his favorite side and she to the other. When he said to go, they both raced quickly to the top. Kendry was like lightning. Her catlike moves allowed her to snake with ease through the branches without any problem. Hendrick stayed at least five feet behind her, the whole time. He never caught up. When she reached the top, she pulled herself up on the branch to sit and relax. He finished the climb a couple moments later and slid himself to get comfortable on the branch next to her, grunting. She could see he was biting his bottom lip with frustration. She chuckled.

"Why do you put yourself through this torture?" she asked, sincerely curious as to what possessed him to relive the same ordeal over and over again.

"Stop bragging," he responded, obviously annoyed.

"I'm not bragging. I just don't see the point of us competing each time with the same results." She smiled a little too smugly.

He rolled his eyes.

She began to venture back down, glad their competition, which had begun to feel like some sort of strange duty, was over. She was looking forward to talking to Tarah before starting her shift at the tavern in a bit.

Hendrick's gruff sighs following from behind, annoyed her. She glanced back at him to glare with frustration but was just in time to see his leg slip from a branch above her. His body slid down, with one arm catching a thin branch, keeping him from falling to the ground. The branch sunk, not able to support his weight. Instinct took over as Kendry sprung her body across the tree and wrapped her legs around his waist, as he dangled by one arm. Swinging her upper body hard, three times, she was able to launch him close enough to reach a stronger branch. Once he was secure, she straightened out her legs and put both hands on the branch below. She continued on back down as if nothing had happened.

Hendrick hung there for second taking a deep breath. Slowly he positioned himself to sit on another branch and allowed his racing heart to slow down. They were over thirty feet up. He could have easily died. And now he'd have

Kendry to thank for saving his life. There's nothing he'd rather enjoy doing less. It probably would've been better to just die.

Hendrick looked down at Kendry who was already back on the ground chatting away with Tarah. His jaw clenched with frustration. Kendry got everything. She was the sweetheart of the town and most saw her cockiness as confidence, but in Hendrick's mind she was super annoying. He just didn't understand why he couldn't beat her. He practiced on that tree every chance he got. There were times where he was sure he would beat her and he wouldn't even come close. How was she always capable of anything put in front of her? Hendrick thought of himself as just the opposite. He was clumsy and could never seem to do the right thing. Growing up without his parents had been tough. Old Mister Carter was great to him and he was appreciative that the kind man took him in after his parents' death. But it wasn't the same as having your mother or father around.

Hendrick had learned the blacksmith trade from Mister Carter. Not that they had a lot of business. Most travelers going through, if they had any sort of issue, would continue on to Glenville or Galvenland. But if someone needed a new horseshoe, Hendrick and Mister Carter could sure give them that. If one of their tires on their cart fell off, Hendrick knew how to replace it. His job was pretty boring. He would wander off into the forest to be alone many times. He secretly envied Marvin who would be going to the Army soon.

Hendrick didn't think there was any way he, himself, would ever make it into the Army. He wasn't athletic enough and didn't have good enough hand-eye coordination. He wasn't smart enough. He had experienced very little education. Only what Mrs. Jamison could provide for him through some tutoring sessions. Kendry, though, was so spoiled. She got to spend every day at the Academy! Hendrick would've loved to be trained the way she was. It was so unfair. He wasn't even allowed into the Academy.

Hendrick took his time climbing back down the tree. By the time he got to the bottom he realized none of his friends had even noticed his almost spill to death, nor had they probably cared. Kendry and Tarah were talking fast. They always talked fast. He found them difficult to understand. They were discussing saving their tips from the tavern to try to purchase a horse together. Hendrick thought this was the stupidest thing he had ever heard.

21

Tavern's End had three horses. He was charged to take care of them most the time, though a couple of Shalia's younger brothers helped him out sometimes. Anyone could borrow them if they needed them. But they were rarely needed. They were only used to go to Glenville and Galvenland to get goods. Kendry was allowed to use the horses at the stables at the Academy anytime she wanted, too. He was sure she was probably a better horse rider than he was, and thinking this made his stomach tighten with jealousy. But for some reason the silly girls wanted to buy their own horse with their own money. Girls were foolish.

Hendrick looked around, disappointed once again that Shalia wasn't there. Just thinking about her brought a slight smile to his face. She was the kindest and prettiest girl in town. But she was also the hardest to ever run into. She wasn't social like the rest of them and always seemed to be working whether at home or at the tavern. He had started spending his breaks from work at the tavern just so he'd have an excuse to see her. But when they had a time to finally relax down at the creek, she was rarely there.

Once Marvin noticed Hendrick striding toward him, he began immediately discussing their plans for the next night. Marvin was really into astronomy and was excited to be doing a campout up on the hill on the northeast side of Tavern's End. He was watching for some sort of comet or something. Hendrick didn't really care. He was just excited to do something different. Plans were always welcomed. He had agreed to be Marvin's watch out. The annoying critters, crenzels, were known for coming out at night in that area. They seem to be curious of fires and both Marvin and Hendrick knew many of them would come investigate if they camped out there. Hendrick's job would be to scare them away which wasn't hard to do since the animals were very skittish and simply beating a stick on the ground would cause them to flutter. But he was committed to going and helping his friend out. Especially since Marvin would be leaving for the Army soon, there wasn't much time left to just spend together.

It had been later that day when Kendry arrived back at the tavern that the note had come. The note that tore her insides out as they read that her father and his men were dead. Now here she was sitting on top of the roof of the tavern looking ahead at her townspeople being carried off when she remembered Marvin and Hendrick's campout!

Scanning the townspeople, she didn't see either of them with the men. They could be safe. She'd have to check on them immediately and then see if she could get them to help her. With three of them, they may have a chance to try to get their friends back, though she didn't have the slightest clue how. If she could get up to the Academy, they could get help from the couple guards left behind and she could grab her archery equipment and some weapons and horses. She doubted there would be time for all this, as her friends were being marched away at that moment.

As quickly as she could, Kendry ran across the roof to the other end and scurried down a pipe on the side. When her bare feet touched the ground, she realized she would have to be very careful not to be seen. If the men came back, they would easily see her footsteps in the mud. She was a pretty experienced tracker herself just from the training her father had given her. She knew it wouldn't be hard for them to discover her whereabouts. But if she took the time it would take to cover her tracks, there'd be no chance to save her friends. She made a split-second decision to leave her prints exposed and she ran as fast as she could toward the spot where she believed Marvin and Hendrick would be camping.

As Kendry rushed up the little hill where they had discussed they would be, she saw their camp fire glowing and remnants of their stuff spread about. But they were nowhere in sight. Her heart jumped. The men had got them, too. First her dad and his men, then everyone at the tavern, and now Marvin and Hendrick. She'd have to go straight to the Academy. Lieutenant Trent wouldn't have a clue what was taking place and he and Officer Lew would still be on duty. They would help her! Immediately, she turned to run towards the forest. But then she heard something.

She wasn't sure where the sound came from but her instincts told her to hide. She ran to the nearest tree and began climbing. Climbing was her strength. It took very little effort and she swung herself from branch to branch and hid amongst the leaves. She quietly looked out over the clearing below. Where had the noise came from? Were the men who took her friends here? She froze. Through the quiet wind, she could hear...laughing.

CHAPTER FOUR

The laughing was getting louder and Kendry would have been scared except she recognized it. She looked across at a tree not far from the one she hid in, and there sat Hendrick. His legs resting over the branch and belly laughing hard.

"Scared you, didn't I?" he asked between laughs. She quickly scanned the area and realized there was no one else there.

"Hendrick, you won't believe what happened."

Then, talking as fast as she could, which to Hendrick was superfast, she explained the events of the night to him.

Before she even finished, he was climbing down the tree. His face had turned white and serious. She took off down the tree, as well. When they both reached the bottom, she finished giving him information and answering his questions. Hendrick looked like he was in shock, staring blankly past her.

"Where is Marvin? Did they get him, too?" she asked, desperately.

"No, Marvin just went back to the stables to grab the horse," he managed to force himself to say. After taking a deep breath, he added, "We decided in the morning we'd go down to the bay to go fishing and we wanted to get an early start. Figured we'd get the horse tonight since we were both still awake."

Kendry could hear the fear in Hendrick's voice. Marvin very well may have been taken. But they were both relieved when they heard the horse coming at them. Until the thought hit Kendry that it might not be Marvin.

"Hide," Kendry whispered to Hendrick. They both found a tree to hide behind and waited until the horse got closer.

Marvin's voice carried above the clamor of the horse, letting Hendrick know he was back. Hendrick came out from behind the tree, relieved to see Marvin.

Kendry ran out from behind another tree scaring Marvin so much he almost fell off his horse. They rushed to explain to him the summarized version of what had happened.

"What's the plan?" Marvin asked, stern and ready to act. Kendry loved that about Marvin. She knew he'd do great in the Army. When a problem arose, he kept a calm head and was ready to act.

"I don't have a plan," she admitted. "My plan was to come here and get you guys. Do ya think we have time to get to the Academy for help and weapons?" They were in the opposite direction of the Forgotten Forest. Kendry knew their friends were probably long gone already.

"Where do you think they were heading?" Marvin asked.

"From what I could tell when I was on the roof, they were heading in the direction of the wharf." The wharf was a few miles away through the woods, toward Galvenland.

"Do you think they might have a boat down there?" Kendry asked.

"Could be," Marvin replied. "How else would they be able to get out of Crestavia unnoticed with tons of prisoners? If they get on a boat in the middle of the night, before dawn, they might have a chance."

"It couldn't be a very big boat," Kendry added. "The wharf is too shallow for anything too large."

"That's how they're hiding it, probably," Hendrick suggested.

"Let me take the horse," Kendry said. "I can rush to the Academy, tell the guards, and get help. I'll snag more horses when I'm there."

"Without us?" Marvin asked. "No way!"

"Okay you can go with me. Hendrick stay here and keep an eye on the fire," she said. Hendrick would just get in the way. He wasn't military-minded and would not be of much help. And then a thought crept in her head as she realized coming back this way to get him would be a waste of their precious time.

"Actually, change of plans," she said. "Hendrick, you go down to the stables and get two of the Tavern's End horses. Marvin and I will go to the Academy and get weapons, horses, and most importantly- we will get help!"

"Where do I go once I get the horses?" Hendrick looked dumbfounded.

"Meet us in front of the tavern. We'll have to go by there on our way toward the wharf."

Kendry and Marvin straddled the horse and rushed as fast as they could to the Forgotten Forest's entrance. Kendry held on tight to Marvin, praying Lieutenant Trent would be at the gate of the Academy and easy to locate. The horse galloped and the wind brushed through their hair, but to Kendry they were going much too slow. She thought about Tarah and Shalia and tried not to let tears form in her eyes.

When they finally arrived, Kendry found it strange that no one was stationed at the gate hidden behind the forest wall. The hair on her arms stood straight up and chills ran down her body. Something definitely was not right. It was eerily quiet and felt still.

They stayed mounted on the horse and slowly steered it through the open gate, both knowing it should not be opened. And then she gasped as she saw them. The guards' dead bodies. Officer Lew was face up, eyes open, but obviously not alive. Another guard, who was face down had blood covering his back, but Kendry didn't look long enough to identify him. She turned her head and closed her eyes.

27

Completely shocked that the men in dark clothes had not only found the Academy but had been able to kill the specially trained guards, she began shaking. This was an Academy for specially trained warfare warriors. Who were the men who had taken her friends? How did they know where the Academy was located? Had they tortured her friends to get that information? Or had they come here first? Had they found the secret passageway in the tavern? None of those things seemed likely as Kendry had watched them come and go. Were these men working for Shadenberg? Had they been spying? Her thoughts swirled around making her feel sick inside.

"What do we do now?" Marvin whispered over his shoulder to Kendry, looking horrified. He'd never seen a dead body. Neither had Kendry, but she was able to throw her sickness aside and focus on their next move.

Kendry led Marvin through the Academy gates and went straight to the artillery room. The door was ajar and she was shocked to find the weapons gone. All of them! The place had been thrashed. The men obviously knew where to look for stuff. There must've been many of them. Much more than she saw at the tavern. How long ago had this happened? She had just been up here yesterday morning.

They quickly made their way to her dad's living quarters. One glance at the destruction and Kendry led Marvin back out. She knew where a few weapons would be hidden among the inner gate in case of emergency. She figured they needed to stop wasting time and head there. Marvin followed behind her without asking any questions. When they got to the back of the gate, she directed Marvin to help her dig through the bushes and slide panels from the retainer wall, exposing weapons and ropes. Kendry handed Marvin an axe and a knife and bundled up lots of rope. She grabbed a dagger and another axe, then they quickly mounted the horse and headed back toward the tavern.

Hendrick had been outside the tavern with the two horses, waiting nervously. He was relieved to hear them galloping toward him. As they approached, his countenance fell.

"Where are the guards? Where's all the help?" he asked looking up the hill behind them for reinforcements.

They didn't answer. He began to ask them again and then understood.

"They've been taken, too?" he asked sadly.

"Not exactly."

He paused and his eyes widened as he realized what she meant.

"What do we do now?" he questioned desperately.

Kendry's head spun. She was not sure where to begin. Surveying her supplies, all she had were a couple of weapons, Hendrick, Marvin, and three horses. Her anxiety started to build, but she suppressed the worries and slid back into survival mode.

Jumping off the horse, she hurried over to the tallest tree nearby. Quickly, she climbed it as far up as she could. If she could get high enough, she knew she could get an even better view than she had when she was on top of the roof. The moon was shining bright and there was no fog.

Pulling herself up to the highest sturdy branch, her eyes scanned around not seeing anything. Feeling hopeless, she tried to think what to say to the boys waiting below when something caught her eye. She pulled her body up and stood on the branch looking far off toward the water. Yes, she definitely could see two different groups of people. And, she was pretty sure in the distance, she saw some sort of fishing boat down by the bay that normally would not be there.

Climbing down as quickly as she safely could, she hurried to relay her observations to the boys.

"It looks as if they're definitely taking everyone toward the bay. Lucky for us, they were all traveling on foot. Probably trying to keep quiet with the hostages. I think if we ride as fast as these horses can take us, we have a good chance of catching up!"

"And then what?" Hendrick rebounded.

"Let's ride to a thick portion of the trees leading toward the bay. Then, we'll need to get off and leave the horses so we can walk quietly. Once we get within range, we will climb the trees and form a plan from there?"

Hendrick's mouth dropped open. "Are you kidding?"

"If we had a bow and arrows, I'd have a better plan," Kendry snapped back.

Marvin humbly admitted that he was not a super good shot, though defended himself by adding that he'd been practicing in preparation for the Army.

"Well, I'm an excellent shot," responded Kendry. "But we don't have one. So, we're going to ride toward our friends and we'll figure it out when we get there. I don't want to hear any complaining. Let's go!"

Without discussing any more details, they plunged through the trees on horseback. They raced as fast as the horses could take them. It seemed like forever. When they finally got past a clearing into the thicker trees which they knew led toward the bay, Kendry slowed them down. Eventually they stopped the horses and tied them up.

Kendry looked down at her feet. She was still barefoot. She had never put her shoes on after waking up. Both Hendrick and Marvin had shoes on their feet, so she instructed them to take them off and leave them by the horses. Kendry gave them some quick tips on how to be able to track back to where the horses were, and then they continued on foot toward the bay. Trying to remember anything that could help the boys if they got lost, she pointed out the position of the moon and the stars. She pointed out specific treetops above them that would stand out from a distance. Then as quick as possible, she tutored them on how to be silent as they approached the bay.

Advising Hendrick and Marvin to watch where they walked, she pointed out the crunching of leaves and branches and told them that any trained tracker, hunter, or assassin, would hear the slightest snap of a twig or rustle of leaves. They inched their way closer and closer in the direction where they could see smoke from a campfire.

Hendrick's knees were literally shaking. He couldn't believe they were doing this. Were they really going to stalk armed men who had just kidnapped their whole town? Men who had found the Academy and done who-knows-what to the guards! Kendry was crazy! Yet, internally he battled his anger toward Kendry for leading them into a suicide mission, because he knew they had to help their friends. This town was his family. He couldn't just sit back and do nothing.

They silently took one step after another until, after what seemed like an hour, Kendry signaled to them to climb upward. They each picked a tree and climbed as quietly and quickly as they could. Marvin was not a good climber. He gave up after a few branches and just sat waiting to get intel from the other two. Kendry was up high in the blink of an eye. She looked down on the clearing in the not so far distance below.

It was a broad clearing between a group of trees. There appeared to be about five men in dark clothing. And there, bound and gagged, were their fellow townspeople, thrown into a pile in the middle of the clearing near a campfire. Even with the distance, she could see the fear and desperation in their eyes. It literally broke Kendry's heart. But it also stirred up a desire to fix the injustice she was witnessing. These men would pay!

The men lounged around, smoking and chatting. A few were eating and one, in particular, was frustrated with their hostages and kept yelling at them to be quiet or stay still.

Kendry could occasionally hear pieces of their conversation and could tell that this rampage had not gone as planned. Up ahead were more trees and then another clearing as the beach came into view. Sure enough, there was a large fishing boat on the docks. She could see a couple of guards out front.

Kendry climbed back down signaling for Hendrick and Marvin to do the same. When they got to the bottom, she took a deep breath.

"Okay, I've got a plan..."

But before she could give them any further information, they were all three grabbed by men in dark clothes.

CHAPTER FIVE

It all happened so fast. Kendry hardly had time to wonder where they had come from. They must've been hiding. How long had they been watching them? Stalking them? She was just up in a tree. She should've seen them! But her eyes had been targeting the smoke from the campfire. She'd only looked ahead to the clearing and the docks. She never even thought about looking behind them or scanning their location. So incredibly stupid of her, she thought. She could hear her dad's tactic training saying not to overlook the obvious. Her foolishness is what led them to this predicament!

Scoping out the situation, Kendry's education from her father's training clicked. Only two men and three of them. This was doable. The man who had grabbed her was also holding Marvin hostage with a sword. The second man had Hendrick and a dagger. Hendrick would be useless in helping to battle these skilled men, but Kendry was fairly certain she and Marvin could have a chance of taking control of the situation if no other men arrived. Unfortunately, they were probably within yelling distance of the camp where other men could be called to help. She had to think fast.

Kendry decided the best method was to use the men's preconceived notions against them. She instantly acted like a scared, weak girl. She flailed about, starting to cry crocodile tears. If she had caught the look on Hendrick's face, she probably would have broken into laughter. He was shocked witnessing her performance as the damsel in distress. Kendry sort of fell into the arms of the man who was holding her. He looked annoyed and resituated to have a tighter grasp on her. He never knew what hit him.

Kendry's martial arts came out in full force. She elbowed him in the chin, kneed him in the groin, and socked him hard in the stomach. He fell over in pain. Marvin quickly grabbed him, knocking his weapon to the ground, where Kendry grabbed it and fell into an offensive stance. The other man, holding Hendrick, reacted swiftly placing his blade to Hendrick's neck.

"I'll cut his throat if you so much as move!" the man threatened, speaking in Crestavian so they could all understand.

Kendry didn't flinch. She stared him straight in the eye, quickly swiped her sword at his arm, cutting it before he had the chance to even scrape Hendrick's throat. The man gasped and Hendrick backed away. She charged at him, kicking his forearm and causing the dagger to drop to the ground. Marvin swung around wanting to help, but he was holding down the first man.

"No, stay on him," she yelled.

Kendry had already picked up the dagger, in addition to the sword. The man was obviously impressed. He reached into his pocket and pulled out a knife. He slowly lifted it, analyzing the best way to use it against this girl with two weapons. Without thinking, she instinctively dropped the large sword and grabbed the man's wounded arm, where blood drenched his shirt. She jerked it backwards in an inhumane angle. He writhed with pain and screeched. The knife in his other hand became useless at this distraction of his pain. Kendry kicked as hard as she could into his kneecap. Hearing a crack, she was sure it broke. She wrestled the knife out of his other hand and shoved his battered body to the ground.

"Get the rope," she yelled at Hendrick. Hendrick just stood, shocked. He knew Kendry could fight and had trained with the best special force warriors in their nation, but he had never imagined she was that good.

As he snapped into reality, he stuttered, "Wh- where's the rope?"

Annoyed, Kendry directed him back toward where the horses were and added a command to grab their socks and shoes, too. Hendrick ran as fast as he could, trying to remember the clues Kendry had instructed them to use to find their way back.

34

"Great," he thought, "Now, she's saved my life a second time."

 He was equally annoyed as he was relieved. Eager to do something beneficial for their situation, he grabbed as much rope from the horses as he could, along with their socks and shoes, and rushed back. Impressed with himself that he didn't get lost, he arrived back to see Kendry standing with her foot on one of the men's backs and Marvin holding the other man down.

Marvin took the socks that were inside his shoes and stuck one in each man's mouth as a gag. Hendrick tried not to gag himself when he saw how far Marvin stuffed the socks down each of their throats.

"What now?" Hendrick asked, not knowing what else to do.

Kendry was already climbing the tree again. She surveyed ahead but this time was sure to look down and around them, too. She scanned for movements, colors, or any signs that people could be there.

Quite a distance up ahead, she could see their friends being chauffeured onto the fishing boat that was docked. Her heart raced knowing they needed to save them before that boat took off and they were gone for good.

Doing a quick count of the men pushing her friends onto the boat, and the ones they had just tied up, she knew that there were at least two more men unaccounted for. Again, she searched the bushes down below them, scanned the thick trees, and traced the route from the clearing to where they were currently hiding.

There! She could see footprints in the mud not far ahead. Were those from the two men that had attacked them? Or were others hiding? She squinted and combed the foliage with her eyes, but there didn't appear to be anyone there.

Heart racing, she began to head back down the tree when she noticed a slight movement. It was more than the wind. It was an animal or person. She froze and waited. After a few minutes, while ignoring Hendrick's waving arms trying to get her attention, she was positive she had spotted them. There were two or three men sneaking very silently toward them. These guys were good. They barely moved the bushes they crawled through. They were slow, but steady. She could tell they were armed.

Kendry climbed about halfway down the tree until she could clearly see Hendrick and Marvin who were looking to her for guidance. She mouthed to Hendrick to climb the tree across from her tree and bring the rope with him. Unsure of what was going on, he obeyed. Grabbing the rope, he began up the tree. Kendry paralleled him climbing up at his pace.

She signaled for him to stop and tie the rope tight at the branch above him. Hendrick's hands fumbled as he did his best to find a spot on the branch where the rope would not come undone. He tied a strong double knot on the other end of a stump sticking out of the branch to ensure it would not slide off. He pulled on it to show Kendry it was secure.

He shrugged at her as to say, "Now what?"

She signaled for him to throw the rope to her. Hendrick lassoed the end and swung it above his head a few times before letting go. He didn't release early enough with enough power and the rope fell a yard before Kendry. He could tell she was rolling her eyes, but quickly pulled the rope back up, hand over hand, to try again. His second attempt was successful and Kendry caught it.

Kendry pulled the rope tight and secured it on her side. She flicked it to ensure it was snug. Then, she quickly crawled back down, signaling to Hendrick to do the same.

On the ground, she whispered for both boys to help her slide their hostages to a specific point between the two trees that she and Hendrick had just climbed. They put the men face down and tied their feet to their hands behind their back. All the while, Kendry was continually looking toward the direction she knew the men would be coming from and listening for hints that they might be getting closer.

Kendry knew time was almost up. She instructed Hendrick and Marvin to hide behind trees on the opposite end and made sure they both had weapons. She looked Hendrick in the eyes.

"Do not hesitate if we need you to use that sword," she demanded. Then she disappeared.

Hendrick's anger fumed. Kendry, with her self-righteous bullying, was not what he needed right now. He hid behind the tree and started shaking. They were about to die. He was pretty certain that their friends were probably already dead. That's probably what Kendry saw up in the tree, not that she told them anything. He could tell she had looked scared, though she wouldn't ever admit it. And if Kendry was scared, then he was definitely scared.

He couldn't see Marvin but knew he was also hiding behind a tree. Were they waiting to be ambushed? He glanced up and could glimpse Kendry at the top of the tree above the men they had bound.

And then he heard them.

Three men very quietly snaked their way through the trees. When they noticed their friends in the clearing, face-down, they all pulled weapons. They took a few minutes to survey the area but didn't come close to where Marvin and Hendrick were hiding. As soon as they reached their friends, the one who appeared to be in charge yelled to the others to cut the ropes.

The other men put down their weapons and pulled out knives to begin sawing the ropes. Hendrick looked up. Kendry had monkey barred her way across the rope and was hanging up high between the two trees directly over the man in charge. His heart raced. What was she thinking? If she fell from that height, she would definitely die. He watched in horror as she positioned herself carefully and then purposely opened her hands and fell.

CHAPTER SIX

Hendrick gasped. Kendry fell for what seemed like forever. Her feet hit the men below in a premeditated motion, tweaking the neck of the leader in an unnatural position. He fell to the ground and blacked out. The other two fell forward on top of their detained friends and moaned. Before they could regain their composure, Marvin was already over them. He knocked one of the weapons out of one of their hands and swung his dagger at the other man who started to charge toward him. The dagger cut the man's face, but it was Kendry who stopped him from lunging forward.

Hendrick had come out from behind the tree. He was shocked to see Kendry alive and on two feet. She had her arm around the neck of the man who had just received the cut in the face. It appeared she was suffocating him. Eventually he collapsed as well. She mumbled something about how he'd have a horrible headache when he awoke.

The guy without his weapon was on the ground facing Marvin who held the sword at him. Kendry barked an order to Hendrick to tie him up. They all three busily began wrapping up the man's hands and feet with rope. Then, they moved on to the two unconscious men. Using two more socks, they gagged the others. Kendry sat down and collapsed back, leaning onto a tree.

"Are you okay?" Hendrick asked her, genuinely concerned.

"Yes," she uttered very unconvincingly. "I practiced that many times... falling into a pile of rag-filled cots. That was much more painful." She stretched her feet and legs.

Marvin approached them grinning ear to ear. "What next?" He asked eager, to move on.

"I hate to be the voice of reason here," Hendrick began. "But what are we expecting to do? Slowly take them out one at a time, because I think at some point, we may get outnumbered."

"Actually," Kendry said, thoughtfully. "I think it's time we go on the offensive."

Hendrick groaned a little.

Kendry ignored his reaction and sent him up the tree to do a little recon and get some intel while she rested. Marvin guarded over their pile of hostages making sure they were all gagged and bound tightly.

At some point Kendry broke the silence from her moment of recovering. "The other men are going to come looking for them. We need to be prepared."

"I got a better idea," Marvin responded. "Why don't we get the heck out of here and leave them behind?"

Hendrick came back down to share his intel.

"Everyone must be on the boat. There are two guards out front but I don't see anyone else."

Kendry did the math in her head. They had five hostages and there were two guards in front of the boat. But there was at least two other men that were unaccounted for. They were either on the boat, inside, or they are venturing out to find their lost men.

"Okay here's the plan," Kendry said. "You stay here and babysit our hostages. Whatever you do, stay on alert because we've got two men who could approach at any moment." She paused and turned her attention to Hendrick.

"You should climb a tree and look down continuously for unnatural movement.   Marvin, you should stay hidden nearby with weapons ready."

"Where are you gonna be?" Hendrick asked, curious.

"I'm going to go rescue our friends."

CHAPTER SEVEN

Kendry looked out over the small bay. She had swum across here many times. Her father had always said it was the best exercise and they both enjoyed the aquatic training. She was an excellent swimmer. But all the times she had swam it, she'd never had to worry about being quiet. Would she be able to swim to the back end of the boat without the guards seeing? Seemed impossible. Especially since it was almost dawn.

She went the long way around the beach, running through the trees so she wouldn't be spotted. When she reached a spot on the curved coast where the men's backs were finally to her, she snuck out into the open. Praying that there was no one watching, she quickly sprinted into the water and dove in. Though it had been a somewhat warm night, the water was still shockingly cold. She swam as quickly as she could without making too much of a scene. She quickly found it was much more difficult swimming in her full clothes than in a swimsuit.

Finally, she came to the stern of the boat. It was a pretty good-sized boat for a fishing vessel. She approached a ladder and clasped the rail. Loud footsteps sounded in her direction. She dropped from the ladder and sunk under the water, swimming under the boat. Holding her breath, she hid as long as she could until she had to come up for a breath, purposely in the darkest shadow at the back of the vessel.

Quietly, she peeked above the water and was relieved not to see anyone. Too afraid to go back toward the ladder, she instead did her best to latch onto the side of the boat. It took all of her upper body strength and luck with finding siding to grip, in order to pull herself up onto the deck. Exhausted, she knew she could not afford a second to rest. She rushed into a dark shadow and froze. Water dripped off her forming a puddle around her feet. She shook with chills from standing still in the shade, soaking wet.

After a few moments of quiet, she began inching forward. Eventually, she managed to skirt around the side to a point where she could dare peek toward the boat's bow.

One guard with a burly beard wandered off the boat onto the beach for a smoke. Another guard, smaller and half asleep, leaned against the front of the boat. Kendry waited until the guard on the beach was fairly far away. She jumped out at the other guard covering his mouth, trying to muffle any sound he could make to alert the guard on the beach. Luckily the lapping waves and wind helped to cover the muffled groans the man made. She could tell she shocked him, and he was ill prepared for an attack. She was able to choke him to unconsciousness. She struggled a bit sliding his body off to the side while crawling, herself, in case the other guard happened to look back. Then, she quickly ran onto the deck below not knowing what she would find.

Drawing her knife out, she entered prepared for battle. She scanned for guards and found there were none. In fact, it was quite vacant except for a door. Relieved, she took her time approaching the door. If there were guards in there, she might be smarter to wait them out. By hiding, she could jump them as they exited. But, the guard on the beach would come back soon and find the other guard unconscious. Or the unconscious guard would wake up! Either way, she had to act fast!

Knowing her father would disapprove, she grabbed the handle of the door and, half-surprised to find it unlocked, swung it open.

Kendry jumped at the response from all those who saw her. There was her whole town, crammed into a room much too small for them all. The air smelled thick with sweat. At first, they were surprised and then they looked discouraged. She quickly realized that they thought she had been caught, too.

Immediately, she tried to hush them. They were making a ruckus and she couldn't afford to be noticed. She even raised her voice a bit to get them to be quiet and calmly and quickly explained she was there to rescue them.

Madame Lansing, though hands tied together, was holding Kendry's arm tight, relieved and terrified, tears in the corners of her eyes. The old lady looked like she had been through the ringer. Kendry patted her hand as she told them all that there were guards out front and it was not going to be easy, but she was going to get them out. Mrs. Jamison asked about Marivn and Mister Carter threw out Hendrick's name. Kendry quickly blurted that they were safe. Then reminded the group they needed to hurry and get out of there.

The group was eager to escape, but the men were even more eager to have the ropes that bound their hands cut. Kendry knew it would take too long to saw through all their ropes, so she focused on the men that she felt could be the most help against the guards outside. Frederick was probably the strongest of the young men and Mister Carter, Mister Lansing, and Shalia's father knew how to fight. She wanted to sever the ties on the Tinminn twins, too, but knew time was up. She told the rest that they would have to wait, and to follow silently. The men fell into her lead, assuming she knew more than they did. The women looked terrified, but desired freedom too much to hesitate. Shalia's parents worked to keep their kids calm.

 Kendry led the charge and quietly rushed out of the tight little room and up the steps to the top deck. The guard she had choked was still unconscious, but the one with the beard who had been smoking was reentering the boat as their group become visible. Without hesitation, Kendry ran straight for the guard. He was unarmed and taken back. She shoved him to the ground. He got up to fight but he was no match for her, backed up with the men from town. They had him immobilized.

Kendry didn't have any rope with her, but Shalia's father held the man tight and Frederick and Jim Tinminn each had one of his arms in case he broke free. Mister Carter and Mister Lansing stood over the other guard. He was starting to come to, but had little strength. They quickly pinned him down. Both guards' mouths were almost immediately gagged by material ripped from someone's sleep clothes.

Tarah and her dad, Mister Lansing, led those holding the guards back into the little room down below, where they had been held hostage. They showed Kendry a box that they had been sitting on, while in there. Eventually, they were able to shove both guards into the large wooden box, though with all their squirming, it took many people to help. Mister Carter used his belt to keep it closed tight. He gave Kendry a smile as if to say 'well done'.

Even with the belt holding the box shut, it still opened a gap and their gagged screams could be heard, though they were muffled. They exited the room and shut the door latch as they joined the others on the top deck of the boat. Some of their group had already ventured out onto the beach. Kendry took a breath of relief for the first time since she had woken to Madame Lansing's screams that night.

Kendry hugged Tarah, whose hands were still bound. She leaned in to Kendry trying to hug her back, so thankful for the rescue. They joined the others out on the beach. Kendry explained that she thought all the guards were accounted for, but was not positive, so they needed to be extra alert as they ventured back to where Hendrick and Marvin were guarding the other men.

Before heading back into the trees, they paused to spend some time sawing the ropes off the remaining townspeople. Mister Lansing had retrieved a knife off one of the guards so he helped Mister Carter, who had Kendry's knife.

The group of them then headed back to where Marvin and Hendrick were, with Kendry leading and reminding them to be alert. It wasn't time to celebrate or catch up. They could still be in danger, though if there were any men left hiding, they would be outnumbered. Kendry's friends were prepared this time. Nobody was going to be taken by surprise. Yet, she would have loved to know for sure if they were safe.

When they arrived back to where the boys were with the hostages, there were hugs and homecomings. The five men were still bound and gagged. Kendry found she couldn't focus. She had a feeling there might still be another man or two out there somewhere. She decided to climb back up one of the tall trees to search. She scanned and scanned but couldn't find

46

anything and knew her friends below were eager to head back to town to round up weapons and help.

After discussion, it was decided that some of them would bring the hostages down by the boat and keep an eye on all of the men they had caught. The other group, mostly the women and children, would head home. Marvin decided to lead them. They put the few older women on the three horses, which Hendrick had rounded up and brought to them.

As the others headed back, Kendry, Mister Lansing, Hendrick, Shalia's father and one of her brothers, Farmer Tinminn and his twins, and Tarah, dragged the five men back toward the wharf. They debated getting all the men tied up on the boat, pulling the anchor, and pushing it out to sea. But they decided heading to the neighboring towns for reinforcements and then riding all the men to Crestavia Capitalia would be the wiser decision. In the Capital, the King could see to their punishments.

These men were obviously slave traders and King Gadden hated the slave trade business. In fact, when the neighboring nations of Shadenberg and Breckenride grew stronger and more powerful off the backs of their oppressed slaves, King Gadden made the choice not to compete economically by joining their slave trading, but instead condemned it. Kendry knew that the battles her father was famous for were due to the slave trade business and King Gadden's attempt to stop it. For slave traders to become so bold as to enter towns so close in vicinity to Crestavia-Capitalia, it would be seen as a direct attack on the king, himself.

As they walked the men closer to the beach, Kendry's heart sunk with pain. She wanted her dad to be there to see what they had accomplished. She knew he would've been outraged over these men entering their village. She needed him to come back. She wondered if the ambush on him and his men had been in relation to the slave trading business moving into Crestavia. Though, she still didn't believe he was dead. He'd be there when they got back to help them deal with all this. He'd have to. She just couldn't accept the alternative.

As if knowing the thoughts in her head, Mister Lansing stepped aside from the man he was helping to drag, and motioned to Kendry that he wanted to talk with her privately.

They walked off to the side and ahead a bit. She knew Mister Lansing was going to give her a pep talk. That's what he did. He was always an encouraging, kind man. But he was also extremely patriotic and tough. She wondered if he believed that her dad was actually gone, or if somewhere in that compassionate heart of his, he actually believed as she did.

"Kendry, there's something I need to show you," he began. The tone in his voice caused her stomach to tighten. He sounded like he was walking on egg shells and afraid to reveal something painful.

He slipped his hand into his pocket and pulled out a necklace. Her eyes widened. It was her father's medallion locket. It never left his neck. Ever. It was a medal he had earned after helping King Gadden win the war against Shadenberg that kept them away from Crestavia for the next twenty years. A friend who was a blacksmith had altered it to become a locket of sorts. With great force it could open and reveal a tiny slot. He had also had it put on a chain. General Walbrek always wore the medallion. Kendry had never seen him without it. Only once, had he shown her that it opened and what was inside.

"Kendry, this piece of medal is the most important non-living thing in my life," *he had told her. He used his strength and pried it apart until a crack became* *obvious. Kendry had been around twelve and had asked him if she could wear* *it for her birthday dinner.*

"Inside here is a lock of your mother's hair. The only thing, besides you, I have *left of her. In addition, I put a small lock of your hair the day she died in here.* *That way, no matter where I am, I will always have a piece of both of you with* *me." His usual thundering voice was calm and slow as he explained this. She* *could tell that it was very sentimental to him.*

"So...I guess that means I can't wear it?" she asked, still hoping.

"Unfortunately, Kendry, the only time you will ever get to wear this necklace is *after I have passed on to the eternal kingdom. Once my body lives no more,*

you can wear it proudly, remembering how much I loved you and your mother."

Looking at the medallion in Mister Lansing's hand, Kendry started to shake.

"Wh-where did you get that? It wasn't with the letter from the king…"

"No, it wasn't."

Mister Lansing swayed back and forth, nervously looking for a way to respond. "When you attacked that guard and we were putting him into that wooden box, I thought to search his pockets for weapons. It was…it was in his pocket."

"No," she whispered. There was no way her dad would've allowed anyone to take that medallion and live. It was his most prized possession other than her. Her arm started trembling.

He was dead.

He had to be. She couldn't hold it in. Tears started trickling down her cheeks. Mister Lansing placed a hand on her shoulder and then turned toward Tarah hinting for her to come comfort Kendry.

Kendry walked off as Tarah started heading toward her. She walked for a while, toward the beach and plopped herself down on the sand, wanting to be alone. Tears were now streaming down her face. Anger bubbled up inside her. She wanted to scream. She shook her head and forced herself to gain control. Right now, wasn't the time to mourn. She needed to stay alert and focused. But her heart felt like it had just been cut out. She suddenly desired to get her hands on the neck of the man who had her father's necklace in his pocket! He was still alive in that wooden box. She would get answers from him!

Kendry looked over her shoulder and saw that her friends were taking the two men they had locked in the wooden box back toward the other bound men. Tarah gained the courage to come toward her. She took a deep breath and sat down next to Kendry. "Let's leave the men to take care of the rest of this. You and I can head back on our own and talk."

Kendry didn't feel like talking. She needed answers. She stood up, ready to face the men.

Tarah got up, too, and walked past Kendry to her father to let him know they were ready to head out. She completely missed the fact that Kendry had other plans. Hendrick walked up and filled the void where Tarah had just been.

"I'm so sorry, Kendry," he started. "I..." He was interrupted by Tarah's scream.

It all happened so fast. Two men appeared out of nowhere. They killed Shalia's father, stabbing him right in the heart. They grabbed Mister Lansing and swung a sword at his neck. He collapsed, blood everywhere. The whole group was down in the blink of an eye. Shalia's brother, Farmer Tinminn, and the twins lay unmoving. Only Tarah still stood, shocked and frozen. The men were already untying the seven other men.

Instinct took over and Kendry and Hendrick ran. They ran fast. They kept running. Kendry's wet clothes slushing in the breeze didn't slow her down. Once in the thick of the forest, they finally stopped.

The men hadn't gone after them.

Kendry started to climb up a tree so she could get a look out and see where they were. Unfortunately, as she began climbing, they heard other recognizable screams. Shalia's scream. Mrs. Jamison's scream. Madame Lansing's cries. Even Marvin's voice yelling.

Kendry paused as her heart felt like it was going to burst from the pain of hearing those screams. She forced herself to continue climbing. She could see out to the wharf. There were more men who were dragging all the women and children back onto the boat. From Tavern's End, the only men that seemed to be alive were Marvin, Mister Carter and a badly hurt Frederick. They were outnumbered and being put back onto the boat with the women and children. The other bodies were being dragged onto the boat, as well. She watched for a few minutes, until the boat pulled its anchor and took off into the bay.

Kendry slowly climbed down. Hendrick, eager with anticipation, looked at her.

"What's the plan?" he asked. "How do we get them back?"

Kendry just stared into the distance.

"We don't."

CHAPTER EIGHT

The walk back to the tavern had been painfully quiet. The horror of all that happened threatened to drown both Kendry and Hendrick. There was nothing left to be said aloud. They both knew it was hopeless. Their friends were either dead or gone. They forced one foot in front of the other, trudging through the forest.

Kendry couldn't stop thinking about her dad. And each time she did, hopelessness sunk over her.

She was already feeling guilty that she hadn't run toward Tarah as she was screaming. She had let her friends down. But, deep down she knew that if she had run back toward seven men, some of which were armed, she would be on that boat captured, as well. Or dead. Yet, she should've tried. Guilt was making it hard to breathe. The feeling of not knowing if she could have helped was worse than if she had been killed.

Hendrick wasn't quite as numb as Kendry. His emotions were raging with questions about what came next. Anxiety rising above any shock, he had to stop a couple of times to ensure he didn't pass out. He couldn't believe all he had witnessed and selfishly wished Kendry had never found Marvin and him at their campout. What would they do now? They'd reach out to Galvenland or Glenville and let them know what happened, but then what? Someone would take them in, right? Would Hendrick try to stay and run the stable by himself? There would still be people passing through that would need help.

Would others come and take over working at the tavern? Would the king send more men to the Academy? Where would Kendry go?

The questions plagued him, though he didn't ask a single one aloud. For now, he wanted to go home. He wanted to feel safe. Though he wasn't sure he'd ever feel safe again back at the small cottage he shared with Mister Carter. His chest physically hurt as he thought about Mister Carter. He'd never see the kind, old man again.

Continually looking over his shoulder as if he expected more men to jump out of nowhere and attack them, Hendrick followed Kendry through the forest. He knew, realistically, with the boat gone, the threat of attack was probably gone, too. It was morning now, and very unlikely that slave traders would come back.

They finally arrived at the tavern, hesitant to enter. The door was left wide open. Finally, they dared to go inside and Kendry began looking around. She headed upstairs and checked to make sure there were no signs of anyone or that anyone else had been there. She checked the kitchen and made sure the trap door to the tunnel leading to the Academy was still hidden.

Hendrick collapsed on a sofa in front of the fireplace between the dining area and the downstairs inn quarters. He lay there, eyes closed, trying not to think. His lean body was beyond exhausted and he just wanted to sleep for a few minutes. Kendry saw him lying there, and decided that closing her eyes for a moment wouldn't be such a bad idea. She sat down in a big fur armchair and lay back, trying to hold in tears. Time passed and she eventually fell asleep, too.

The door creaked and somewhere in Kendry's dream-like state she knew she was being watched. She jumped up, heart racing, and found herself face-to-face with a big man with an aged face and unruly gray hair.

She took a deep breath of relief. It was old Mr. Ordin from Galvenland.

"What's going on?" he asked, perplexed at the scene before him. "The tavern closed today?"

Kendry collapsed back down into the chair. Hendrick was awake and she looked to him for help. Communicating was not going to come easily for her today. Hendrick calmly explained that they had been attacked by slave traders, most likely from Shadenberg, and that only the two of them had escaped.

"The whole town's gone?" the man asked as if he thought they were crazy.

Kendry nodded, since he had turned his attention back to her.

"Oh, hay barrels! Wait until King Gadden gets word of this! Mister Lansing? Madame Lansing?"

"Gone," Hendrick barely mumbled. Kendry was glad he hadn't mentioned that Mister Lansing was gone in more than the sense of having left on a boat. She couldn't bear to think about how she had witnessed his murder.

"Mind if I grab a drink?" Mr. Ordin asked as he headed toward the bar. Kendry rolled her eyes. Her whole world was just destroyed and old Mr. Ordin had to get his alcohol fix before attempting to show sympathy for the hell she and Hendrick were experiencing. She thought about what Tarah would've thought if she told her about this, as they both shared a ton of inside jokes about Mr. Ordin and all the other regular customers that came through. But, thinking of Tarah just caused a stab in her heart and she closed her dark green eyes and rested her head back on the chair.

He came back with a mug full of ale and sat down in a chair opposite Kendry.

"Well," he began. "Guess I'll have to head back to Galvenland and get the word out. Everyone will need to be on alert. We'll have to send word to Glenville, too. You two won't be safe here, alone. You'll probably need to come back with me. Got horses?"

Kendry looked at Hendrick. She had no idea where the horses were that Marvin had led the townspeople back on before they got ambushed. She knew there were plenty of 'secret' horses at the Academy. But she wasn't planning on leaving anytime soon.

"We'll stay here today and sleep here tonight. Got to close up the tavern. Lock things up around town. The slave traders left by boat. They'd be crazy to come back so soon with everyone on alert. I think we're probably safer here than anywhere," she explained.

"Hmph," Mr. Ordin responded while nodding. "Prob'ly true. Well, let me know if you need anything. I'll send some of the women out tomorrow to help you sort through stuff and some of the young men to help board things up. There might be someone to step in and help out at the tavern until it runs out of supplies."

"We can manage here for a few days," Kendry stated matter-of-factly. She didn't need a bunch of people from Galvenland flooding Tavern's End with their sympathetic looks or covetous eyes. She could just imagine them picking apart their small village. Tavern's End would be no more.

Old Mr. Ordin wasn't in much of a rush to leave and sipped his drink while another customer arrived. Kendry went and found the 'closed' sign to post outside. She didn't feel like serving drinks or rehashing the night's events to every person wandering through town. Mr. Ordin and Hendrick, though, seemed up to the task and updated the other man that arrived.

The rest of the day continued with people popping in to give their condolences and asking questions. Everyone wanted to know as many details as possible. Kendry's head was spinning. She was thankful that Hendrick seemed to have his wits about him and was able to handle most the conversations. At some point in the day, she made her way upstairs and sunk onto a bottom bunk ignoring conversations that trickled in from downstairs. She ran her fingers over her dad's medallion. She had been wearing it since that morning, but hadn't really had time to examine it. It was beautiful. Brushed silver metal with a lion stamped into it. It reminded her of her incredible father. He was brave, courageous, and strong like a lion. He even sort of resembled the beast with his unruly thick, long hair and broad, muscular build.

A couple of men laughed down below. It made her sick that customers still came in and grabbed drinks and socialized while her pain was drowning her. She wished they would all just leave.

Her wish came true in the late evening. The last passerby finally exited after telling them how sorry he was for their losses. Hendrick rounded up some food for them to eat. They ate in silence, both staring out into space. After dinner, they collapsed back in the foyer and fell asleep, drained. Somewhere in the middle of the night, Kendry awoke. Numb to the emotions suffocating her, she just lay there staring at the ceiling. She realized that she and Hendrick would need to go up to the Academy and bury the bodies of the guards that were dead there. The thought literally made her sick to her stomach.

She shook her head wishing she could just undo everything that had happened over the last couple of days. What she wouldn't do to see her dad again! Or even give Tarah a hug. The injustice of knowing her friends were taken against their will, to who knows where, left her so agitated she had to sit up. Her fists were balled up in anger and she had to forcefully calm herself down.

Forcing herself to lay back down, Kendry rehashed the many times she heard her dad and Malark discuss the evil slave trading business. People would be taken from their homes, in the middle of the night, never to be seen again. They would be sold to the highest bidders at auctions in border towns like Regaria or Frankton. Those towns were targeted by King Gadden for years, but when spies out of her dad's Academy spent time there, they found the corruption went far past the tiny border towns. Shadenberg funded the criminal activity and the lack of law and order encouraged gangs of criminals to create their own mini militias to keep the business running. The border towns became hubs for black markets, illegal gambling, prostitution, and drug trafficking. Bounty hunters and bookies were commonplace in border towns, too.

General Walbrek had fought many battles against this corruption decades ago trying to stop the evil practices from spreading to neighboring nations. The way Kendry understood it, the nations surrounding Crestavia had gotten very strong and powerful due to the kidnapping of innocent people and turning them into slaves. The slaves had mined coal and minerals, worked the lands, and built cities, causing Crestavia to fall behind in economic power.

King Gadden had been pressured to join in the slave trade practice in order to compete, but stood strongly against it. Instead, he and General Walbrek had used the Academy to train up an elite group of spies from Crestavia that were sent to live in all the neighboring nations. Over time, many of the spies became trusted servants of the other nations' kings and leaders. They incited rebellions when weaknesses were discovered in the nations where they were stationed as spies. Once riots and rebellions spread, King Gadden would send in General Walbrek and the army to take over the nations.

King Gadden had succeeded with many victories. Some of the nations they overcame, joined Crestavia. Others, created their own new governments with King Gadden overseeing their safety. All slave trading in these places had been stopped and the goal was to let people go back to their homes. This was one of the reasons why General Walbrek was famous. Many oppressed people saw him as their hero. He was the symbol of the freedom they had received from their slavery. But, other nations, such as Shadenberg, saw King Gadden and him as instigators who attacked and destroyed small towns and nations. And, slave trading still happened throughout lands outside of Crestavia's reach. Over the past ten years, General Walbrek had retired from leading the army and had settled down at the Academy permanently. Obviously, slave trading was on the rise again.

It was no coincidence that the men that killed her father and targeted his spies were slave traders. Word had been brewing that a war was coming with Shadenberg. In fact, it was all Kendry heard about while working at the tavern for months. Seemed every person passing by had information to share or request regarding the attack everyone assumed would be coming. Kendry knew word would spread fast to King Gadden that Tavern's End was attacked and King Gadden, knowing the Academy was secretly located there, would understand that this was more than a random kidnapping. In addition to the news that General Walbrek and his men were dead, King Gadden would surely push for war.

It hit Kendry for the first time that the note from King Gadden was probably code. King Gadden was probably aware of the real way her father and his men had been attacked and it definitely was not from bandits. This was a planned coordinated attack. Kendry shook. Without her father there to lead, would Crestavia win?

Something moved outside the window. Kendry froze. She slowly looked over at Hendrick. He was still asleep. She hadn't imagined it. She had definitely seen something outside the window move. But what she saw was too tall to be an animal. It was probably another traveler who got close to the tavern before realizing it was closed. She stood up and carefully looked out the window. There was no one there. No horses. No movement. Completely empty. If it had been a traveler, she would see them leaving down the cobble stone path. But there was nothing.

Goosebumps rose on her arms. Something inside told her to get a weapon. She grabbed a sword that had been resting behind the chair she had been sitting in. Quietly, she walked past Hendrick, not wanting to wake him, and put her hand on the door latch. Slowly and silently, she slid it to unlock the door. Then, she carefully placed her hand on the handle and pulled the door open. It creaked a little and the breeze from outside rushed in. She peeked her head out and looked around. No one was there. She boldly stepped out and made her presence known to anyone who might be hiding.

"Anyone there?" she said quite loudly. No response.

She walked out a few steps and looked around more. The cold air sliced through her thin shirt. Her eyes scanned the area in front of the building and along the path ahead. She finally got up the nerve to walk to the end of the tavern and look along the side. There was no one around. An owl hooted off in the distance and some critter scurried in a nearby bush, but otherwise she was alone.

Kendry relaxed a little. Her mind was playing tricks on her. She decided to go back in and thought it would be a good idea to go upstairs and sleep in one of the bunks, since her neck was sore from the chair. Her ankle still ached from where she had fallen on it when she landed on the men, and lounging around all day had stiffened it. She limped back toward the entrance, but abruptly stopped.

She slowly walked toward the window that looked in on where she had been asleep. There, in the mud under the window, was a fresh footprint.

CHAPTER NINE

The next morning Kendry got tea started for her and Hendrick. She was completely exhausted as she had never fallen back to sleep after finding the footprint. She chose not to tell Hendrick about it. Whoever had been there was gone now. Hopefully it was a traveler who just looked in the window and quickly left. Something told Kendry that wasn't the case, but she was choosing not to dwell on it now that the sun was up.

They had decided they wanted to leave the tavern early before people started to drop by. She left a note letting travelers know that they were closed and would be back that evening after working to secure their town. Their plan was to go to the Academy first and dig graves for the guards.

They traveled through the secret tunnel, but it felt eerie. Hendrick made small talk to help keep their minds distracted. He had only been to the Academy once before when he was younger. His father had taken him before he had passed. He told Kendry that his father had been friends with her dad before either of them had moved to Tavern's End. In fact, he got the feeling that his parents moved to Tavern's End at the request of her father. Kendry had never heard that and didn't know why her father would want his parents there, but realized she didn't know much about her dad's social life outside the Academy. She could remember Hendrick's father and her dad chatting at the tavern. Maybe they had been good friends. Hendrick asked Kendry questions about the Academy. Kendry wasn't really in the mood to chat, but she responded politely until they arrived.

"We'll need to get shovels from the shed outside the stables. I'll show you where I think the best spot to dig will be," she instructed as they headed toward the gate to enter. She knew from when she and Marvin had been there that it was going to be hard to see the bodies of the men at the gate. She warned Hendrick, hoping that it wouldn't be so shocking if he knew what to expect.

But, when they got there, Kendry froze. Eyes widened, she stuttered something.

"What?" Hendrick asked, confused by her actions.

Kendry looked all around. They were gone. The bodies were gone. There was no evidence that they had ever been there. She kicked around the dirt where she knew Officer Lew's body had been. She found evidence of blood buried under it.

"They're gone!"

"What?"

"The bodies. They're gone!" she exclaimed. "This is where they were. They were dead. Here. They..are...are gone..." She ran through the gate and desperately began looking behind things and under stuff.

"What does that mean?" Hendrick asked, suddenly looking afraid. "Does that mean someone's here?"

Kendry paused. No, that wouldn't make sense. Would it? Her brain scrambled trying to understand what was happening. When she and Marvin had come that night to get help and weapons, the bodies were here. Now they weren't. Would the slave traders have come back for them? Maybe they were trying to hide evidence that Shadenberg had discovered the Academy? She ran her fingers through the top of her unbraided hair, fumbling for words to say. None of this made sense.

"Let's get out of here," she said. Hendrick was quick to agree. They ran out into the forest, choosing to take that route back instead. It was't worth the risk of revealing the hidden tunnel to an unseen onlooker. Kendry's stomach growled. It was loud enough for Hendrick to hear. They had wanted to get such an early start that they had only drank tea and skipped breakfast.

"Why don't we go back to my place, next?" Hendrick suggested. He knew they had food available and he was eager to see if there was any struggle left by Mister Carter when he had been taken. They both stayed on alert, not knowing if they were actually alone in town or not.

Arriving at the house, Hendrick got choked up realizing he'd never see Mister Carter again. The kind blacksmith had taken him in when both his parents died of the same sickness. He had always been wonderful to Henrdrick, training him as an apprentice and giving him a place to sleep and food to eat. There was no reason why Mister Carter should've taken on the responsibility of caring for him. Usually, it would've been a woman in town to adopt that responsibility, but Mister Carter saw the advantage of teaching Hendrick a skill and Hendrick believed the man enjoyed his company as much as Hendrick benefited from his care.

Kendry followed behind Hendrick. She had never been past the front porch of Mister Carter's cottage, though she'd been in his blacksmith shop and the stables plenty of times. The house was tiny. There was one main room about half the size of the loft Kendry slept in at the inn. The room consisted of a kitchenette area and a small table with two chairs. An open doorway led to a fork opening to two more rooms. Each tinier than the one prior, the rooms barely fit a bed and desk.

Hendrick was busy overlooking everything, trying to look for any inconsistent alignment or placement of furniture or items to tell some sort of story of what had happened there. But he concluded that everything looked pretty much normal. A drawer was open in the kitchen that normally would've been closed, but there was no way to know if he or Mister Carter had just left it open. Kendry wandered into Hendrick's tiny room. The desk was covered with hand-drawn pictures. There were charcoal and blank scrolls of paper spread about the floor around the desk.

"These yours?" she asked.

"Yes," he answered. "Mister Carter likes to read in the evenings and I'm not very good at reading. So, he's encouraged me to draw." Embarrassed, he tried to scoop up some of the pictures, but Kendry was already flipping through piles of them. She couldn't believe what she was witnessing. They were very detailed portraits of everyone in town.

"They're so life-like," she exclaimed, amazed. "You drew these? I can't believe I didn't know you could do this!"

Hendrick's face heated up with embarrassment. He had never told anyone about his talent for drawing. Artistic abilities weren't really praised in a town that found its identity in elite military training.

"Thanks," he mumbled as he cleaned up around his room.

"These are just unreal," Kendry added. "She looked at the drawing of Tarah and had to control her emotions. "Can I have this?" she asked desperately.

"Yeah, sure," he said actually flattered that she liked it and glad that it would memorialize Tarah. Then, she turned to the one of her father. A tear slipped down her cheek as she stared at it. It looked exactly like him. The portrait even showed the medallion around his neck. She ran her finger across the page and felt such a surge of pain wishing she could see him again. She looked up at Hendrick and he nodded. She took the portrait out and set it aside with the one of Tarah. She continued flipping through the pictures, amazed at each one.

"Hey," she said sounding annoyed. "Why don't you have one of me?"

"Huh?"

"There's a picture of every single resident of Tavern's End...except me."

"It's there. I've done one of everyone. Mister Carter challenged me to do the whole town. I did everyone our age first. They're all in that pile," he said pointing to the group she was looking through.

"Well, it's not here," she responded. She was a bit frustrated because she wanted to see if it would look as incredibly life-like as everyone else's portrait. Giving up, she moved on to Mister Carter's small room, examining the books he had on his desk.

Hendrick went through every single picture in the pile. Kendry was right. It was not there. He flipped through them again, this time taking each one and placing it on his bed. The portrait of Kendry was missing. He racked his brain. Would he ever have moved it? Did Mister Carter ever look at it? No. It was always here. Kendry's portrait should've been right by Tarah's. The fact that it was missing bothered him. He moved into Mister Carter's room and begin searching in and under things.

"What are you looking for?" Kendry asked.

"Your portrait," he responded, a bit distracted. He moved into the outer room and searched there. "It's really strange that it is missing."

"Well, I doubt anyone broke in and stole a picture of me," she said a bit sarcastically. But Hendrick was thinking that maybe someone did. There was no way that picture would've disappeared on its own.

Kendry was getting bored of the little cottage, knowing there was so much more to do and a chance that there could be danger lurking anywhere in Tavern's End. She suggested they go to widowed Farmer Tinminn's next, since it was close by. Thinking about the twins made her sad. Hendrick took one last look around and agreed. He went back into his room and opened his desk drawer. Fumbling through his few possessions, he took out the only portrait he had of his parents. He didn't know who had drawn it, but Mister Carter told him it was most likely his mother as she was a very talented artist. He folded up the portrait and put it in his pocket. He grabbed a bag and stuffed it with some clothes and things. He figured he'd rather stay at the tavern for the time being.

They spent the rest of the day going from home to home, searching for anything out of place and locking up residences. They also boarded up windows and took valuables back to the tavern with the intention of eventually hiding them all at the Academy. Walking through each home was haunting. There was something eerie about knowing that the people who had lived there left their residences so suddenly and would never be coming back. Mrs. Jamison's slippers were still by her bed and the sheets were opened up as if she had planned to slip right back in. Quite a few times Kendry and

Hendrick found themselves overwhelmed with emotions and had to sit down and just process all that had happened.

Finally, as the sun was setting, they went back to the tavern. They both took their spots in the sitting area where they had slept the previous night and just sort of pouted. Collectively, they were mourning the loss of their town. One of them would bring up someone or something from the daily life in Tavern's End and the other would comment. Then it would be silent until someone had another thought to share. They laughed at the silly way Shalia's mother was always shouting at one of her kids and never seemed to know where they all were. They cracked up over pranks the Tinminn twins had committed and the time Mister Lansing finally turned the tables on them and they ended up from head to toe in horse manure. They both agreed that Shalia was one of the sweetest souls to ever live and Marvin would've had a great career in the army.

They were reminiscing about Farmer Tinminn's harvest traditions when the sound of a horse galloping interrupted them. It came right up to the tavern. They were both up on their feet looking out the window as Abigail hopped off the horse and burst through their door.

Abigail was a friend from Galvenland. Her parents ran a convenient store where all the citizens of Tavern's End shopped and got supplies. Kendry had expected at some point that Abigail and her parents would come check on Kendry and Hendrick, but it was odd that she was arriving like this at this time in the evening.

"You have to go!" she yelled at them. "Now!"

CHAPTER TEN

What's going on?" Kendry asked eagerly.

"You have to leave NOW! The king's soldiers are coming to arrest you. You don't have much time!"

Kendry looked at Hendrick, confused. What was Abigail talking about?

"What?" Hendrick asked.

"Look, all I know is that soldiers sent from the king are in Galvenland. They stopped at our shop and were getting a drink at the pub. They said they were on their way to Tavern's End to arrest Kendry for aiding and abiding slave traders for profit. They said that they have proof that you were working undercover with Shadenberg and are the reason why the town was kidnapped."

"What!" both Hendrick and Kendry yelled. "That is insane!" Kendry added.

"I know," Abigail responded looking out the window. "My parents and, well, everyone in the pub for that matter, tried telling them that. It makes zero sense. My mom thinks King Gadden isn't ready to go to war yet, so to save face he is blaming the kidnapping on you, trying to make it seem like an isolated event because you accepted bribes to help them."

"This is crazy!" Kendry responded. "There is no way the king believes I did something like that! And there is no way anyone else would ever believe it either, right?" She turned to Hendrick for a response.

He shook his head, but looked out the window behind Abigail concerned that soldiers might arrive any second.

"Look, Kendry, I rushed here. But they were finishing up their drinks. They have a warrant for your arrest and said you are to be taken to the palace for sentencing. They are calling you a traitor to Crestavia. I honestly don't think they are going to listen to common sense. You need to get out of here!"

At that, they all fell silent. But the silence was broken by the sound of horses in the distance.

"Thanks, Abigail! Get out of here so they don't try to implicate you!" Kendry commanded her. She then looked at Hendrick and they both ran to the back of the kitchen. The king's soldiers might know about the Academy, depending on their security level. But the Academy was the only place they could think of to hide. They quickly ran through the tunnel after securing the trap door in place. Unless they knew about its location, it would not be discovered under its attached carpet.

Out of breath, they arrived at the Academy. The last time they had been there, they had been quick to want to leave. But this time, there didn't seem to be another choice.

Hendrick helped Kendry push the gate closed and they bolted it. He followed Kendry, eyes darting right and left, as she ran to her father's quarters. Ignoring the destruction done to the place she used to feel safest on earth, she quickly pushed a small bookshelf away from the wall. Sliding her hand down, she counted the bricks following a pattern she had memorized. Once a particular brick was located, Kendry shoved it as hard as she could. She asked Hendrick to help. Confused, he helped her push. Finally, she decided to kick it instead. It loosened just enough. She wiggled it and eventually was able to dislodge it. Behind it was a lever. Taking a deep breath, she pushed down on the stiff lever. A noise popped across the room. She quickly put the brick back in place and shoved the bookshelf back in front.

Next, she grabbed paper from her father's desk, a feather pen, and an ink well. Keeping an ear out for noise evidencing anyone finding them, she scribbled a note down. It read:

Dad,

I am heading to Aunt Thelma's for safety. She's agreed to hide me. Don't worry I can handle the hike through the Cascadia Mountains. I don't plan to come back. When you are home safe, send for me at Thelma's.

Love, Kendry.

She shook the parchment to help the ink dry. Then folding it neatly, she placed a wax seal over the fold, rubbing it with her thumb to secure it. She carefully penned the word 'father' on the front and left the note on her dad's bed, tucked under his pillow.

Kendry then rushed across the room to a small rug in front of a desk. She pulled up half the rug and pulled a panel from the floor.

"We're going to hide down here," she said to Hendrick. He was relieved to see they had a hiding place. He'd been concerned soldiers could burst through the door at any second. He climbed down through the hidden hole. Kendry followed him into the darkness.

"Don't worry. Even if they were to find this spot, there is no way in without pulling the lever hidden in the bricks. My father had this hide-out created for us in case we ever needed to be kept safe. Only he and I know about it."

Hendrick put his arms out in front of him and felt around. It was dark, but spacious. Upon investigation he found weapons and even jars of food and bottles of water. General Walbrek had been prepared.

They sat there in the hidden basement for almost an hour. Hendrick began wondering if they should leave, but Kendry knew there was nowhere else to hide if what Abigail had said was true. They pondered the information Abigail had given them. Neither of them could understand how word had spread to the palace about the slave traders or how that information had gotten reinterpreted to say Kendry had something to do with it. It just made no sense.

"How far is it to your Aunt Thelma's?" Hendrick asked.

"Huh?" Kendry responded. But then she realized he was referring to the note. "Oh, I don't have an Aunt Thelma. And my father is dead. That note was simply to throw the soldiers off our trail. Maybe they'll read it and think I've ran off. Hoping it will cause them to head into the Cascadia Mountains and throw them off my scent."

Hendrick was impressed. Kendry really thought of everything.

"Off OUR scent," he said.

"What?"

"You said, that it would throw them off YOUR scent. I was just correcting you. It would throw them off OUR scent. There are two of us, ya know?" Hendrick stated.

"Yes, but when I go on the run for my life, it will just be me. I'm not risking your life. You will be able to stay here or live in Galvenland or Glenville. Apparently, I'm going to be a fugitive and an orphan."

"You are not leaving me here," he said seriously and with more boldness than Kendry had ever heard from him. "I have nothing left here. My family is gone. My friends are gone. My life as I knew it is over."

Kendry felt bad that she hadn't thought about Hendrick's hurting, at all. He was an orphan, even before this. And the man who had cared for him was now gone.

Hendrick continued, "Look, you and I haven't been the closest of friends, but we are friends. If the king's soldiers can't find you... they could suggest I had something to do with kidnappings, too. I'm not safe staying here, either. You have to let me go with you. Wherever it is you're going...I'm assuming you have a plan?"

"Not exactly," she said. "And...your life will be in danger if you come with me, Hendrick. I think you should really reconsider."

"Kendry….DO NOT leave me behind. Do you understand me?" The seriousness in his eyes held her gaze. He looked as hopeless and helpless as she felt.

She nodded. They were in this together.

Just then, they heard a noise. They hushed each other and sat perfectly still. Yes, more noises. And more. There were definitely people up above. After a few moments it became obvious that they were in her father's room right above them. There was talking and furniture being moved. Hendrick's heart raced so loud he was sure Kendry could hear it. Kendry stared up at the ceiling, frozen in anticipation of what would happen. Feet stomped overhead. They weren't leaving. More boots pounded entering the room and someone in charge ordered the others with a loud yell.

"Open it!" he exclaimed. Kendry and Hendrick braced themselves.

CHAPTER ELEVEN

The order from one of the soldiers was loud. He was telling the other men to open the trap door. Or was he? After torturously waiting to see if they were found, Kendry realized he was ordering them to open the note. They listened as intently as they could, but it was muffled and difficult to decipher. The conclusion Kendry came to was that the men had discovered and read the note. It appeared they must've believed it, because the sound of their boots headed out of the room.

Kendry and Hendrick stayed in silence for at least fifteen or twenty minutes after the last footstep had left. Finally, Kendry whispered that they should sleep there. It was late evening and if they were going to be on the run, they needed rest and time to be sure the soldiers were really gone.

Hendrick found a cot in the corner and realized Kendry was making herself comfortable in another one. She tossed him a wool blanket. The General really had thought of everything. Hendrick cozied up in the cot and closed his heavy eyes. What in the world were they going to do when they awoke? Not having a plan was killing him, but he was so exhausted from the emotional day and finally felt safe down in this bunker that he allowed himself to pause on worrying and fell into deep sleep.

Kendry kept one ear open for quite a while, listening for any strange noises above. Finally, she forced herself to get some rest, too. Before drifting off, she thought about the day her dad had showed her that secret bunker. She had been very young. He wanted to be sure she understood that the hidden room was a secret from everyone and that only the two of them would ever know about it. He had told her that he had made many enemies and that if any of them ever retaliated, he needed to know that Kendry could hide and be safe.

At the time she had thought it was mysterious and exciting that she and her dad had their own secret place to hide. Never, over all her years, did she really think she'd ever need it. First off, her father was loved and respected by everyone she'd ever met. Secondly, she didn't expect that she would ever be accused of a crime.

Her eyelids fluttered closed as she thought about King Gadden. She had never met the royal highness, but had heard plenty about him when her father and Malark spoke politics and business. They both respected the king and rarely had anything bad to say about him. It didn't make sense to her that he would think she was a traitor.

Kendry rolled over in the cot. She felt restless. There were so many questions. She'd need to find out what was true and what wasn't. How did her father really die? What was King Gadden's plan regarding Shadenberg and the slave traders? Why did he believe she would've helped them? None of it made sense. But, for now, there was no solution except to sleep. So, she did.

A few hours later, Kendry woke. She was still extremely sleepy but her mind started racing and once that happened, she knew it was useless to stay laying there. It was the middle of the night and probably the best time for she and Hendrick to leave town. She couldn't believe that she would be leaving Tavern's End. She wasn't even sure where they would go. But, as of now, they needed to be prepared for anything.

Mentally, Kendry started to make a list of things she would need to gather and pack for them. They would most likely be traveling for weeks in order to get far enough away to lose the interest of the king's soldiers. She wondered about traveling into a border town like Regaria or Frankton. She knew they were rough places and didn't know how she or Hendrick would do there. But, if they could travel through unnoticed and unharmed, they could escape to Mestode or Sedonia or somewhere they would be safe from King Gadden's men. She needed to go somewhere that she knew enough of their language and customs to get by. Thankfully, she was raised at an Academy that taught these things, but never did she think she'd actually need them for her residence somewhere.

While Hendrick slept, she placed in a pile two bows and quivers of arrows that were in the corner of the hidden room. She was thankful her dad had weapons hidden away. She also grabbed a dusty bladder for water that was in a crate with many other things. Hendrick heard her moving around, but dreaded getting up. He kept his eyes closed, pretending to sleep, so that he could deny what lie ahead. The unknown.

After a while Kendry realized Hendrick was awake and suggested they venture upward and see what the king's men left behind. She warned that they may have left a guard stationed to lookout for them. Hendrick was nervous, but knew they couldn't stay hidden in this small room forever. He nodded and helped her open up the trap door using a tool that was leaning against the wall.

Slowly, they creaked open the hatch. Kendry stepped up on a crate and peeked out. Everything seemed calm and quiet. She continued to open it until her body could fit through. She gently pulled herself up and sat on the floor in her dad's bedroom, alert and scanning every corner. Hendrick handed her the bow and an arrow. Now armed, she walked around the room and looked out the doorway. Satisfied there wasn't immediate danger, she came back and helped Hendrick up.

Everything was thrashed. The room looked as bad as she felt. She closed her eyes disturbed at the scene before her. Nothing would ever be the same again and she knew it.

After verifying that the note was no longer under the pillow where she had left it, they quietly made their way through a few of the living quarters to collect items Kendry knew they would need. They grabbed duffle bags and backpacks. They loaded up clothes and supplies.

Kendry decided it was time to change her own clothes and went to her old wardrobe in the room winged off her father's quarters. She'd been wearing the same outfit since she was working in the tavern and Lieutenant Trent

75

handed her that note. She had run upstairs crying and collapsed in her clothes, going to sleep in them. She hadn't changed out of them for the last two days. It felt good to put on fresh clean clothes and strap on a well broken-in pair of boots. She packed a wide assortment of clothes not knowing where they would end up or how they'd need to be dressed.

Before leaving her room, she glanced over her dresser and looked at the memorabilia she had collected over the years. So many memories. She picked up a bracelet made of white stones and slipped it over her hand. It lay softly on her wrist, just below her crescent shaped birthmark on her inner forearm. Malark had collected the stones for this bracelet on one of his deployments. He told her that the natives there believed the stones would protect people. He had them make into a bracelet for her by a jeweler in Glenville and gave it to her for sixteenth birthday. She needed protection now more than ever!

Leaving her room, she went back to the main room of her father's quarters and revealed his hidden safe behind a huge shield on the wall. She knew the combination and was able to take out stashes of money in many different currencies. She placed the money in a leather pouch and tied it to her belt, tucking it into her thick long skirt. Unfortunately, it caused a noticeable bulge. Hendrick pointed it out and she agreed they needed a different method to hide the money. After visiting many different rooms, she came back with a few different pouches. She kept the majority of their current currency in the leather pouch in her skirt, but divided out the other money into the other pouches. They each put one in their duffle bags. Kendry told Hendrick to hide one in his pants. The others, she said, they could keep under their horses' saddles in pouches that were there for hidden items.

Next, they rounded up a few more weapons and tools and ropes from the area where Kendry and Marvin had got the axes the night prior. Unfortunately, most weapons still seemed to be missing. She led Hendrick to a storage room of sorts where they each grabbed a make-shift tent bundled up and a small sleeping pack. Their last stop was the cafeteria. They went through the back into the kitchen and packed up as much food as they could find and fit in their backpacks. Skins of water were attached to their packs as well.

Next it was time to go to the stables and find horses. Hendrick was blown away by the stables. He instantly wished he could have worked there instead of at the Tavern's End's stables. There were rows after rows of the most magnificent horses he'd ever seen. Kendry explained that these were 'extras' as most the horses were taken by the men when they left for the training exercise.

They each picked a horse and began loading their items on, which was no easy task. Hendrick picked a beautiful black mare which he immediately named Midnight. Kendry chose a brown horse that she had ridden many times. His name was Chester. Together, Chester and Midnight took Kendry and Hendrick out of the Academy and into the forest where they quietly searched for guards as they began their venture away from Tavern's End.

CHAPTER TWELVE

They'd been traveling for a few days when Kendry made an unusual request. They had only been hiding deep in the forest and as far away from towns as possible, so when Kendry suggested Hendrick go shopping at a supply shop in a village across the valley, it took him by surprise. She orally made a list of supplies she thought they would need moving forward and figured this was just as good an opportunity as any, to get them.

"We're far enough away from Tavern's End that it's less risky than other villages we've passed," she began, trying to convince him that this was a good idea. "That village is on the cross paths of many trails. You won't stick out as being foreign as they are only used to foreigners shopping at their store."

Hendrick reluctantly agreed as long as Kendry promised to stay hidden. It didn't take long by horse to arrive at the quaint supply shop. Hendrick intentionally planned on making this a short shopping trip, so he quickly located the supplies needed and hurried to leave. The only thing he did not get was Kendry's request for caddonberries. He thought the request was ridiculous. They needed to save their money for essential things and caddonberries were a luxury. The dark, sweet berry was eaten as a dessert and definitely was not essential. They were pricey, too. So, he had purposely left that off his mental list as he paid for the other items.

He found it strangely nice to be amongst people again after the past three days hiding out in the forest, though he was extremely nervous they'd get caught. His anxiety had risen with each day they'd been on the run. He desperately wanted to hear a plan or know what their destination would be. What would their future look like? But, Kendry was in survival mode. No decisions were made and no plans were even discussed.

They'd both been rather fragile in regards to their emotions. Their friends were on a fishing boat somewhere heading for who knew where. They'd never see them again. Kendry hadn't even had a chance to process the loss of her father and Malark, who was like an uncle to her. Then, she falsely got accused of being a traitor to Crestavia, causing them to have to leave everything they knew behind. Everything that could possibly be wrong was wrong. At night, Hendrick could hear Kendry's muffled cries. He acted as if he didn't notice because he was trying to stifle his own tears. Heartache and hopelessness swept over both of them.

Maybe that was why when she first had asked for the caddonberries, it had sort of made him angry. It was such a high maintenance request. Their circumstances were dire and she wanted a treat. But as he wandered out of town alone, he reasoned with himself. Maybe caddonberries would cheer Kendry up. Maybe they would give her a glimpse of hope. He realized she needed something to make her smile and this was a simple way to do that. So, when he saw a fruit stand selling caddonberries on his way back toward the forest, he paused, turned toward it and shoveled out the money to buy some for her.

When Hendrick had taken off on Midnight, Kendry had stayed in the outskirts of the forest hidden back behind trees. She was thankful for the alone time to think without Hendrick staring at her. She knew that they needed a plan, but what would that plan be? Her father had been killed and she was dying to know the truth behind his death. King Gadden had issued a warrant for her arrest based on the belief that she had been working with slave traders from Shadenberg. Who would have told him that? What evidence would he have had? If she turned herself in, could she get enough witnesses or find enough proof to convince him of her innocence? She wrestled with question after question until Hendrick arrived back with their supplies.

After packing everything up, they headed back deep into the forest. In the evening, they found a spot to settle. Hendrick set up camp while Kendry took the bow to go hunting. She came back later with a rabbit that they prepared

80

and roasted. Hendrick then took the horses down to a stream to get them hydrated before settling in for the night.

When he came back to their campsite, Kendry was inside her tent. He tied up the horses and announced he was going to go to bed. In response, she exited her tent.

"What do you think?" she asked hesitantly.

Hendrick jumped a little. He was taken back. Kendry's strawberry blonde locks had been died dark brown.

Caddonberries.

She hadn't eaten them. She had squeezed out their dye. She also had cut her hair about half its normal length. He couldn't believe she was the same girl he used to race to the top of the trees. She looked so different with dark hair.

"Good idea," he replied. "You don't look at all like the girl they will be describing to people."

Though he smiled and nodded as he said it, inside his heart was breaking. Even Kendry, the Kendry he knew, seemed gone. It seemed that everything from their old life was dead. He went to bed that night feeling more depressed than he had since the whole thing had begun.

The next morning Kendry awoke extra cheerful. She seemed motivated to get them on the road again and Hendrick noticed the difference immediately.

"Do we have a plan?" he asked, sure that a plan was the only thing that could have put a spring in her step.

"We do, indeed," she responded matter-of-factly. She began rolling up her sleeping pad.

"Do I get to know what it is?"

"I think it would freak you out."

"Well, now I'm definitely freaked out." He stared at her waiting for a response. She just kept packing and moving things around, purposely ignoring him.

"Kendry!"

She stopped what she was doing and looked at him.

"We're headed to Crestavia-Capitalia."

His mouth dropped open in silence. He shook his head. She must be joking.

"Are you insane?" He couldn't believe he just heard those words come from her mouth. "King Gadden's got a warrant out for your arrest! He has soldiers searching for you...and, you wanna march right into the Capital and help him out?"

"We'll be hiding in plain sight," she responded with a smile.

"I'd rather not hide in plain sight," he emphatically countered.

"It's the last place the king would think to look for us. Plus, I need answers. Being in the Capital will help us to hear what is going on. I need to know. Are we close to war with Shadenberg? What are people saying about my father's death? I need answers. And, we'll be able to get jobs in the Capital. We can take care of ourselves and make money. We can continue camping out in the edge of the forest and save up our money..."

"So that's the plan?" he interrupted. "Get jobs and take care of ourselves! Are you kidding? And try our best not to get caught by the king's soldiers...while we're camping and working! This is nuts! You want to just move on and forget our past lives at Tavern's End!" He yelled angrily.

"Of course not!" Kendry responded, obviously annoyed at his anger toward her revelation.

She sat down on a log near her packed-up tent. She looked at him square in the eyes, understanding the anger, frustration, and fear he was feeling at her suggestion to head to the Capital.

"The night our friends were kidnapped I heard the men talking at the tavern, Hendrick." She paused and then continued. "I recognized their language and now that I think about it, I know exactly who they were."

She had his attention. He sat down on a large rock and urged her to continue with the look in his eyes.

"They were speaking Regarian. The language used mostly in border towns. I think the men were bounty hunters, not slave traders from Shadenberg. King Smolden of Shadenberg may have hired them. I don't know. Maybe they were being paid by someone to try to capture my father. He's always told me he has plenty of enemies out there. Or, maybe they were part of the ambush that killed him and after killing him and his men, they thought grabbing a few hostages to sell as slaves would be extra profitable. I know there may be no truth to this theory, but I am choosing to believe it for one reason," she paused to study the expression on his face. He seemed intrigued.

"If it was really Regarian bounty hunters that took our friends, then there is actually a chance we could get them back. They may have been taken to Regaria before being shipped out to whomever bids on them. In Regaria, anything goes. We could try paying bribes for them to be ransomed. And, if they are taken to Regaria by boat, it will at least a month for them to arrive there by sea because they'd have to go down around the Eastern Peninsula. But, by land, we could there in a number of weeks from the Capital."

He looked at her with exhaustion. He had experienced a quick burst of hope, but now realism sunk in.

"Kendry, even if it was Regarians that took them, they probably were taking them straight to Shadenberg...not Regaria. Only King Smolden would want slaves from the kingdom of Crestavia. No one else would be willing to chance a war with King Gadden. Going to the Capital and trying to save up our money to purchase our friends back from hypothetical bounty hunters isn't realistic. Even if by some miracle we had enough money and made it to Regaria without getting killed by bandits or taken by slave traders, there is no way we'd be able to find our friends. Your plan has so many holes in it, it may as well be a sieve."

Kendry shooed away his negativity. "Look, I at least want to go to the Capital and see what the mood is there. I want to get a feel for the latest news. I think getting jobs for a couple of weeks, at least, would be beneficial. We can move on if we don't gain any useful information. But, don't rule out Regaria. If we could get there before harvest season, we might beat that fishing boat back."

Hendrick objected, "That fishing boat could not keep that many people on it for a month. They wouldn't have enough food or water on board. If anything, they were traveling to another sea vessel somewhere. But honestly, I think they were taking our friends back to Shadenberg. Everyone knows King Smolden is picking a fight with King Gadden. He wants Crestavia to attack him so he can obliterate us. Word is Shadenberg's gotten very powerful from the money they've made off all those slaves' backs. He's itching to destroy Crestavia once and for all. King Gadden is the only one standing in his way of spreading his slave trade over the whole continent."

Kendry sighed. She knew he was right. But she clung to the little bit of hope that she might see Tarah and the others again someday. And, she had to do something in the meantime. Running far away with Hendrick to save her own skin was not going to work for her. That is what she did the night the men took their friends away in that boat. She was done running away. If her friends were alive, she had to have a plan to do something to help them. If King Gadden knew anything helpful, she had to discover a way to find that information out. She had no idea what exactly that plan would be, but she knew it began at Crestavia-Capitalia...the capital city.

She clutched the medallion hanging around her neck. In honor of her father, she would not run away.

"I'm going to the Capital, Hendrick," she stated without allowing an argument. "You can stay or come with me or run away or do anything you want. But I am going."

"*WE* are going," he said. Resigned to stick with her, he feared what this meant. But at least they finally had a plan.

CHAPTER THIRTEEN

With an actual plan, both Kendry and Hendrick were more motivated during travel. They made great time finding themselves reaching the Capital in only a few days. Before entering town, Kendry had to change clothes. She knew her village pants and long-sleeved blouse would stand out like a sore thumb in the Capital. At the Academy she always wore pants and modest shirts. But here, those clothes would flag her as a foreigner, for sure. They were trying not to gain attention since the king's men were looking for her, so she put on a rather fancy long skirt that she had packed. She had only worn it once before, to a festival in Glenville. It would be more in line with the fashion in the Capital.

Kendry frowned as she lifted the bottom of the hem of the skirt to get her shoes back on. It was not easy climbing trees with a skirt down to your ankles. But worse, was the shirt. It was fitted and sleeveless except for the capped shoulders. She had also worn it to the festival, but only because her father was away on travel.

General Walbrek would only let Kendry dress modestly at the Academy. He didn't want the men there to get distracted by her. But when at the tavern, she could dress less strictly. For years she would change out of long sleeves to work her shifts there. But then on one occasion, a customer had grabbed her wrist while she was pouring his drink. He took his calloused thumb and rubbed her forearm lightly, encircling her birthmark. She was completely shocked. Looking back, she knew she could have knocked his lights out for touching her. But, at the time, she was trying not to be rude or make a scene.

Knowing what he was doing wasn't right, she tried to pull her arm away, but he tightened a grip around her. He then complimented her reddish blonde hair and pale skin tone. Her inability to move away from him gained the attention of Madame Lansing behind the counter. At the same time, Malark had entered the tavern and noticed what was happening.

Before Kendry could blink, Malark had the guy in a choke hold and was dragging him out of the tavern. She was positive Malark probably beat the man to a pulp although all he said when he came back in was that the man would never come bother anyone at Tavern's End again. Then, rudely, he told Kendry to go put a sweater on. She was frustrated that he implied it was her fault that the perverted and twisted man had assaulted her. But she did as told. From that point on, she'd often put a sweater on when men she didn't recognize visited the tavern. Wearing a shirt now that was so lacking of material made her feel nearly naked. But this is what people wore on hot days at the Capital and she didn't want to stand out.

Flattening the pleats on the skirt and buttoning the neckline of the shirt, she finally came out of the tent. She felt embarrassed, but knew she'd better get used to it. She tried to think of it as a costume worn by a spy as they infiltrated another nation.

Hendrick was shocked to see her looking so different. He still wasn't used to the dark brown hair that had been cut just below her shoulders, and now in those clothes, she just looked so....girlish.

His heart fluttered a little and he looked away.

"How do I look?" she asked hesitantly.

His voice cracked as he answered, "Fine." He busied himself with drawing in the mud with a stick and then added, "No one would ever know you were the same Kendry from Tavern's End."

The statement hurt both of them a bit since it seemed to be concluding their old lives were gone.

The first day in town, they just rode around the Capital checking things out. Hendrick had never been there before and it had been years since Kendry had visited. The sheer amount of people and shops was exhilarating and overwhelming to Hendrick.

They toured the busy downtown area, looking at stores and businesses. They discussed ideas for where to search for work and made note of areas of town that weren't safe for loitering. In late afternoon, they headed back into the forest to try to find a place to 'live'. They knew they might have to move camp often so they wouldn't be discovered. Camping in the forest for travel was acceptable, but living there as a nomad was discouraged by the king's guards. They liked to remove any riffraff from the forest and place them in vagabond camps or refuges.

They found a spot close enough to a water supply, but far enough from the city to feel safe. They discussed everything they had seen and heard through the day as they pitched their tents.

"I don't think it will be difficult to get a job as a stable boy," Hendrick began, not sounding thrilled. "I saw lots of 'help needed' signs at stables outside businesses."

Kendry was roasting a squirrel over their campfire and nodded to show she was listening. She had not had as much success in the job search. She wasn't sure where to begin. She wanted desperately to work somewhere that would lead her to information that would be beneficial to them. But, applying to work at the palace would not only be stupid, but would be useless. Being a servant in the lower ranks at the palace wouldn't exactly afford her an audience with the king. She figured she'd have to see about being a maid for a noble family or for one of the families residing in the wealthier side of town. Working ten hours a day behind the scenes at some aristocrat's house didn't encourage her in her quest to find her friends. It was all feeling useless.

"It's depressing to think that we spent all day in town and didn't hear anything about Shadenberg or my father or anything," she said sounding defeated.

"Did you really expect we would?" Hendrick asked with a tone of rudeness. This plan never made complete sense to him, but he knew Kendry needed to see for herself that being at the Capital wasn't the answer. Plus, the whole time they were in the Capital, Hendrick worried they would be recognized.

The fear of being there all day had worn him down, causing his politeness to wane.

"I had hoped," she responded. The two sat and ate their dinner in silence while the sun set.

Kendry climbed into her tent and Hendrick used a stick to move around some of the burned wood in the fire. Without warning, something leaped into view from behind Kendry's tent. The cat-like animal bared its teeth and hissed at Hendrick. It looked like it was ready to pounce. Hendrick's heart jumped at the initial surprise, but now he froze in terror. Wild cats were not super common in this part of the woods and this one looked desperate for food. Desperation made animals extremely dangerous. He still had the stick in his hand and he lifted it, holding the bottom tight with both hands. His arms shook as he prepared himself to swing at the creature if it lunged at him.

Kendry's head peeked out of her tent and stared at the back of the ferocious feline. The wild cat heard her and whipped its head quickly in her direction. Then it turned back to Hendrick. It showed its teeth again and hissed louder. It was positioned much closer to Hendrick, but didn't like that its back was to Kendry, so it kept uncomfortably twitching in her direction to hiss at her, too.

Kendry slowly stood up. The animal took a step forward and another to its side so it could face its body as much as possible toward both of them. Kendry side-stepped from the tent at a slow and steady speed toward Hendrick. The cat kept hissing. It faked a step forward a couple of times, but didn't leave its spot.

Kendry quickly took the last huge step closer to Hendrick and grabbed the stick from him. As soon as she had it, she yelled loud and jumped toward the wild cat. It leapt with fear backwards, making a crying noise and then took off darting fast into the woods.

Hendrick sighed with relief. The cat was gone. Kendry tossed him the stick back and walked toward her tent.

"Next time, don't wait," she instructed. "Just scare it before it gets a chance to size you up. That one wanted you for dinner," she half-chuckled and slid into her tent to go to sleep for the night.

Hendrick just stood there. He was relieved, of course. But he was getting sick of Kendry saving his life and really sick of her know-it-all attitude when it came to survival.

The next morning, they rode back into the Capital. Hendrick was right about finding work and landed a job easily. He was hired at a stable outside of a busy pub and across from a trading post. There were lots of horses to tie up and release to their owners and plenty of manure to scoop. It was very low pay but the man who overlooked the stables was nice enough and occasionally Hendrick received a tip from a wealthy customer.

It took Kendry a few days longer to gain employment. She discovered that most maids were hired by word of mouth and recommendations. She lucked out one afternoon when she entered the Capital's library to give herself a break from the frustrating job search. As she wandered through the main entrance room, she was shocked to run into a huge replica of her father! There was an exhibit about the great General Walbrek. She read the carefully printed scrolls posted on the wall around the statue. They shared information she had never learned.

"The Great General Walbrek is a symbol of freedom and power to all those in Crestavia. He grew up outside Lumeria in a small town called Skvorton. Showing incredible aptitude for physical challenges, he joined the men of his town in the logging business at age 12. At age 17, he was recruited into the Army. Soon thereafter, Walbrek fought in the Battle of Meadowlark. He quickly rose through the ranks and became a commander in the king's elite sniper teams. After the fall of Cedarloop and the historic win at Folerton, he was promoted to general. At that time, Shadenberg and Breckenride were rising to power through their exploit of hostages turned to slaves. King Gadden made a monumental stand against the slave trade industry and put General Walbrek in charge of ridding the nations of this abuse. General Walbrek organized secret spy missions and gained intel that was used to incite rebellions and create protests against leadership in many nations such as Lumera, Vestacia, Sedania, and Wedorna. The great successes of these rebellions allowed General Walbrek, himself, to lead armies into each nation and destroy their governments. He never lost a battle and was feared by the nations he attacked.

General Walbrek is known for personally releasing hundreds of slaves to go back to their own homelands. Monuments to him have been created and displayed throughout cities all over the continent. General Walbrek is also rumored to have fought five men at once and have won without a scratch upon him. He is believed to be one of the best fighters Crestavia has ever known.

Walbrek's personal life includes growing up in Skvorton, being a logger, and losing both his parents at a young age. At age 20, Walbrek married his sweetheart, Svarkina, but she died at sea while he was away on assignment. From that time on, he focused all his attention on his career. He and King Gadden became close friends.

Sixteen years ago, General Walbrek retired from his post and moved to an unknown location to marry and raise a family. Crestavians have seen him out and about when they stop at a pub for a drink or bet on a horse at the races. He's hailed a hero and will always be Crestavia's favorite fighter!"

Added below on a newer scroll was another inscription. It read:

"A couple weeks ago, General Walbrek's body was found in the forest outside Crestavia. It's believed bandits killed him while he was sleeping. Crestavia honored his life at a memorial service which King Gadden, himself, read the eulogy. This statue was made in his honor and presented at his memorial by King Gadden."

Kendry's head spun from the information she had just read. But, before she could process and question the material, she was interrupted by a man who worked there.

"Can I help you with something?" he asked in the most proper dialect.

"Uh, no, thank you," she responded, politely. She took a few steps toward another exhibit and acted like she was reading the inscription above a tribal head covering.

"That says that the Bulendurian chiefs wear those at their tribal rituals," he began, assuming she couldn't read.

"Yes, I see that," she said annoyed that it was assumed she was illiterate. Then, showing off, she read the Bulendurian inscription in their language that was engraved across the flap that would lie on the forehead. "Savage We Might Be; Stupid We're Not."

The man's head jerked back in surprise. "You familiar with the savage tribe of Bulenduria?" he asked.

"No," Kendry said and then walked away.

Out of the corner of her eye, she could see the man wander over to a woman across the room. The lady had a tight grayish-black bun and a few wrinkles showing her age. She nodded as the man talked to her and then headed Kendry's way.

"Great," Kendry thought to herself. *"I made a scene. Just what someone on the King's 'Most Wanted' list should not be doing. I better get out of here."*

The lady purposely stepped in Kendry's way and introduced herself. She was the librarian and shared with Kendry that her main sponsor had told her that Kendry could read Bulendurian. She wondered how that could be?

Quick to improvise, Kendry explained that she grew up in a traveling circus. She said that her parents were acrobats and she was a tight-rope walker. She figured it wasn't exactly lying as she could walk tight ropes at the Academy from time to time. Just not as a performer in a circus. She mentioned that her parents had died the year prior and she had come to the Capital looking for work. She explained that growing up traveling she had learned many languages and customs and been to many places.

"Certainly, you haven't been to Bulenduria?" the woman asked. "They prefer to kill outsiders that bring 'culture' to their backwards tribe."

"No, we never performed there," Kendry added. "But we did perform in areas nearby, and many people spoke that dialect as well." She hoped the lady would believe her lie. But, just in case the woman pondered her response too long, she redirected the lady's attention to the exhibit of her father.

"I just got to town a couple of days ago. Could you tell me about General Walbrek? I see he died recently. Does anyone think it was in connection to

Shadenberg's threats against Crestavia or the slave traders that captured those poor people from Tavern's End?" She hoped her bold question would gain her information about the rumors going around in Crestavia, but not cause suspicion.

"Oh, those are good questions, my dear," the lady said smiling a bit. "You are very educated, aren't you? Your parents must've given you tutors while you traveled."

Kendry nodded and then waited for a response to her questions.

"Well, it's no secret that Shadenberg has been threatening Crestavia. But rumor is King Gadden was crushed from the news of Walbrek's death because he had hoped Walbrek would lead his troops against Shadenberg. People think that King Gadden was trying to call Walbrek out of retirement and maybe that was why he was in the forest when he was killed. He may have been traveling to see the king." She took a breath and then continued. "But it turns out the people kidnapped from Tavern's End were part of an inside job by a Shadenberg spy who had been working as a handmaiden at the tavern there. She made a bunch of money off those poor people and then took off into the mountains. I'm sure she'll find her way back to Shadenberg someday, but what an awful thing for those people to go through!"

Kendry had to breathe slowly to calm herself. She wanted to yell that it was an awful thing that happened and that 'those people' were her people. Instead, she tucked the scarf around her dyed hair tighter and tried not to make herself stand out more.

"Thank you," she replied. "I'm just going to peek over some of these books before I leave."

But instead, she found herself talking with the lady for another twenty minutes about her pretend education by tutors and imagined travels with the circus. Using her knowledge learned at the Academy of different cultures and places, she was able to pass off that she had visited many nations. She could tell she had the lady convinced and interested. Before she knew it, the librarian was offering her a job there at the library. Her skills in language and academics, but position as an orphan, made her the perfect employee because they could pay her next to nothing, but use her talents to their benefit. She introduced herself as 'Kelly' figuring it was close enough to her real name that she would hopefully remember to answer to it. She gladly accepted the position and began right then by shelving scrolls and books.

With both Kendry and Hendrick working that day, they had little time to interact that evening. They were both hungry and tired. Kendry was glad for the excuse of exhaustion because she really just wanted to lay quietly in her tent and process all she had read about her father.

How much of it was true? Had her dad really been a logger? Why hadn't he ever mentioned that? She knew his parents had died when he was young of illness. She definitely had never heard that he had been married prior to her mother and that his 'sweetheart' had died at sea. That was crazy! It was so strange to think of him having a whole other life before she was ever born.

The library did not seem to know about her mom dying in childbirth or that she existed. She also found it interesting that nobody seemed aware that the supposed traitor from Tavern's End was actually General Walbrek's daughter. The exhibit's explanation of his death must've been crafted by King Gadden himself. She was angry to find that they had a memorial service for him and she hadn't been there. The whole thing led to a mess of emotions.

Trying to get a reign on her feelings so she could clear her mind enough to sleep, she rolled over in her tent. She could hear Hendrick's loud breathing as he slept. Well, they had gotten jobs like she had suggested. They got information, as she had hoped for. Now what? Was this what their future was going to be like? Working and camping. Not a bad life except for the fact that Tarah and their other friends were probably slaves somewhere. That's if they were even still alive. Kendry worried secretly that the men who took them might've just thrown them overboard. Tears welled up in her eyes. Why didn't she do more to try to stop them? Why did she and Hendrick run?

She wished there was some way to know where they had been taken. Were they all split up and sold to different nations? Would they all end up in Shadenberg? Were the men who took them Regarians working for King Smolden or bounty hunters searching for her father? Still so many questions, but it hit her that none of the answers really mattered. When it came down to it, the ending was always the same. Her father and Malark were dead. Her friends were gone. She and Hendrick were in the Capital with jobs and no one realized she was the accused traitor from Tavern's End. How long would that last? What if someone who knew her from Galvenland or Glenville came to the Capital and ran into her? Would they turn her in? Did people back home actually believe the king's lies or was Abigail right and they all knew there was no way Kendry would have done that?

She tried to force herself to relax, but could hear Hendrick up moving around outside his tent. Annoyed, she silently wished he'd go back to bed. Whenever he was up moving around, she felt like she needed to keep an ear out for his safety. Then she realized he was still breathing heavily and sounded asleep. Someone else was outside the tent.

CHAPTER FOURTEEN

Kendry knew the second she sat up in her tent, whoever was outside of it would be aware that she was awake. She listened for a moment and tracked their steps in her mind. Whoever it was, was slowly walking around their campsite. Kendry's duffle bag and backpack were in her tent with her and she knew Hendrick's were with him. The only items lying around the campsite were a few tools for cooking and some clothes hanging to dry. If it was a bandit, they should've been gone by now with the couple of items they could grab. That's when she heard the horses' hooves clobbering around from a distance.

Midnight and Chester were tied up on a tree across their fire pit. If some bandit was trying to take their horses, she was not going to let them! Kendry jumped up and slid out of her tent grabbing her bow. In a flash she had an arrow pulled back and was pointing it at a man who was indeed untying Chester. The man looked at her and slowly placed his hands in the air to show his surrender and that he wasn't armed.

"Step away from my horse!" she said emphatically, emphasizing every syllable. Hendrick was out of his tent now.

"Kendry," he said shakily.

She glanced at him and saw why he sounded scared. Another man, armed with a dagger, had it across Hendrick's throat. He stared down Kendry with complete composure.

"Why don't you drop the bow, Missy," he said condescendingly. "You might hurt someone with that thang."

Kendry kept her aim on the man near the horse. She knew she couldn't swing it around quick enough to aim and shoot the man threatening Hendrick without him killing Hendrick first. The man pulled the blade tighter to Hendrick's throat causing Hendrick to squirm and shudder.

"Okay, okay," Kendry said trying to get him to loosen his blade from Hendrick's throat. She slowly put the bow and arrow down in front of her.

"Good," the man said sounding satisfied. He turned back to his friend who finished untying Chester. He started walking the horse over toward the other man and Hendrick.

The man removed the dagger from Hendrick's neck and gave Hendrick a shove toward the campfire. That was the split second Kendry needed. The moment Hendrick was safe, she charged the man. It took him by complete surprise. He lifted the dagger but Kendry had already kicked his forearm with full force. The dagger flew out of his hand. She punched him square in the face. He moaned and covered his eye.

The other man stepped forward and yanked Kendry's arm. She bent her elbow and wrapped her other arm behind his neck, pulling it down and jabbing her knee into his face. He gasped in pain and let the tightness of his grip on her arm loosen enough that she was able to pull it away. She kicked him in the groin with all her force. Then, turning back to the first man, she kicked him in the groin, too. Both men cowered in pain but looked angrier than ever. Kendry stepped back to retrieve her bow and get a safe distance from the men, but her foot slipped between two tree roots. Not being able to move her foot caught her off guard and she tripped. The men seized that opportunity to take the upper hand. One grabbed the dagger and the other got on the horse.

Kendry knew she couldn't angle her body to get a good enough aim to shoot an arrow at either man, so she instead scooped up the bow and tossed it to Hendrick. She pitched him an arrow and yelled, "Shoot!"

Quickly, she then tried untying her strands keeping her boot on so she could try to slip her foot out. Why hadn't she taken her boots off when she had laid down to relax?

Hendrick, confused by the speed at which everything was happening, attempted to get the arrow poised onto the bow. He lifted the bow and aimed toward the man on Chester. The other man saw him with the bow and quickly hopped on Chester's back, too. The two men galloped away, with Kendry yelling at Hendrick again to shoot and him trying to figure out his aim.

Everything went from hectic to silent in an instance. Kendry stood there staring at Hendrick and he with the bow aimed at nothing. The men were long gone.

As Kendry continued unstrapping her boot and trying to remove her foot, she started yelling at Hendrick. Each sentence got louder and louder.

"Why didn't you shoot? All you had to do was shoot! Did you want them to get away with our horse and a lot of our money? What is wrong with you?"

Shame poured over Hendrick. He was not an expert at a bow. He had done his best to try to quickly aim it so he could shoot, but had simply run out of time with his hands shaking so much. Kendry continued to rail on him.

"Can't you do ANYTHING to help us out here? I have to do EVERYTHING! Would it have been so hard to shoot the wretched man that just held a dagger to your throat? It's YOUR fault our money is gone! And it's YOUR fault Chester is gone! Don't think you are ever riding Midnight again- he's now MY horse!"

Anger poured out of her. All her emotions from the past week swam to the surface. The new information she had received about her dad and missing him, Malark, and Tarah rushed to the forefront of her thoughts. She was angry. Not necessarily even angry at Hendrick. Just angry at everything! So angry. And, Hendrick's idiotic decision not to shoot just gave her an opportunity to let that anger come flowing out. She groaned and refused to even look at him as she finally got her foot out from between the roots.

But then something happened they both didn't expect. Hendrick got angry back.

In a voice so loud and fury filled, it took Kendry by surprise that it was even him, he began yelling at her.

"I am SO sick of your holier and mightier than thou, better-than-everyone-else attitude! Yes, you can fight! Yes, you can hunt and camp! But you are one of the most awful human beings I have ever known! You think the world revolves around you! You are bossy and prideful and just a plain 'ol brat! So, let me tell you something, Queen Kendry," he yelled with sarcasm. "Not everyone cares what you think! I don't care one bit that you are mad at me for not shooting those guys. I am not an expert at a bow like you are! I haven't been trained by the world's best warriors for years on end! I tried the best I could to get the arrow ready to launch and you know what," he took a breath before continuing. "It didn't happen. Not everything we want to happen, happens! I didn't want Mister Carter got get dragged away on that boat! I didn't want Marvin to get beat by those men! I didn't want to get stuck here with you! But it has all happened anyway! And so now, I am going to make something happen that I do want. I'm going to rid you of my annoying presence. I'm done here."

He began packing up his tent and shoving some stuff in his duffle bag. Kendry was still a little taken back by his outburst because it was so outside his character. She stood there while he continued.

"By the way, here's the money you accused me of losing!" he threw a pouch at her. "I thought it wasn't wise to leave it in the horse's saddles while we slept. I realize your mighty warrior friends do that, but I actually removed it and slept with it on me."

She glanced down at the pouch, relieved it wasn't stolen and a little embarrassed that she had accused him of that.

"Chester is gone," he continued. "So, you can keep Midnight. I'm leaving on foot and I'm not going to miss you or your royal attitude one bit!" With that, he marched off into the forest. Kendry just stood there for what seemed to be an eternity. She was just too shocked by the day's events to even know how to react. Finally, she collapsed into her tent and cried and cried until she ran out of tears.

CHAPTER FIFTEEN

The next morning Kendry woke exhausted, not sure how much she had actually slept. She got moving immediately and started tracking Hendrick. It was easy to follow his footprints and paths of broken brush. She climbed a tree and looked out and could see the little makeshift campsite he had made for himself. She quietly snuck up on him and sat down on a log behind his back. He was stirring a small bowl of berries and didn't notice her.

"I'm sorry," she said quietly. He jumped a mile.

"Darn it, Kendry! You scared the life out of me!"

He calmed himself down, and turned back to stirring his mushed berries, trying to ignore her.

"You are right, ya know?" she began, pausing before continuing. "I did have a unique upbringing and I forget that not everyone has been trained as I have. I know I can be a bit..." she paused looking for the right word. "...bossy....over-bearing..."

"You berate people and make everyone feel like they're the size of an ant," he added completing her thoughts.

It was quiet for a second and then she responded. "I really am sorry."

They both sat there quietly for a while. She continued talking to the back of his head.

"Our families, our friends, they are all gone. I haven't been handling it the best. I've treated you unkindly," she said humbly. "But, Hendrick, you are my friend. And I need you right now."

"You said I was useless," he mumbled back.

"I didn't mean it."

"Yes, you did. We both know it's true. I can't hunt like you. I can't fight like you. I can't shoot a bow and arrow like you. I can't even beat you to the top of a big brandy tree!" His voice raised a bit as he added the last part. She could tell she had bruised his ego. He then concluded with, "You don't need me, Kendry. You really don't. And, I'd like to figure out how to survive without you. I'm sorry, but I'm done putting up with your condescending attitude. Tavern's End is gone. All of it."

She bit her lip, sitting quietly for a moment more. Finally, she stood up and took a step back toward where she came from. "Fine, Hendrick." She took another few steps and then turned back toward him. "But you know what I think? I think that I am trying to take responsibility for my rude attitude toward you and that you should humble yourself a little, too. Maybe you don't think I need you, but our friends need both of us. If you could swallow your pride and forget the fact that I can climb a tree faster than you, maybe we could get past our character flaws and work together. "

Without turning around, he shrugged.

She started heading back deep into the forest, but paused one last time to shout something at him. "By the way," she yelled. "The only reason I can climb that brandy tree faster than you is that I have been trained to do so. I've trained daily. If you listened to instruction, instead of rolling your eyes at advice, you could beat me, too. You are stronger than me and very talented at climbing."

He half-laughed at her attempt at a compliment.

She continued, "You need to stop looking at the next branch ahead of you and instead look ahead two or three branches. Your focus is too shallow. If you changed your focus and practiced that way, you would beat me," she concluded. And with that, she left.

He sat there for a long time, frustrated that she was able to find him so easily. Mad that she thought a simple apology would change anything. She had no idea what it was like living in her shadow with the rest of them. She got everything she wanted and more. Her life was perfect! Or...it was...until her father and Malark were killed. Until the Academy was done for. Until their townspeople were kidnapped. Until the king put a target on her head. She had been through a lot. Maybe he should've received her apology with more compassion.

He got up and walked around until he found a good climbing tree. He took his time scoping it out and climbing each branch slowly. Then he made his way back to the ground. He was good at climbing. That's why it was so frustrating that he could never beat her. He looked back up at the tree and slowly took a couple of breaths. As fast as he could he raced up the tree, hand over hand, branch over branch, but he was sure to look ahead a few branches the whole time. When he reached the top, he shook his head. She was right. He knew he was faster using that method. He smirked wishing she had told him that bit of advice long ago. But she was as competitive as he was and was not going to take her edge away by disclosing her secret. He still wasn't sure she needed him, but one thing was for certain. He needed her.

Later that evening after working at the stables all day, he found his way back to Kendry's campsite. She was sitting on a log massaging her sore bare feet. She looked up at him blankly.

"You here to forgive me?" she asked bluntly. "Or to try to take Midnight back?"

"Forgive you," he said. "If you forgive me and..." he walked over to the fire pit and sat down across from her. "...and if you teach me to fight."

Her eyebrows raised.

"I mean it, Kendry. I never want to be in a situation again where I see people I care about taken and I don't know what to do to help them. I don't want to feel helpless if Shadenberg attacks Crestavia. I want to know that if I shoot an arrow, it will hit the target. And I want you to train me the way the men at the Academy were trained. You know their methods and exercises. I know I'm not as physically built or coordinated as the trainees at the Academy, but anything I can learn will help."

She opened her mouth to respond, but he interrupted.

"Don't tell me it will be useless or you can't. Don't tell me it's a waste of time or we have no time. Don't give me any excuse. I need to learn!"

"I know," she said. "I know."

His eyes widened. A smile crept across his face. "So, you'll do it?" he asked anticipating a positive answer.

She nodded. "We both need to be ready for whatever lies ahead. We'll start tomorrow."

He stood up so excited he wanted to jump or scream or something, but instead just sort of paced back and forth, grinning. "Good then. I'm going to go get all my stuff."

Hendrick headed out to find his other campsite and relocate back with Kendry. Not able to stop himself from silently celebrating, there was a definite skip to his step the rest of the day.

CHAPTER SIXTEEN

Their shifts working at the stable and library were not consistent. Hendrick had lowest seniority and only worked when not enough stable boys showed up. It happened often enough to keep him busy. But the capital's library was open on random days and so Kendry's work schedule sometimes conflicted with Hendrick's time off from work. Yet, anytime they were both in the forest together, they trained.

Kendry started Hendrick's training with archery. It was something he could easily practice on his own while she was at the library. He improved almost immediately due to simple tips of instruction from her.

They both had an exercise regimen for the morning and then Hendrick added his own routine of archery and axe throwing. Kendry was impressed with his stamina and commitment. He really did want to learn and was willing to put in the work.

The most difficult skill for him to tackle was sword fighting. He had never practiced with his dad as many of the young men would do growing up. He was awkward in his stance and the way he held the sword made Kendry cringe. They only had one sword between the two of them so they did a lot of mock fighting with a thick stick, but it lacked the reality of what was needed to truly teach him to sword fight.

In addition, Hendrick needed to learn weaponless combat. Kendry decided to have him focus on balance and speed exercises as well as martial arts. They sparred each morning and evening and every time she was able to show him a new move or teach him a new defense strategy. He would often get frustrated with himself for not perfecting moves fast enough, but Kendry reminded him that she had been doing this her whole life.

One evening, after they'd already been working all day, Hendrick pleaded with Kendry to spar with him. Kendry just wanted to sit and relax. But he was relentless, so she gave in. During their sparring, she was able to swipe his leg out from under him. It caused him to fall face first in the dirt. Angry, he got up and had to take a few breaths to calm down. She was hungry and wanted to get dinner cooking on the fire, but he wanted to redeem himself and keep fighting. At her refusal, he groaned and picked up a rock. She could tell he was frustrated as he launched the stone into the forest.

Kendry was irritated. It had been a long day and she needed to discuss something with him that she had learned at the library that morning. She had been trying to find the best way to approach the subject, as she wanted him on her side in regards to her opinion. But, looking at how frustrated he was, she knew this would not be the best time to bring it up.

"I'm going to take Midnight to get some water," he said as he untied the horse. They both knew that sometimes it was best for them to get some space from each other. When he got frustrated, going for a walk was a good idea.

Kendry stayed and cooked a fish for her dinner. Time ticked by. When Hendrick still didn't arrive back, she started to get a bit worried. She followed Midnight's hoof prints down toward the creek. Eventually she found the horse tied up to a tree branch, and looking unruffled. It seemed odd that Hendrick would've left Midnight. She called Hendrick's name and got no response. So, she did what she always did when she was trying to find someone. She climbed a tree.

From high up, she was relieved to see him in a clearing between some trees a ways ahead. He was just kicking branches and throwing rocks. She found it a bit humorous that he was still pouting, but was annoyed because tonight was not going to be the night to bring up what was written on the scrolls she spent all day posting at the library. He wouldn't be in the right mood for her to share the information.

Resigned to climb down and head back to the campsite without him ever knowing she had followed him, her eyes caught something in the distance. Approaching Hendrick, without his awareness, were a couple of men. She could see their horses standing still in the distance. These men could hear Hendrick and were stalking him.

Kendry yelled, hoping she'd surprise the men enough to run away or get Hendrick's attention. But, none of them heard her. She watched in horror as they snuck up behind Hendrick and grabbed him.

She focused in on the men. Now she could see who they were. They were kingdom guards. They were most like patrolling the forest for vagabonds, bandits, or those up to no good. She could see they were talking to Hendrick, one of them holding each of his arms. Then they looked around the clearing. The one not holding Hendrick walked about searching in bushes. They were probably trying to find his campsite or figure out why he was out there. Would he direct them back to Midnight? If so, she was in a tree above the horse.

 Kendry stayed glued to the scene far off and watched as eventually the men escorted Hendrick back to their horses. They put him on the back with one of them. Before they could ride off, Kendry was flying down the tree. She rushed to the ground and hopped on Midnight. The horse took off toward where she knew the guards' horses had been. She had to find out where they were taking Hendrick. Were they arresting him? Would they go back to the campsite?

Slowly she tracked them from quite a distance. On more than one occasion, she had to climb up a tree again to see where they were after she had lost them. Eventually she followed them into town. It was late evening now and the streets were not super busy, so she did her best to try to stay inconspicuous. A few times she had to act like she was going somewhere other than the direction they were going in, but ultimately located their horses up ahead again. Finally, the guards stopped outside a wooden building. They parked their horses and took Hendrick by the arm inside.

Kendry casually rode down the street. She approached the wooden building and turned to read the sign. *Youth Refuge.*

Kendry had heard of Youth Refuges. These were places where kids on the streets or orphans were taken. The king would supply the funding for these refuges and rumor was the men that lead them would often pocket the money and cheat the youth out of their provisions. Youth staying at a refuge might starve or be beaten or lack medical attention. She'd also heard that King Gadden had gotten better at sending officials out to monitor these places, so they probably weren't all bad. But, the idea of Hendrick being at a refuge made her hair curl.

With the number of kids and teens Kendry saw living on the streets, she wondered why only certain ones ended up in a refuge. What made the guards choose certain people and leave others to scrounge and beg on street corners or live in alleys? What were the odds Hendrick would end up in one? Kendry wondered what story he must've told the guards. He kept them away from their campsite, most likely because if Kendry was discovered she could end up arrested. He didn't even tell them about Midnight being tied up down by the creek.

Content with the knowledge of where the guards took him, she turned around and rode back to her campsite. There was nothing she'd be able to do at that moment, so going to sleep was in her best interest. It was strange being alone again and yet, she knew that it wouldn't be for long. She would find a way to get Hendrick away from the Refuge. She slept horribly, keeping an ear out all night in hopes of hearing Hendrick come back, though she knew that wasn't possible.

The next morning, Kendry rose early. She was planning to pass the Youth Refuge before heading to the library. She wasn't sure what she was hoping to see or find, but knew she had to figure out a way to get Hendrick released. Her goal at the library that day would be to read up on everything in relation to the Refuge that she could find.

But on the way there, she passed the stable where Hendrick worked and saw him scooping up manure in the back. She couldn't believe her eyes! Acting like she was a customer shopping at the trading post, she paid to have

Midnight boarded. Then, when no one was looking, she snuck around to the back of the stable and approached Hendrick. He saw her coming and dropped his shovel.

"Kendry! Oh, I'm so sorry! Wait until I tell you what happened," he began. "I got caught by kingdom guards on my walk last night and they took me to…"

"…the Youth Refuge," she said finishing his sentence. His expression showed his surprise. He nodded.

"I followed you there," she said. Confusion showed on his face, but she didn't add any further information. "Let's get you out of here," she said. "I'll grab Midnight and we can take off to the forest to pack up and then we'll need to keep moving, I guess."

"No, Kendry. I was actually hoping to find you after work and discuss this. I think this is a good thing. See, at the Refuge they feed us for free. They also give us a small allowance of funds for supplies and personal needs. From what I could tell last night, the guy in charge is a dope. He doesn't even seem to know what is going on. I think we should both try to stay there for a while and save up our money. We can work twice as much because we won't have to fish or hunt for food, which will save us time."

"You want to be held prisoner at that place?" she asked completely stunned.

"No, not exactly. See, I've been thinking…" he paused, took a deep breath and continued. "I think we do need to go to Regaria. When I was cleaning the stables the other day, I heard a couple of the guys talking. One of them had come from Regaria. He was saying how if you pay people enough money there you can gain any information you want. People sell each other out continuously and there is no loyalty."

"Okay…" Kendry responded not knowing what that had to do with anything.

"If we save up enough money, we could go to Regaria and try to bribe someone to let us know where the townspeople from Tavern's End were sold. Everyone has to know about townspeople from Crestavia being kidnapped and if they did, in fact, come through Regaria, as you suspect, we might be able to find out where they are now. I know that knowing where they are won't exactly help us get them back, but it's something. I just need to know if they're alive, ya know?"

"So, now you want to go to Regaria?" Kendry interpreted.

Hendrick nodded. "But what they also said is that in Regaria people don't mess around. You need to be able to stand up for yourself and it's really dangerous. They said it was no place for a lady."

Kendry was offended but before she could defend herself, he continued. "Don't worry. I don't think of you as a lady." He smiled, showing the comment was made in jest. She smiled back.

Hendrick peeked around the alley way to make sure that no one he worked with could tell he was skipping out on his duties to chat with a girl. He turned back to her, relieved that no one was around.

"I have a better idea. Or, at least a different idea," she corrected, trying not to sound like she was dismissing his plan. "I saw something when I was working at the library yesterday. They had me posting up scrolls about a competition. It turns out King Gadden's son, Prince Casper, is hosting a competition of sorts in honor of his sister, Princess Gendella. It's for noblemen and it's a tournament to see who is the best of the best. The winner will receive title of 'Regency Advisor" for the king and will have the opportunity to court the princess."

"Okay...so?"

"There's more. The competition is only for noblemen as, of course, only a nobleman could have a chance to marry the princess. But I think the king is really looking to scope out the talent to find someone to replace my father in the position of leading in battle. The competitions of the tournament are all events a general would excel in and be an expert at. Since the best fighters are rarely noblemen, it is no surprise that the tournament had a portion for everyday citizens, too."

Hendrick tried to follow what she was telling him, but he was already confused. As if she could read his expression, she clarified.

"Everyday peasants and citizens of Crestavia can compete in a mini competition before the tournament. The top three winners will get to join the noblemen in the larger tournament in the fall. But, in order to entice peasants and everyday workers to compete, King Gadden is rewarding them with a very large amount of money." She paused and then emphasized, "Hendrick, it would be enough money to bribe anyone in Regaria or even try to ransom back our friends. I think you have to try for it!"

"What?" he asked. "You think I should compete for that tournament?"

"Yes! You don't have to worry about the big tournament in the fall, but try to win this mini competition and the monetary prize that goes with it. We could keep training. The competition is in a few weeks. If, by some chance you won, we could quit our jobs and go straight to Regaria. If not, we can keep working and save up or just chance it and go to Regaria anyway. I feel like we're just wasting time in the Capital, now. I feel like we need to do something!"

He leaned his head back and took a deep breath, obviously deep in thought. "I agree. I'm getting antsy here. But I don' t think I'd have a chance at winning that competition, Kendry. What kind of events are there?"

"The scroll didn't say anything about the competition, but plenty about the tournament in the fall. As for training, we can focus on the events listed for the fall: archery, sword fighting, racing, obstacle courses, boxing, martial arts, and so forth. There's no way to know what they will test you on or make you compete in."

It was a lot to think about, but it was logical to at least try. He suggested he could quit his job at the stable and spend all his time training. He'd want Kendry to keep her job, in the meantime, so they could bring in some money. She nodded enthusiastically.

"There is a cost to register," Kendry added. "But we took enough money from the Academy for that. You will have to pay the fee and you have to sign an application stating that you would be willing to give your life for the king. Then you are given an immediate physical evaluation to see if you can even compete. If approved, you show up for the competition in a few weeks."

Hendrick was slowly nodding as he processed all she was saying. It made sense to try, though he really doubted he had a chance. Kendry seemed to always believe in longshots and he wanted to kick some reality into her brain, but at the same time they didn't really have many other options. Plus, it felt nice to have her believe in him.

"It's a plan," he agreed.

She nearly jumped up and down with excitement. Just the thought of having something to look forward to pumped life back into her. A goal. A mission. A plan.

"We can talk more about it later," Hendrick concluded. "I got to get back to work."

"Let's talk about it tonight," Kendry said and then realized there was still the very large issue of Hendrick being caught by guards and staying at the Refuge. "I don't have any interest in staying at that refuge, though," Kendry added. "I've heard horrible stories about those places and the way they treat youth and kids getting locked in. I am staying in the forest where I am free to do whatever I want."

"I thought the same when the guards were taking me there last night," he began. "I planned to try to escape as soon as I could. But I got to talking to my bunk mate last night. Nice guy named Kenan. He filled me in a bit on the Refuge."

Kendry's attention piqued. Her eyebrows rose encouraging him to continue.

"See, there are lots of refuges all around the Capital. Most are awful because the directors running them pocket the money from the king and starve the kids there. They keep them locked up and are even known for abusing them."

Kendry cringed.

"But this one is for older teens about to enter adulthood. And the director is a whiny, weak old guy with no guts. He knows half the teens in his refuge could kick his butt if they wanted to. So, he basically leaves everyone alone if they keep curfew and keep their bunks clean."

Kendry's expression told Hendrick she didn't buy it.

"No, really. It doesn't even seem that bad there. Most everyone prefers it to living on the streets."

"At least on the streets, you are free to do what you want when you want," Kendry rebutted.

"Maybe, but the streets don't have bathing rooms, warm beds, and hot cooked meals."

"True," she had to admit a bath not outside in a cold river would be heavenly and a warm bed would be the frosting on the cake.

"There are two overseers employed. One on the boys' floor and one on the girls' floor. The one on the guys' floor is a big guy and I wouldn't want to anger him. But, with only one of him and about thirty of us, he keeps pretty hands-off with the guys. If anyone misses curfew or causes problems, they lose privileges and gain extra chores. If they continue to cause issues, then they are thrown out onto the street."

"I'm sure some of them wouldn't mind that," Kendry responded.

"Usually, kids at refuges want to get thrown out, Kendry, and their directors don't want them gone because they want the dues from the king to care for them. But at this place, everyone is about to age out anyway. And most seem content with the free food and room and board and do their best to behave. Kenan told me that my bed opened up because the guy who was there before mouthed off one too many times."

"See, I don't like that," Kendry emphasized. "I don't want to have to follow their rules."

"I know, but look at all the benefits. We don't have to worry about bandits, wild animals, or the king's soldiers finding you in the forest and putting it together that you are the traitor from Tavern's End."

"Shh," Kendry hushed him looking around to make sure no one heard.

"Plus, we don't have to waste time hunting, skinning, cooking meals. We get money just for staying there, though it isn't much. I was told by the director that we are all expected to work every day and pay taxes weekly to the king through him. So, we can even keep our jobs. Or, I can pretend to be going to work and really go train in the forest since we have enough money on hand for me to give him toward taxes."

"He probably over charges for taxes and pockets the extra," Kendry hypothesized. "Younger kids don't work but the teens do, and so they can make money off of us that way!"

"So what?" Hendrick replied. "Overall, it's a good place to call home for a couple of weeks while I train for the competition. I will pretend to go to work every day and train in the forest. When you are not working you can help me. The only bad part is that if we miss curfew even once we can never come back. But then we just go back to the forest, so it's really not a big deal!"

"I...guess..." she said hesitantly. "I'll try it for a few days but if I hate it, I'm running away."

Hendrick smiled. "Good. Because I already told the director about my 'sister', Kelly, and he's expecting you there tonight. Lucky for you, a bed opened up on the girls' floor because a girl got really depressed and refused to go to work or clean up her area. They kicked her out."

"Oh, goodness," Kendry said, not liking the idea of the Refuge at all. "I'll tie up our duffle bags and tents in the highest branches of the tallest tree I can find. What items do you want with you?"

"I don't think we should have anything with us at the Refuge except hygiene items and clothes," he stated. "The floors are open to everyone and people get jealous of those who have any good belongings. Kenan warned me that everything gets stolen so I even slept with my shoes on last night."

"This place sounds great," she said sarcastically.

CHAPTER SEVENTEEN

Kendry's bunkmate was probably the most annoying girl she had ever met. The girl had a strange obsession with appearances. From the second she saw Kendry she began bugging her about wanting to fix her hair or try makeup or lotions on her. Kendry could not believe people so shallow existed. Who was this girl that she spent her whole allowance on colored powder for her eyes and wet dyes for her lips? The answer was that she was a girl named Dola. And Kendry realized quickly she wanted to avoid Dola at all costs.

The Refuge consisted of four floors. The bottom floor had a common room for the teens and a dining area. The second floor was a huge room housing thirty beds for the girls. The third floor was the same as the second, but for the boys. The fourth floor consisted of a first aid room, bedrooms for the two overseers, and the director's office and quarters.

On the girls' floor, Kendry was not allowed to really be anywhere but on her top bunk. The other beds all belonged to other girls and so she was to stay in her own place. All her clothes and personal belongings had to fit on her bunk with her. But she didn't like to be on the bed because Dola spent all her time on the bottom bunk with her mirror talking to Kendry about eyebrows, eyelashes, lips, and cheeks.

Because of that, Kendry spent every moment she could outside the Refuge, either at the library or in the forest with Hendrick. But after curfew, which was too early in Kendry's mind, she preferred being down in the commons room.

Hendrick had introduced her to Kenan who introduced her to his twin sister, Kina. Kendry immediately liked Kina. She had a kind demeanor and a funny personality. She was very friendly and had lots of friends at the Refuge so it helped Kendry to meet people. She forgot how much she missed having friends. Hendrick was fine, but he was a boy and their personalities had never exactly drawn them together before they were forced to count on each other.

The first night at the Refuge, Kina was showing Kendry the ropes. She explained that the girls' overseer, Mildra, was not very maternal, but was a fair person and not one you'd have to worry about unless you planned on breaking rules.

She also informed Kendry that the guys' overseer, Brutt, didn't like the girls and looked for any excuse to try to have them punished or thrown out.

Kina walked Kendry to the dining area and showed her where they got their trays. They were very limited on the amount of food they were allowed to have and were expected to eat everything on their trays with no exceptions. Then, they had to clean their trays and tables and ask to be dismissed by Mildra or Brutt.

Kendry was actually enjoying the mush that she thought would be disgusting and the berry flavored drink she served herself from a barrel. It was nice to eat something different than what she caught or hunted outdoors. She decided maybe Hendrick was right about staying there for a couple of weeks. It didn't seem it would be too bad. It would allow them more time for training, as well as provide some variety in their menus.

"So, Kelly, Hendrick tells us that your family were circus travelers and that you walked the tight rope while he was behind the scenes loading and unloading things. What a crazy life you must've experienced!" Kenan looked up at her with interest.

Kendry choked on her drink. So, Hendrick had decided to use that lie with the director. She wondered how he was able to sell it since she was the one that knew all about the places they supposedly had traveled.

"Yes, it was a crazy life. Not nearly as fun and adventurous as it sounds. Just a lot of work," Kendry said convincingly.

They continued small talk and she found out about Kenan and Kina's past. They were dropped off by an aunt at a refuge when they were six years old. They'd been through some horrible refuges and ran away a couple of times. Kina mentioned living on the streets but didn't say too much about it. She explained how they felt very lucky when they got thrown in this refuge with Director Druble.

Another girl at their table, Molly, shared her sad story of being abused by neighbors who took her in when her parents died. They eventually moved her from Tegola, where she was born, to Breckenride, where she became a servant to them. Later, they had moved to Crestavia. When she was of no use to them anymore, they dumped her in the streets. Eventually she got picked up by guards.

Hearing their stories broke Kendry's heart. She had such a great upbringing, but most people her age had already been through many horrors. Eventually someone changed the subject and they started talking about Dola being Kendry's bunkmate which made them all giggle. They had lots of crazy Dola stories to share, leaving Kendry's side aching from all the laughing.

As they were talking and chuckling, Kendry noticed a boy across the way carrying his tray to the only open seat left in the rather small dining area. What caught her attention was that the boy looked really nervous to sit down. He was sort of small and thin and looked a little shaky. Kendry's eye caught that he was searching for anywhere else to sit, but finally took his place in the only empty chair.

Immediately, a big good-looking guy at that table called attention to the boy. He started challenging him for his choice of seats and when the boy apologized for sitting there and started to get up, the big bully mocked him.

Kendry was out of her seat so fast she didn't even know what hit her. She could not stand a predator mocking his prey.

"What's your problem?" she asked bolting toward the bully and his table of laughing buddies.

The good-looking guy looked genuinely surprised by her question. "What's YOUR problem?" he asked back, then looked back and forth at his friends trying to figure out if he was missing something.

"Why are you being such a jerk to that boy?" she asked, pointing behind her. The boy was red in the face and looked like he wished he could disappear.

"Why don't you mind your own business, princess!" he answered.

"Did he do something to you? Or are you just a bully?"

At that, the bully slowly stood up. He was very tall, very strong, and definitely handsome. He stared at Kendry, not saying anything. When she refused to be intimidated, he finally responded.

"I don't like that twerp because he's the definition of a loser. But I'm guessing that's why you're standing up for him, huh? Losers like to stick together." His friends chuckled a littler under their breath.

Mildra had been in the commons area, but was starting to wander toward the dining room. She looked at the bully and the way he was looking at Kendry.

"Druvan, do I need to call Brutt in here?" she asked in a stern voice.

"No, we're just becoming introduced," he responded and then smiled fakely at Kendry. He sat back down and completely ignored her.

She walked back to the table with the girls. Molly's eyes were huge. "No one ever stands up to Druvan," she said quietly.

"Well, Druvan's a jerk," Kendry said back.

Kina laughed a little. "We all think he's a jerk, Kelly. Thing is, he beats up anyone who challenges him or shows animosity toward him. So, next time you are outside the Refuge, watch your back. He won't care that you're a girl. I've seen him mess with girls before."

"I can't wait for him to try," Kendry said and took her last bite of mush.

Druvan and his friends got Mildra's attention after cleaning up their trays and table and asked permission to be dismissed. As they filtered out of the dining area, Druvan purposely passed close to Kendry. He leaned over her shoulder and whispered, "You are going to be sorry you opened your mouth at me, twit!" With that he left.

Kendry's face turned hot with anger. Who did he think he was? She would show him! She could not wait to get him alone in an alley and kick his rear end to the high heavens.

The incident at the dining hall caused Kendry to earn quite the reputation. The girls were all talking about it on their floor and apparently the boys got wind of it on their floor, too. Hendrick was quick to warn Kendry that Druvan had it out to get her. He wasn't too worried because he'd seen Kendry fight and knew that there was little chance Druvan had been trained by top martial arts experts like Kendry had. But he still didn't like the idea of her having another target on her back. And, they were supposed to be keeping a low profile and not making trouble. If Kendry got in a physical fight with Druvan and beat him badly it would cause people to take notice. If word got back to the king's guards, someone might put it together who she really was.

Kendry and Hendrick found that staying at the Refuge really did give them much more time to train. Hendrick stopped taking shifts at the stable and instead went straight to the forest each morning. Kendry didn't start working at the library until it opened mid-morning, so she was able to train with him before work and then again, after. They made sure they were back at the Refuge for dinner and curfew.

With more time to train, Hendrick's improvement increased greatly. Kendry couldn't believe how much better he was getting at every skill. Well, every skill but sword fighting. Only having one sword and his lack of natural talent made it difficult. But he was getting faster, stronger, and his aim with weapons was much more accurate already. He even managed to beat her in a race up a tree! It was probably the proudest moment of his life and Kendry smiled big letting him enjoy his moment of victory.

Kendry got her own practice in when they sparred. She enjoyed boxing but Hendrick favored martial arts, so they practiced both each day. Sometimes he would hunt, as target practice, and then sell the animals at the market on the way back to the Refuge in the evenings.   Then, they would head back to settle in at the Refuge for the night.

 Kenan and Hendrick hung out with two other guys at the Refuge. Mavo and Thron were always part of their foursome. Kendry saw them together every night and morning. They ate meals together and played logic games in the common room. Kendry was happy Hendrick had made some friends. Kina, Molly, and Kendry would join the boys in the evenings for discussions about politics and trivia.

Kendry liked Mavo. He was always very positive even if whatever topic they were discussing was inherently negative. She could've seen her father and this dark-skinned, muscular-built teenager talking battle and planning war strategies. Mavo had a knack for seeing things outside the box. When they discussed Shadenberg's inevitable attack on Crestavia, Mavo always had great ideas that Kendry thought King Gadden himself should hear about. It was like Mavo was a born war strategizer. He wanted to fight and didn't want Crestavia to sit around and do nothing.

Kenan, Hendrick, and Thron, on the other hand, all hoped there would not be a war. Mavo would suggest Crestavia attack first and the other three boys would shake their heads in disagreement. Kendry was pretty sure that's what she liked about Mavo. He was not willing to sit around and wait for something to happen. He wanted to jump in and spark the fire.

Thron was quite opposite of Mavo. He tended to be extremely negative and Kendry nicknamed him Grumpy-Thron behind his back. But he and Hendrick clicked which was good to see. Kendry knew Hendrick had missed Marvin and the other guys from Tavern's End. It must've been nice for him to have some comradeship again.

One evening, the seven of them were chatting in an area of the common room, when Druvan and his buddies entered in their direction. The common room was large and usually they didn't mix, but he was heading straight toward them.

Thron looked up and tilted his chin in Druvan's direction to get all their attention that trouble was coming their way.

"Kenan, Mavo, when did you guys start hanging out with this garbage," he asked pointing his finger at Kendry.

Hendrick started to stand up. Thron pulled him back down before his legs were straightened.

"Hey Druvan. What's up?" Kenan responded politely, pretending like he hadn't just insulted Kendry.

"I heard Brutt's sick," Druvan answered. "Throwing up in his room upstairs." Druvan mimicked vomiting. Kendry rolled her eyes. "That means there's no one to watch over our floor tonight."

The sentence hung there for a second and then Kendry responded. "So, who exactly are you threatening?"

Druvan just smiled and then signaled to his buddies it was time to leave and they all walked away.

"He'd never go on the girls' floor," Kina said to Kendry. "He's just trying to stir everyone up."

"Yep, he likes people to sleep with one eye open," Thron said. "He enjoys threatening and watching you squirm. But, really, he's a wimp."

"I don't know," Molly said. "I've seen him beat a couple of people real good in the past."

"I have, too," Mavo piped in. "He can fight. And he has a horrible temper."

Seeing Mavo's respect of Druvan's skill worried Kendry a bit. Mavo was a big, strong guy, himself, and he obviously tried to avoid upsetting Druvan.

"Someone needs to teach that guy a lesson," Hendrick said. They all nodded. "Be careful tonight, Kelly."

"You, too," she said to her pretend brother.

As time ticked away, everyone made their way up to bed, but Kendry hung out down below hinting to Hendrick that she wanted him to stay, too. They needed to talk. When they were finally alone, she whispered to him.

121

"Director Druble is away on business. Brutt is sick. Well, that's if what Druvan said is true. That just leaves Mildra."

"Leaves Mildra for what?" Hendrick asked, confused.

"When the guards first brought you here, did they take you to Druble's office?" she asked. Hendrick nodded. "Did you notice the large sword above his desk?"

Hendrick thought about the office and there had been a sword on the wall.

"We need a sword, Hendrick. I've been thinking about it non-stop since I saw it there. The only way we are going to get you better at sword fighting is if we have two swords. We need to get it from his office!"

Hendrick felt sick to his stomach. He actually liked it here. He was happy for the first time since Tavern's End. Maybe even more so than in Tavern's End. And, Kendry wanted to get them kicked out.

"No, we're not risking it," he said matter-of-factly. "We'd not only get thrown out, we'd also get arrested for theft. We'd end up in the king's dungeon, not on our way to Regaria to try to get information about our friends."

"Don't be silly," she responded back. "I wouldn't suggest it if I didn't think it was easy. Director Druble leaves his big window open up there on the fourth floor. He's been gone since yesterday and I noticed this morning...it is still open."

"A window?" Hendrick asked.

"Yes, you don't notice the window unless you walk behind the Refuge. You can see it from the back-alley or the side yard on this side of the fence. You can't see it from the street because it's on the other side of the building. And, it's wide open."

"Why would he leave it open?"

"It's hot up there and no one can get to that window up on the fourth floor. Well, no one but a tight rope walker," she added, smiling.

"What? No! You're not going to walk across a rope into his window, are you?"

"Nah, I don't need to tight rope walk anything. This old wooden building would be easier to climb than the tavern back home, which I've climbed a million times. I've scoped this place out. I will have no problem at all getting in his office."

Hendrick's head was spinning. She was crazy.

"My only concern," she said slowly. "...is that I'm not sure how to get back in my room in the Refuge that is locked without anyone noticing an obviously large sword. And, I'm afraid some of the kids that live in the alley way will see me and give me away to a guard."

"Exactly. That's why we are going to pretend we never had this conversation," Hendrick concluded.

"If I could climb out a window on my floor without anyone noticing...but there always seems like someone is awake or rolling around. But, if I could...I could climb up to the fourth floor and get that sword. Then, I'd need to get back down to my floor and I guess hide the sword in my bed. It wouldn't be foolproof. Anyone could wake up at any time and see me. "

"Which is why you are NOT going to do it," he stated firmly.

"Except..." she said in a sly voice. "I noticed something tonight. While we were all in here talking, Mildra opened that back window. Probably because it is such a warm night." She pointed to a window in the far corner of the commons room. "Director Druble or Brutt always go around and close the windows in the evening. They are the ones to make sure we are locked in. I saw Mildra lock the front door but I don't think she thought about that window."

Hendrick's stomach was turning. He could see where she was going with this.

"If I hurried, before Mildra remembers she left the window open, I could scale the building and get the sword. I could hide it in the bushes behind the Refuge and hope and pray that no one sees it there tonight. Then, in the morning, we could grab it and take it to the forest!" Kendry was ecstatic with this idea. Hendrick was not.

"No. Too many things could go wrong. Plus, if we're both not in bed in the next half hour we are going to get a grievance."

"Then, we need to go quick! And, before anyone else wanders downstairs or wonders what we're doing down here." Kendry walked over to the window. Hendrick couldn't believe she was doing this.

"No, Kendry, please don't. I don't want to get kicked out of here."

"Then, go to bed. It'll just be me that gets kicked out and I don't mind living in the forest. I've got to do this. We need that sword."

"No, we don't. I actually think you just like to create drama or something," he said frustrated.

But she was already climbing out the window and there was nothing he could do to stop her.

CHAPTER EIGHTEEN

Scaling the back of the Refuge was not only easy for Kendry but actually fun. She loved the challenge of climbing something new and it was a bit of a thrill to do it at night while trying not to be seen. She could hear kids and teens in the alley way and saw their campfire smoke rising, but she was silent hidden in the shadows.

She arrived at the fourth-floor window quicker than expected. Climbing in was a little difficult because Director Druble had a collection of stuff on the window sill. She almost knocked over a knick-knack of a soldier and caught an ashtray before it fell to the ground. Slowly, she put her first foot on the ground and then rotated her other leg to join it. The window was in the far corner of the room so she looked around surveying the area, thankful for the moonlight shining in.

The office was smaller than she remembered. A magenta seating bench against the wall was dusty and the matching sofa in front of the director's desk was faded. There were shelves of books filling the far wall. Lots of scrolls and papers were stacked on the desktop. A small round table stood next to his desk. It had a serving tray with glass containers full of liquid and crystal looking chalices. There was a woven rug on the wooden floor which Kendry was thankful for, because it softened the sound of her footsteps. And, there, behind the director's desk was a silver sword.

The sword had gotten Kendry's attention when she was 'enrolling' at the Refuge. It was finely made and beautiful. She wondered the significance of it.

She could not envision Director Druble ever using it. It must've belonged to someone important or been used in a special duel or battle for him to want to hang it on his wall. She walked over and ran her finger along the flat smooth side of the sword. She couldn't wait to use it while training with Hendrick. She reached up and took hold of it with both hands, planning on lifting it up out of the braces that were holding it on the wall. But, as soon as she touched it, she heard a noise.

A key was turning in the door knob! Kendry fell quickly to the ground. She hid behind the big oak desk. The chair was in the way so she couldn't climb under it. She bit her lip. Her heart was racing. She stayed as still as she could as the door creaked open.

Listening, she heard footsteps approaching the desk. She could hear someone picking up the glass pitcher and pouring themselves a drink. Was Director Druble back? They hadn't expected him to return for a couple more days.

"Don't think I don't see what you're doing," Mildra's voice said pointedly. Kendry closed her eyes tight. She'd been caught. She started to crawl out when she heard Brutt's voice answer Mildra.

"Just needed some brandy to get me through the night."

"You still sick?"

"Very," Brutt managed to say. "But I can't sleep. Hoping the brandy will help me with that. How are things downstairs?"

"Fine," Mildra responded. Kendry heard Mildra's muffled footsteps across the rug toward Brutt. It sounded like she was pouring herself a drink, too. "We better clean these chalices before he returns. He won't notice the brandy gone but he will notice if his chalices are used."

"Hmph," Brutt replied. It was quiet for a while and Kendry assumed they were both drinking the brandy. She stayed frozen and tried to will herself not to breathe loudly. Her feet were starting to tingle from the cramped position she was in. She wanted so badly to resituate and give them some blood flow but she was in too close to them to chance it. She willed herself to not think about the pain and uncomfortable feeling of pins and needles.

126

After what seemed like forever, Mildra left, reminding Brutt to lock the door. A moment later, he left, too. Kendry waited patiently until she heard the key relock the door and footsteps dwindle away. She uncramped her body and pulled herself up. Taking her asleep foot out in front of her, she practiced putting pressure on it until she could walk. Then, she turned her attention to the sword and without delay, slipped it off its hooks and headed back toward the window. She wouldn't be able to climb without using both hands so she slipped the sword down the back of her blouse and tucked it through her belt. She then tightened her belt and prayed it wouldn't fall. This would be interesting.

Back in the commons room, Hendrick was freaking out. Kendry had been gone a very long time. He knew he needed to get in bed and quick. The tension of waiting with no sign of her was wearing him down. He kept looking up out the window and then pacing the room.

"Hendrick?"

Hendrick jumped. Kenan was coming down the stairwell. "What are you still doing down here in the dark?" he asked.

"Oh...uh...I was just...uh, I fell asleep on the couch. But I was just coming up," he glanced over his shoulder at the window. Still no sign of Kendry. Kenan made his way down the last steps and walked toward Hendrick.

"Man, I know you are probably scared of Druvan, but it's much worse to corner yourself off somewhere alone than to just come up to the sleeping quarters and pretend to be asleep."

Hendrick nodded. "Yeah, I was on my way up." But, before he could even take a step toward the stairwell, they both looked up to hear steps coming down their way.

There were three of them. Druvan and two of his buddies. They were whispering loudly about something and when they saw Kenan and Hendrick standing there, they smiled like they had won a prize.

127

"Well, what do we have here?" Druvan asked snarkily. He laughed a little and shook his head at his friends. Then he rubbed his hands together like he was anticipating a delicious meal.

"We were just heading to bed," Kenan said.

"You WERE, but you're not anymore," Druvan rebounded. "We're going to have a little...chat."

Hendrick took a deep breath. He glanced over his shoulder again and happened to see Kendry plop down in front of the window. His heart raced with fear as to what would happen to Kendry if Druvan saw her outside that window. Wanting to make sure Druvan and his buddies didn't notice her, he did the first thing that popped into his head. He swung a full-force punch right into Druvan's face.

From there erupted a huge brawl involving all five of them. Kendry had positioned herself to climb back in the window after hiding the sword in the shrubs. Her eyes widened with surprise when she saw the boys fighting. Her instinct was to jump in and help, but as she climbed through the window, she found herself hiding behind a loveseat and watching with admiration.

Hendrick was amazing! His training had really paid off. He was dodging blows and whipping around and kicking down guys while punching others. It looked so smooth and calculated. Kenan would get a punch in now and then, but it was pretty much Hendrick against three guys and Hendrick was winning. Occasionally, Druvan would get a good blow at Hendrick and Kendry would cringe at the thought of the pain, but overall, it was Druvan and his friends that were going to be covered with bruises and black eyes.

They were so involved in their fight that they didn't hear Mildra walking down the stairs. She yelled at them to get to their rooms immediately. They all stopped fighting and bolted. Kendry stayed hidden. She was fairly sure Mildra wouldn't mention the fight to Brutt. But, Mildra probably would be checking beds on both floors. As soon as Kendry was sure she was gone, she snuck up the stairs. After watching Mildra pass the second floor to go up to the boys' third floor to check on them, she slid quietly into the girls' quarters. Kendry climbed up onto her top bunk, thankful everyone was asleep, and smiled. As long as no one took the sword from the bushes, her adventure had been a success! And, after seeing Hendrick in that brawl, she really felt like he had a chance at doing well in the upcoming competition.

CHAPTER NINETEEN

With two swords at their disposal, they planned to focus on improving Hendrick's sword fighting skills. But the first time they Kendry and Hendrick met in the forest with this mission in mind, they were taken back by something unexpected. As Hendrick arrived and he and Kendry began discussing the plan for the afternoon's training, Kendry hushed him. She heard something. Someone was there. They both froze and looked around.

"Come out," Kendry yelled toward a wall of trees in the distance. "We know you're there." She held the sword in fighting position and Hendrick slowly picked up the bow and an arrow that they had set out for training.

From behind the tree, peeked Kina. "Hi," she said shyly. "Just curious where you two run off to all the time," she said sounding apologetic. But, then out stepped Kenan, Thron, Mavo, and Molly.

"Crud," whispered Hendrick. They'd been caught. How were they going to explain why they had a ton of weapons out in the forest?

Mavo, Molly, and Kenan smiled, looking embarrassed that they'd been caught spying on them. Thron looked curious and walked over toward Hendrick. He picked up an axe. "What in the hay barrel is going on?" he asked, abruptly.

Kendry looked at Hendrick. He shrugged.

Mind spinning with the perfect lie to coverup their situation, Kendry finally decided some honesty might work best. She explained that they were desperately in need of money for some friends that were out of town and that they had decided to enter Hendrick into Prince Casper's competition to join the tournament in the fall. They all seemed to know what she was talking about but looked surprised.

"We've been training and practicing so Hendrick can be ready," Kendry said hoping they were buying it.

"Cut the hogwash," Thron said rudely. "Kenan told us how Hendrick fought like a Shadenberg ninja against Druvan. How do you know how to fight like that?"

Hendrick looked back at Kendry. She took a deep breath. "Our dad was in the Army. He was an expert at martial arts and fighting. Unfortunately, he never taught Hendrick how to sword fight. I learned some from our uncle I visited once for a summer, but we were going to focus on getting Hendrick better at it."

"Where'd you get the swords from...and the rest of the weapons?" Thron asked, suspiciously. Kendry was getting tired of Thron's questions.

"They were our father's," Hendrick answered. "We knew we couldn't bring them to the Refuge and they have sentimental value to us. Plus, with Shadenberg threatening to attack, we want to be prepared."

"Glad you mentioned that," Mavo said. "We all want to be prepared if war breaks out. What would you think about letting us train with you?"

Kendry's heart raced. How could they get out of this? Hendrick started mumbling about how they had a goal to win the competition and didn't want to have to worry about competing against friends or getting distracted. But then it hit Kendry. Why not? Why couldn't they train, too? It would help Hendrick to have others to spar with and sword fight. In fact, it would help them both to have others to race against and compete in exercises. Mavo would be the hardest competition and that would be good for them.

"Sure," Kendry said, talking over Hendrick. He stared at her in disbelief. "It'll be good for you to have more competition and others to train with. As long as everyone understands that in two weeks Hendrick is competing in Prince

Casper's competition and that is our main focus right now. They all nodded in response.

So, for the next two weeks, training changed quite a bit. The seven of them began working together to help Hendrick improve. It became obvious to the others, fast, that Kendry knew more than any of them. Thron was the most suspicious about it. The others just seemed to think she was skilled from unique circus training and an uncle that spent time instructing her one summer. But Thron wouldn't let it go, often asking pointed questions. Kendry found herself avoiding him as much as possible.

Back at the Refuge, the seven of them also stuck together. Druvan was red hot with anger whenever he saw them, but Brutt and Mildra managed to keep him in line. Director Druble never made one comment about his missing sword. Kendry couldn't understand it. She wondered how often he went in his office or if he had even noticed it missing. Regardless, she was thankful it couldn't be traced back to them.

Finally, they reached the morning of the competition. Hendrick and Kendry went down to the Army barracks and paid the fee and she helped him fill out the application. They had him enter the barracks for an evaluation. Kendry stayed outside and got worried when she watched many men leave angry that they hadn't passed. Most of them looked to be in pretty good shape and so she wondered what sort of evaluation it was. When Hendrick finally came out the gate, she looked up at him, hopeful. He smiled.

"Easy," he said. Kendry breathed out in relief. He would be heading that evening to the Military Training Center for the competition. She gave Hendrick a huge hug and congratulated him.

When they got back, their friends were all at work and Kendry had to head to the library for a few hours. Hendrick decided to take off to the forest for a while to train some more. Kendry was ecstatic as she filed books and scrolls that afternoon. She prayed that Hendrick would somehow win. If they had that prize money, they could go to Regaria and see if they could find someone to bribe for information.

The thought of leaving the Refuge sort of hurt a little. Aside from Dola's annoying nags to make over Kendry's beauty and Druvan's threatening looks, it had become a place she equated with friendship. She would miss Kina and Molly. She would miss Mavo and Kenan. She wasn't sure she'd actually miss Thron. He always seemed like he was trying to find fault in Hendrick and her. But Hendrick liked him so she dealt with his presence in their group. Still, saying goodbye would be hard. Would they even say goodbye? They'd probably just sneak out.

When she arrived back at the Refuge, she told Kina the good news. Kina shared it with Kenan and Mavo who were thrilled for Hendrick. She was pretty sure Mavo was a little jealous. He had wanted to try out, himself, but couldn't afford the entry fee. Thron, surprisingly, was impressed and happy for Hendrick, too. Kendry headed upstairs to find Molly.

Molly was lying in bed. She looked sweaty and pale. Kendry was immediately worried. "Are you feeling, okay?" she asked.

Molly shook her head. "Kendry, I have a huge favor to ask you," she began and then started coughing. Concerned, Kendry waited patiently for her to stop coughing and continue. "I'm supposed to work tonight at a big fancy house party for a nobleman. They are having important guests. Kina is working it, too. If I don't show up, they will give my position away and I won't have work. I need this job."

Kendry squeezed Molly's arm. "It'll be okay. You just need to focus on getting better."

"Would you fill in for me? The host won't know you aren't me. She's never met any of us. You could just introduce yourself as Molly. None of the other girls will tell on us. Kina's already coached some of them to go along with it."

Kendry delayed answering for a second. Tonight was the competition. She wanted to be there cheering on Hendrick. Of course, she was not allowed in the training center so in reality, she'd just be waiting outside. It made sense that she might as well be helping Molly out while waiting for news about Hendrick.

"Sure, Molly. Of course," she answered.

Within an hour, Kendry was putting on Molly's servant dress and hiding her hair in a thick scarf. Her strawberry golden roots were starting to grow in and some of her locks were beginning to show her natural color through the fading brown caddonberry dye. She would need to find more berries soon and re-dye her hair, but scarves had been doing the trick in the meantime. The outfit fit her perfectly, but she wondered aloud what the Capital had against sleeves. This outfit, too, was sleeveless and she felt so exposed.

Kendry and Kina arrived at the dinner party just before dark. The huge house was actually a mansion. Kendry had never seen anything like it. Though she would spend most of her time in the back kitchen and downstairs preparing things, she took in every detail she could. The ornate decorations and elaborate architecture took Kendry's breath away. The place was really something amazing.

The large mansion was owned by a rich nobleman who was rumored to be good friends with Prince Casper, the son of King Gadden. The dining hall opened up to a large outside veranda with a beautiful garden surrounding it. Kendry admired the large decorated, pillars that held the veranda up. It was a beautiful night and she was actually glad to be there serving instead of sitting outside the training center worried about Hendrick.

The girls working the event at the mansion were given permission by Mildra to be late for curfew. Hendrick had been given an exemption, as well, since the tournament was expected to go late. Kendry spent the whole time at the dinner party praying for Hendrick's success. Most of the night she was in the kitchen, helping the cooks prep the food and assisting others with the presentation of the food on trays. Occasionally, she'd be asked to bring a platter into the dining hall.

The dining hall's table setting was exquisite. Everything from the candles to the cloth napkins were superb. The table was attractively lined with gold tablecloths embroidered with delicate swans. The large pillowed chairs the guests sat in were royal blue with the finest grade of golden lace bordering the cushions. Kendry would've loved to just stand and stare at the beauty. It would have been lovely to take it all in. But the servants were constantly rushing and she barely had a chance to take in the grandeur the few times she was allowed in the hall.

The night was coming to an end and Kendry was asked to refill glasses along with a few other servant girls. She began at the head of the table, refilling the host's glass. She moved on to the person to his right, when she heard a familiar laugh coming from far down the table. She looked up. There, at the far end, enjoying conversation and ale, was Malark.

CHAPTER TWENTY

Malark was alive. He was right there at the other end of the table. Her father's best friend was guzzling ale and laughing at someone's comment. She was in shock. The lady awaiting her glass to be filled cleared her throat to get Kendry's attention. She apologized and filled it to the brim. She continued down the line, having difficulty taking her eyes off the man who had been like an uncle to her. He was alive. How could it be? Did that mean her dad was alive, too? What was going on? She had to talk to him. Now.

Malark had already been served more ale. In fact, the other servant girls had already attended to his side of the table, but she had to get his attention. This dinner party included a few of the King's officials. One of the men she knew to be a personal assistant to the prince. She had to be careful not to reveal who she was in front of anyone or give them reason to wonder why Malark would know the servant girl.

She walked over to his side of the table and acted like she was checking their glasses. When she got to him, she picked up his glass and held it just long enough for him to glance up to see what she was doing.

"I have plenty, thanks, Hon," he said nonchalantly. But when she didn't set his glass back down, he looked up at her. His expression was one of complete shock. He glanced around the table to make sure no one else was paying attention to his reaction toward a servant girl. She set the glass back down and signaled with her eyes for him to meet her outside.

He half-nodded and then joined back in the conversation around him. Kendry returned to the kitchen and put down the pitcher. She turned to Kina and said she needed to excuse herself for a moment, indicating she was going to relieve a full bladder, but instead took a long, out of the way path to end up out on the veranda. She hid in some bushes in the garden and waited. She knew it would be illogical to expect Malark to be able to excuse himself without suspicion. He would probably have to wait until the meal was over or there was a lull in conversation. But he wandered out onto the veranda much sooner than she expected.

"Pst," she signaled to him that she was in the bushes. He wandered over in her direction, continuously looking around him to make sure no one was following. He finally slid into the bushes and led her further into the garden. Then, he wrapped his arms around her and hugged her so tight she started to cry tears of joy.

"Kendry," he said with such relief as he pulled his arms away and looked into her eyes. "What are you doing here? Are you okay?"

"I'm fine," she whispered.

"They tried to convince me you were a traitor. I showed up at the tavern right as the king's men arrived. I told them it was preposterous to think you would have anything to do with Shadenberg or slave traders, but they claimed they had orders from the king to arrest you. They brought back a note they said you left written to your father about traveling to your aunt's place. That was very clever of you. As soon as I saw it, I knew you were somewhere safe. But this is the last place I expected to find you!" He hugged her again.

"So glad to see you! Malark, we were told that you were dead. That you all were dead. But, you're alive!"

"It was a lie, Kendry. We discovered that Lieutenant Trent was a traitor spying for Shadenberg. We needed him to believe that something happened that would lead the king to tell you all we died. That way we could follow him to his contact and lead Shadenberg to believe our forces were down. You all at the tavern were only supposed to think we were dead for a few hours. Your father and I were there outside the tavern when they brought you the

138

message. We waited outside the Academy with some of our men and tracked Trent as he took off."

"My father!" Kendry said. "He's alive!"

Malark paused. He looked like his emotions were going through turmoil as he tried to squeeze words out. "He was. He might be. Kendry...I'm so sorry, but I do believe he's gone for good."

"What happened? Where is he? Tell me everything."

Malark looked over his shoulder. There were voices out on the veranda. He whispered, "He was alive, Kendry, but the king sent him on a mission and..."

"Then, he's alive!" she said, positive of it. "He wouldn't die on a mission. He's undercover somewhere. He wanted everyone to think he was dead for some reason," she said as she touched the medallion hanging under her blouse. "But I will never stop until I find him, Malark! My life mission will be to find him! I don't care where I have to go or what risk I need to take." Kendry's passionate personality was pouring out of her. Malark gently took hold of her wrists to try to calm her down.

They could hear voices getting closer. Someone may have been admiring the garden. Malark looked down at Kendry's wrist. She was wearing the bracelet he had given her. He rubbed his thumb above it, staring at her crescent shaped birthmark and a tear formed in the corner of his eye.

"Guards! Here! Hurry!" he yelled toward the veranda. Kendry's face changed from one with a mission to one completely confused. She turned around and heard footsteps running toward her. Malark's light grasp on her wrist turned into a tight grip. "I'm sorry," he mumbled, avoiding eye contact.

Everything happened so fast. Men rushed toward them. Her head spun as the recollection that Malark was betraying her sunk in.

Instinct took over. She knew Malark well and she knew his left knee was painful and weak. It was the reason he didn't go on missions or join battles, anymore. So, she kicked it as hard as she could. He fell in pain, trying to take her down with him. But she was too fast. She started to run and saw two soldiers coming at her. Malark yelled at them to grab her. The first soldier advanced, but he must've assumed she was just an average girl because he didn't use any urgency or caution in his attempt. Kendry had him down on the ground before he knew what had happened. The other soldier took notice. Malark yelled that she was the traitor from Tavern's End and must be brought to the king alive.

The soldier on the ground pulled himself up. The other guard was already analyzing Kendry. She faced him, ready to fight. The guard took out his sword thinking a weapon might make her think twice before lunging at him. Instead, she was calculating how she could use them against each other. She darted behind the guard that she had first knocked down, who was already sore from her punches and kicks. She swiped his leg while elbowing his face. He tripped in front of the guard with the sword, giving Kendry just enough time to run. She darted to a pillar at the end of the garden. As if it had been a staircase, she flew up that pillar and climbed onto the roof. Edging her way to the back of the roof, she balanced, and walked along a limestone wall until she was outside the property. Then, she scampered down and ran for the house next door. Scaling a wall, she made it up to that house's roof. She crawled to stay out of sight until she found an alcove hidden under the peak of the roof. Hiding in the shadow, she sat there for what seemed like an hour. Her body was freezing.

Commotion had broken out in the garden next door after she ran away. It sounded like they had called more guards for help. She could hear yelling and people scurrying around. She made herself comfortable and stayed put. At one point she actually heard Malark yelling at someone that if Kendry didn't want to be found, she wouldn't be found. He encouraged them to give up the search. This made her smile, knowing that he recognized her ability to perform the skills she watched him train others at the Academy, year after year. But the smile wasn't one of satisfaction as she still couldn't believe she was using those skills to hide from Malark who had just betrayed her.

Getting back to the Refuge was the hardest thing she'd ever done. There were guards all around the city searching for her. She had to be very careful and methodical. She knew she'd be locked out of the Refuge by the time she finally got there. It was almost midnight when she did make it to the alleyway behind the Refuge. She tried to blend in with some of the kids asleep on the street until she was sure no one was around the Refuge. She decided her best bet was to climb the back wall and sneak in the window on her floor. She knew she'd be discovered by some of the girls who might be awake or wake up, but it was worth the chance.

Getting lucky, because no one saw her enter the window, Kendry decided to bypass going straight to bed and attempt to venture downstairs to see if Hendrick was possibly still awake, awaiting her return. She snuck quietly down the steps and was ecstatic to see Hendrick waiting up by the window, searching for her. She ran and gave him a huge hug. Her emotions hit their tipping point and she began to cry. Hendrick didn't know what was going on, but he stroked her hair lightly and tried to calm her down.

"Shh. It's okay," he said gently. Finally, she pulled her head away and looked up at him with tear-stained cheeks. He continued, "Kina said there was some sort of problem at the dinner party and they were looking for a criminal. I was so worried when you didn't come back."

Kendry just shook her head slowly. He had no idea that she was the criminal.

He smiled. "Do you want to know about my night?" he asked. And without waiting for her to respond, he blurted out, "I won! Kendry, I won!"

She had totally forgotten about the competition. "What? Oh my! What happened?"

"The first event was a race. Plain and simple. Hundreds and hundreds of us took off across the training field. There were some obstacles to climb over and some to climb under. I came in seventeenth. They kept the top twenty and sent everyone else home. The next event was...you're going to laugh...sword fighting! We all had to fight four others. They had these crazy armor things on us and the swords had some kind of painted tar on their blades. If you were able to tap and mark your opponent in a spot on their armor that could kill someone, you got a point. You had to have at least three points to move on."

He smiled again, bigger this time. "I got four points!"

She smiled back.

"Only eight of us moved on to the last event. It was a huge pole with fake limbs sticking out. The event was simply a race to the top and back down. We did it one at a time and they would time us. They had an hourglass of sand going and when you made it back down, they poured the sand you used into a bowl. The winner was the person with the least sand. And...my bowl looked empty compared to everyone else's!" He was so excited that Kendry couldn't help but hug him again.

"So, what does this mean?" Kendry asked. "Did you get the money?"

"No, not yet. But this is why I was waiting up for you. I leave tomorrow for the palace. It was me and two other guys that officially won. The three of us, and our servants, will be hosted at the palace for two days. We will get to dine with the king and meet the princess. Then, we will begin a journey with the prince and his officials to see the layout of battle preparations for war between Crestavia and Shadenberg at the Military Base near the Great Divide. They want to get our feedback on military operations...isn't that crazy? I'm going to be giving feedback to Prince Casper! We are to get our monetary prize somewhere during this, I believe, because they said we'd then be back in the fall to participate in the tournament with the nobles."

Kendry was trying to take all the information in. She was still reeling trying to process the fact that Malark was alive and had just tried to have her arrested for treason. She wanted to share that information with Hendrick but felt like she would be stealing his joy. He was the happiest she had ever seen him. Yet, she knew that the king's guards could show up any moment at the Refuge. It wouldn't take long for them to figure out that Kendry was posing as a servant girl and that the servant girls often lived at refuges.

"I'm going with you, tomorrow," she began. "I'm going to be your servant."

He smiled. "I figured as much, but do you really think it is safe for you to be anywhere near the palace? I think maybe I should bring Mavo with me and we can relay everything we learn to you as soon as we get back."

"No one will recognize me," she promised. "I've got to go with you."

He started to argue and so she decided to just blurt it out. "Malark is alive! I saw him tonight at the dinner party."

"What!" Hendrick didn't believe what he was hearing. "Did you talk to him?"

"Yes, until he yelled at guards to arrest me."

"Huh? Malark wanted you arrested?"

"Yes. I don't know what is going on," she said as she paced back and forth. "He was there, alive. I was overjoyed. I hugged him. He told me that the message from the king that everyone was dead was a lie meant for Lieutenant Trent."

"Trent?"

"According to Malark, Trent was a spy from Shadenberg. They figured it out and so they set a trap for him. Malark said he and my dad were there when we got the message and that they followed Trent after he got the news that they were dead. Of course, I have no clue whether or not to believe a word Malark says. He told me my father COULD be dead. That he was sent on another mission by the king. I don't know that I believe it. I mean, Malark is hanging out at a dinner party with the king's officials. He wanted me arrested and he wants me to think my father is dead. I'm starting to wonder if Malark framed my dad for something. Maybe Malark framed me, too. Maybe he wants my dad's position or something. I don't know, I find it all so hard to believe. I have loved Malark my whole life! He's my family!"

Hendrick hugged Kendry, again, as she began to sob. He held her and tried to think of what to say. It was true. Malark had been super close with Kendry and her father. How could he betray them? Not knowing how to respond, he went back to the plan for tomorrow.

"Then, I really don't think you should go with me to the palace. If Malark is around, he will see me and look immediately for you. You have to stay as far from the palace as possible."

"Hendrick, soldiers will be looking for me here, soon. Maybe even now. I can hide in the forest or take off alone somewhere, but that doesn't get me any closer to finding my dad or freeing our friends. You need to go to the palace and get that money. I need to try to meet with the king in private. Maybe Malark has filled his head with lies."

"No. It's a suicide mission. They will find you and arrest you and probably hang you for treason. You will not be going! You are going to head straight to the forest, get our stuff, and get out of town. I will go with you and forget the palace and the money, if you want."

Kendry walked over to a seat and plopped own. She put her face in her hands. She knew Hendrick was right. But they were so close to getting the money and so close to getting answers.

"Okay, I'll make you a deal. Let me go as your servant and I will be as quiet and hidden as possible. I just need to be there. I need to hear and watch things. Please, Hendrick! Please!"

"Kendry, what if Malark or someone sees you?"

"He won't be at the palace! And no one else knows what I look like. I will make sure I am disguised well. Please, Hendrick! Please!" she begged.

"I feel like we're both going to regret this," he said. She jumped back up and hugged him again.

"Thank you! Thank you! I'll see you in the morning. We need to get some sleep. If guards come in the night, I will dodge out the window and hide in the forest. I promise."

Hendrick nodded. He didn't know what else to say.

They both snuck back up to their floors quietly. Kendry climbed into bed, knowing she wouldn't sleep a wink. She needed to do some planning.

The next morning, she quietly woke Dola early. "Dola...I was wondering if you could help me with something?"

CHAPTER TWENTY-ONE

Hendrick was enjoying all the extra attention from his friends after they found out he was going to the palace. Druvan and his sidekicks were annoyed and went upstairs to eat their breakfast to avoid Hendrick's moment in the spotlight. Kendry, Molly, and Dola were still upstairs and hadn't come down yet. The rest of the residents were getting breakfast and lounging about in the commons room. Mildra was keeping an eye on things and Brutt was upstairs with Druvan and the others.

The sound of horses galloping toward the Refuge could be heard over their conversations. Everyone paused when a loud knock banged on the front door. Mildra looked annoyed. She wandered over to the door and opened it. One of the king's officials stood with two guards.

"We are looking for a young woman that we believe might live here," he said loudly, making sure everyone in the commons room and dining area could hear him.

"We have lots of young women that live here," Mildra said condescendingly. "Any particular type I should be checking for?"

The official looked irritated. He pulled a scroll out of a bag on his arm. He unrolled it and faced it toward her. Then he panned it around the room.

Hendrick's mouth dropped open. It was the missing picture! The portrait he had drawn of Kendry. The one that had been missing from his room at Mister Carter's in Tavern's End. How did the king's official have it? His heart started racing. Though Kendry looked a little different now than when he drew that picture, everyone there would be able to identify her.

Most everyone who looked at the picture then glanced at Hendrick. It was like they were waiting for his response to lead them on how to answer. Thankfully, Mildra broke the ice.

"What do you want with that girl, anyway? Did she steal something?"

"She's wanted for treason. She is a traitor to King Gadden and Crestavia. She's the one that got those people in Tavern's End taken as slaves."

Gasps and whispers erupted. Hendrick could feel eyes on him.

"Well, I hope you find her, then!" said Mildra. "But, she ain't at this Refuge. Never seen anyone like that. Any of you?" she asked the crowds of teens. Everyone either froze or shook their heads no.

Hendrick spoke up. "Never seen her before." He knew his statement would emphasize to his friends that he didn't want Kendry sold out. The official didn't look super convinced.

"None of you have ever seen this girl before?" he asked again, staring at each of them in the eyes as he scanned the room. Most of them shook their heads again or looked away. But, then one voice spoke up.

"They're all lying."

Hendrick's heart sunk. He looked over and felt betrayed at the voice that was disloyal to him and Kendry. It was Thron.

"That girl's name is Kelly."

Hendrick wanted to punch Thron square in the face. He held his breath instead, watching the official. How was he going to get word up to Kendry to escape out the window? He was trying to think of a way to excuse himself or signal to Kina to go upstairs without the official noticing.

Thron continued. "Kelly's pretty well-liked which is why no one wants to rat her out. That and maybe some of them don't recognize her in that picture. She's a little older now. But, that's definitely her."

146

The official handed the scroll to Thron. "Positive?"

"Yes," Thron answered. The official started searching the room and then walking toward the stairwell. "But she doesn't live here anymore," Thron continued.

"What?" the official turned and glared at him.

"She left a couple of weeks ago. Ran away in the middle of the night. Her bed's been filled with a new girl. Now that we know she's a traitor, that explains why she took off. Maybe she was afraid someone would recognize her."

Mavo then piped in. "Let me see it," he pulled the scroll Thron was holding closer to him. "Yeah, that is Kelly. I heard her saying something about wanting to see the Cascadia Mountains."

"Me, too," Kina said. "She had family there or something."

Hendrick wondered if it was a coincidence that they picked the same place Kendry had lied about in her note at the Academy as the place she was rumored to run off to, but he hoped they really would focus on the Cascadia Mountains and get out of there.

"I want every single person in this building in this room, NOW!" the official yelled, getting angry. Two of the guards set off up the staircase. Hendrick's blood pressure rose. If only he could get word to Kendry that they were coming. She'd need to escape out the window now.

A few of the teens came down the staircase. Hendrick watched closely. Would the guards have Kendry?

He saw Molly and Dola stepping down the stairs with another girl between them. He jumped a little. He had never seen the other girl before. At least that was his first thought. And then he realized it was Kendry. She looked different to say the least. Her hair was shorter, bobbed a few inches below her ears. It was no longer the faded brown from the old caddonberries, but was instead a dark brown. Almost black. Her eye brows were dyed to match which is what probably made the most difference. Even her face looked different. Somehow her freckles had been removed and her lips looked fuller.

147

Her cheek bones were more defined making her face appear thinner. He stared trying to make sure it was really her. She made no eye contact, but quietly followed the others down the steps and merged back into the corner of the crowd. A few seconds later, Druvan and his buddies came down with Brutt. Finally, Director Druble arrived at the bottom floor and invited the king's official to come to his office. The official declined, but continued scoping out the room.

"If she returns, contact us immediately," he said, leading the soldiers out. Everyone looked around making faces at each other. They all knew Kendry was there hiding in their midst. All except Druvan, his friends, and Brutt who had been upstairs with a few others. Mildra explained to Brutt and Director Druble that they were looking for some criminal, but she must've been at another refuge. Satisfied, they dispersed and told everyone to get to work and on with their day. Kina, Mavo, Kenan, Molly, Thron, Hendrick, and Dola made their way over to Kendry.

"What do you think?" Dola asked. "I really am an artist, aren't I? No one would ever recognize her!"

Hendrick shook his head. No one would recognize her that didn't know her.

"Where'd that come from?" Kendry asked, surprised to see the picture of herself.

"They left without it?" Kina asked. "You better hide that. They'll be back."

Hendrick looked at Kendry. "Maybe Malark took it from Mister Carter's house. I don't know. But the king's officials had it and brought it here looking for you. You're not safe here."

Thron cleared his throat. "Don't you think you guys owe us an explanation? What's going on?"

Hendrick looked again at Kendry. She nodded. She trusted everyone there except maybe Dola and Thron. Meet us in the forest and we'll talk.

Not long after, they filed into the area where they had met often to train. Dola was the only one who had never been there and the group wished that she still hadn't been allowed. She talked non-stop and quickly got on most of their nerves.

"Fill us in," Thron demanded, not willing to wait a moment longer.

"We're from Tavern's End," Hendrick began. "We're not siblings. Just friends. Our whole town was taken hostage by slave traders right after we found out that Kendry's father, an important general, had been killed. The two of us barely, and I mean just barely, got away. Without any explanation, the king's officials showed up saying they wanted to arrest Kendry for being a spy for Shadenberg. We've been on the run ever since."

The others were quiet. Thron spoke up. "Well, that explains a lot. She can fight because she's a general's daughter. But, why in the world would you run to the Capital where the king's men would be looking for you?"

"We need answers," Kendry explained. "Nothing makes sense. Why would the king blame me? And do the slave traders have something to do with what happened to my dad? We're hoping that with the money Hendrick won we could go to Regaria and try to bribe people for answers."

Mavo jumped a little. "Regaria? That's not a great idea."

"I agree," said Kina. "You may never return from Regaria if you go."

"Well, we'll have to figure that out," Kendry added. "Right now, we need to get ready to have Hendrick go to the palace. I'm going to disguise myself as his servant and join him. They plan to travel to the Great Divide and if Hendrick has his money by then, we may try to run off from there and head toward Regaria. I don't know..." she was obviously thinking aloud and Hendrick wasn't sure if he agreed it was a good idea or not.

"Servants need to be male," Mavo said. "They won't let him bring a female servant."

"They might allow it if it was his 'sister'," Molly challenged.

Kendry looked at Kenan, "Got any extra clothes I could borrow?"

CHAPTER TWENTY-TWO

An hour later, Kendry with dark black hair was dressed in Kenan's clothes and wearing one of Thron's hats. Her physique was obviously female so Mavo suggested one of his large overcoats for her to swim around in. Being that servants often wore whatever clothes they could get a hold of, no one would think it was unusual that her clothes were baggy. If she kept the hat on and her chin tipped toward her chest, she did look like she might be a male servant. They all gave her advice about not making eye contact with anyone and staying back in the shadows away from anybody important.

No one seemed to agree that it was a good idea for her to go with Hendrick, but Mildra now knew who Kendry was and any number of the other residents could decide it was worth a bribe to tell the guards Kendry's whereabouts. So, they were careful not to share openly that she was going with Hendrick.

They all wished them well and made them promise this wouldn't be the last they'd see them. It was sad saying goodbye and realizing they wouldn't be returning to the Refuge. Now that Kendry's identity was known, it was no longer an option to reside there, but leaving their new friends was harder than they had expected. Kendry and Hendrick took off for the palace, butterflies in their stomachs.

Upon arriving, Hendrick had to wait a long time outside the front gate. He was told he would need to be verified by the competition's head official and that man was in no rush to arrive. The two other winners of the competition showed up with their two servants. They all made themselves comfortable sitting on decaying logs outside the outer gate of the training center.

One of the other winners introduced himself right away to Hendrick.

"I'm Graeme," he said and asked why they weren't being let in. After Hendrick explained that they had to wait for verification, the other winner showed up. He purposely chose not to socialize with Hendrick and Graeme. When Graeme introduced himself to him, he huffed and turned away. Graeme gave Hendrick a look that almost made him laugh. The third guy was pretty stuck up.

By the time the competition's head official showed up a couple of hours later, Graeme and Hendrick had hit it off and were enjoying themselves in conversation. The third winner stood up and approached the official first. "My name's Ruttin. I'm sure you remember me from the competition. Now, my dear fellow, may I ask why have we had to sit here for so long?"

The official ignored Ruttin. He looked at Hendrick and Graeme. "Your servants?" he asked. They all pointed toward the shadows of a tree across the way. Kendry was sitting quietly about six feet apart from two guys who looked as bored as she felt. When she had first arrived, one of them looked right at her and said, "I didn't know girls were allowed."

Kendry's heart sunk. But she improvised. "I'm his sister." The guy nodded. That seemed to satisfy him. The other servant asked if any of them ever thought they'd see the day where they'd get to go to the palace. Kendry and the first servant shook their heads no. And then none of them spoke another word for the next few hours.

The official finally went and talked to the guards behind the gate. Eventually, a man came out to lead the three winners and their servants inside. The men were taken to a hall and told to be seated. A stern woman came in and gave them a long list of directions and instructions for the next couple of days. They were told exactly what to do and what not to do. Their own servants would be expected to take care of their needs, except at the royal dinner where only the king's servants would be allowed.

Eventually, some royal guards showed up and escorted them by horse to the palace. Entering the large gates felt surreal. They were each shown to their guest rooms. Hendrick's was as big as Mister Carter's whole house. He had never seen such luxury and flopped down on the bed as soon as he was left alone. He couldn't believe his luck! Then, he thought about Kendry. She was being escorted to the servants' quarters. Suddenly, panic gripped him. What if someone recognized her? What if she got herself in trouble? He needed to check in with her.

He'd been instructed that a string by his bed would ring a bell for his servant in her quarters, if he needed anything. He wanted to pull that string right then, but realized she probably hadn't even made it to her room yet. Hendrick hoped she would stay out of trouble.

After Kendry was left alone is a small closet sized room with no windows, she sat on the hard bed that practically filled the whole room. This would be her chance to begin searching the palace. Hendrick was told to rest for the afternoon until he and the other three men would be introduced to the king that evening. Kendry was expected to lay out his clothes, but figured Hendrick was on his own for that. She wasn't going to waste a moment.

She didn't know exactly what she'd be searching for, but deep down she wanted to see the king. She knew that was ludicrous because the king wouldn't just be lounging about in an area of the palace that a servant could easily get to. And if she did see the king, what would she do? Would she walk up to him and ask him why he framed her? Would she demand to know what happened to her father? She knew none of that would be wise. But she couldn't waste her one opportunity in the palace by sitting in a small servant's room waiting until evening.

Kendry slowly opened her door. It creaked and her heart raced. She was in the palace. She could not afford to get caught sneaking around. But, sneaking around was exactly what she was planning on doing. She figured the best way not to look suspicious if someone saw her was to look confident in that she knew where she was going. So, she boldly walked down the long hall.

Over the next several hours, she learned the layout of the main rooms and halls of the palace. Twice she had to pretend to be lost and ask those questioning her identity where to find Hendrick's room because he had rung for her. Two other times, she randomly asked servants for directions and they didn't question who she was or why she was there. Eventually, she started to feel comfortable with the layout and how to get around.

As she was heading back to her room, realizing that it was getting closer to dinner time, she scored the best news of the afternoon. She saw a long curly staircase that had a rail that one could use to jump up onto a beam way above the floor downstairs. She smiled. This is how she could get around unnoticed. If she could get up onto that beam, she could sneak around the outer edge of the huge entrance room and end up on any wing of the palace without having to walk across out in the open.

That evening, Kendry knocked on Hendrick's door. He was so relieved to see her that he hugged her. "Where have you been? I've been ringing that darn bell for hours!"

"Just getting familiar with the place," she said in a calm voice. "I'm fine."

He frowned, but was relieved.

"Let's get you ready for dinner." She helped comb his hair to look fancier than how he normally wore it. She flattened out his shoulder pads and smiled. There wasn't much else for her to do. He had already been dressed in the nice clothes he had borrowed from Thron.

"You nervous?" she asked.

"Nah," he said sarcastically. "I mean I'm sure I'll meet lots of kings in my lifetime." The enormity of the evening hit them both. This was a big deal. She wished him luck and gave him a quick kiss on the cheek. He blushed and without making eye contact left the room.

At dinner, he expected to meet the king, but was told that King Gadden was feeling under the weather. Instead, Prince Casper and Princess Gendella were there to welcome the three men. Prince Casper congratulated them on their success and wanted to hear all about their backgrounds. As dinner began to be served, they were encouraged to share a little about themselves. Graeme responded first.

"I was born in the Valley of Cascadia. Lived in a few different towns there…Trania, Cascade, and Munker. I'm a son of a sailor and so when I came of age, I started helping him with shipments around the empire. I've traveled to most places west of Shadenberg. I can speak many languages. At sixteen, my father died and my family moved to Munker Bay. Mostly logged trees there. Just came to the Capital a few weeks ago. Heard about the competition and thought I would give it a go."

Prince Casper seemed impressed with Graeme's talent for speaking many languages. He asked him which ones and then they made small talk in other dialects. Hendrick and Ruttin had no idea what was being said. Princess Gendella seemed to understand as well and laughed at a joke Graeme made. Hendrick was feeling smaller and smaller by the moment.

Ruttin decided to interrupt and give his background. He was the son of a carpenter and grew up in the Capital. Though not a nobleman, he was sure to brag about every important person he had met or his family knew. He seemed to think of himself superior to Hendrik and Graeme and his arrogance showed. It was obvious to Hendrick that Prince Casper was not impressed with Ruttin.

Last, the attention turned to Hendrick. He was glad they had served drinks by this point because he needed one. His heart was racing and his hands were clammy. He opened his mouth to speak and nothing came out. He cleared his throat and decided to tell the truth.

"I grew up in Tavern's End. Both my parents died of a plague when I was little. I was taken in by a blacksmith who let me apprentice under him. When the slave traders came, I was visiting a friend in Glenville," he lied. "But when I went back, there was nothing left of my small town. So, I made my way to the Capital and got work as a stable boy, living at a refuge."

Ruttin sneered as if he was embarrassed for Hendrick to only have that biography to give. Graeme looked interested and bit into a moist roll. But Prince Caspian was enthralled.

"So, you know the traitor, personally, then?" he stared at Hendrick. Immediately Hendrick wished he had gone with the circus story instead. He just brought a lot of attention to himself which meant bringing attention to Kendry. Thankfully, only the king's servants were currently present at the banquet.

"Uh, yeah. She was a girl in town. Honestly, I can't believe she would do what she has been excused of, no offense, your highness," he added realizing that might have sounded insulting. "Just that she never seemed the type to break the law and I don't know how she would've ever met slave traders in the first place. She worked at the tavern most all the time."

"You any idea where she would be now?"

"I've heard she went to stay with family in the Cascadia Mountains. At least, that's the rumor."

"Yes, I've heard that, too," he said. "But I have reason to believe she has been in the Capital recently. You haven't seen her or ran into her?"

"Oh gosh, no. Wow, Kendry might be in the Capital? That's news to me! Crazy! Why would she come here?"

Ignoring Hendrick's question, Prince Casper continued, "I think this is wonderful the way that fate worked it out for you to be here! I want you to meet with my right-hand man, an official named Sleege. I would like you to tell him everything that you know about Kendry. It is very important that we find her. What she did broke my father's heart."

Princess Gendella squirmed in her seat. Both Hendrick and Graeme noticed. She tried to cover by asking a question, "Would anyone like more stew?" The servants immediately rushed to each of them to fill their bowls.

"So, do any of you have real experience with battle or strategy for battle?" Prince Casper asked, getting back to business.

They all shook their heads no. He looked disappointed. "Well, we are looking for a Regency Advisor to help us create the most powerful army in the world. It will be fascinating to hear your opinions and advice when we show you what we've been working on in the Great Divide. We'll be leaving first thing in the morning."

Dinner continued with many courses of incredible delicacies. Hendrick couldn't believe all the food and how it just kept coming. Graeme complimented the princess on her outfit. She gave him a courtesy smile and then turned to her brother and asked to be dismissed. Once Princess Gendella excused herself, the men continued on with their feast and conversation. When their banquet concluded, Hendrick went back to his room. Kendry was sitting on his bed and jumped up as he walked in.

"How did it go?

Hendrick gave a rundown of the evening. Kendry was disappointed to hear that King Gadden was not in attendance. She was initially perturbed that Hendrick told the truth about being from Tavern's End, but then realized it was a great way to get conversation going about the false accusation against Kendry. She wished he had gotten more information. She wondered what Sleege would want to know about her. Maybe they could twist things to encourage the king's men to search in the wrong direction, again.

Hendrick was exhausted. He had been nervous about meeting royalty, blown-away by the meal, and terrified about giving something away about Kendry or her getting caught. It had been an emotional night to say the least. Kendry decided not to mention to him that she planned to scope out the palace again after she left his room.

They said good night and she promised to be there first thing in the morning. Then, she left his room and went straight to the spiral staircase that allowed her to get footing onto a beam above the main room. Once on the rafter, she was in her element. It felt good to climb. She scaled a couple of other poles and pillars and ended up walking across a giant beam to the other side of the main hall. She saw a couple of servants come and go, down below, but nobody noticed her. Once she got across the room, she climbed down and stuck mostly to the shadows. Eventually, she slipped into the far wing of the palace, where she had not been able to get to during the day.

Though the palace was heavily guarded on the outside, once inside there weren't any guards. Which is why Kendry found it odd that this new wing of the palace did have guards posted. She had to be very careful not to get caught. She went back to what she knew best and climbed up a decorative wall with pillars until she could pull herself up onto the ceiling's rafters. Hiding up in the ceiling allowed her to watch down below and listen without being seen at all. It took her a long time to climb across the room she was in and fit through an air duct hole into the next room, but when she was finally through, she knew it had been worth the struggle to get there.

Down below was Prince Casper, another man who she assumed may be Sleege, and Malark! They looked like they were finishing up a serious discussion. Malark was getting ready to leave. Kendry shook a little when she saw Malark. It was still so hard to believe he had joined the enemy. Or maybe he was the enemy and he was getting the palace to join in on his crazy ideas. She didn't know what to think, but she knew he couldn't be trusted and that she would have to be extremely careful from now on knowing he was in the palace. He would see right through her weak disguise. And, if he saw Hendrick, he may assume that Kendry would not be far away.

As Malark was heading out of the room, he turned back to the prince and practically yelled, "We must locate and apprehend General Walbrek! That is our main objection!"

Prince Casper nodded. "I agree. But the girl is still top priority, too. I want his daughter. It's the only way to get him back."

Malark was getting angry. "I told you! She is gone! She would not dare come back to the Capital! She knows I would have her arrested and your men are looking for her. Sleege can talk to Hendrick all he wants. But if the girl doesn't want to be found, she will not be found! Our focus should be on Walbrek!"

Kendry's stomach stirred and her heart raced. Her father! Alive! She had to make sure they did not get to her father!

Then the man she assumed was Sleege spoke up, stopping Malark before he exited. "We have good intel that says he is in Bulenduria. We've sent ambassadors to talk to the Bulendurian tribal leaders. We're doing everything we can. We will send in Crestavia's best to apprehend him. It will just take time. We need more information to find out where he is hidden."

Malark shook his head. "It's been weeks. If King Gadden were still alive, we'd already have Walbrek here. You are playing things too safe. You need to put our best people on it, now, and prepare for casualties. Walbrek won't get taken without a bloodbath."

Kendry's eyes popped open wide. King Gadden was dead? This was news. So, Prince Casper was running the show. Or maybe Malark. She was confused, but did everything she could to stay still and listen intently.

"I think you should remember who you are talking to, Malark," Prince Casper said with a threatening tone. "You don't tell me how to run my kingdom. The end goal is Shadenberg. War isn't just looming, it's inevitable. We can't lose our best men in Bulenduria. We need them available against Shadenberg. Walbrek is a priority and it will be done when Sleege says so."

Malark grunted and walked out.

When the door slammed and the Prince and Sleege were alone, Kendry watched as they both sat down.

"He's going to become a problem," Sleege said. "Do we need to keep him around?"

"For now, yes. He has sway with the troops and knows a lot about defensive and offensive strategy. He's stubborn, but far from useless." He paused a moment and then continued. "I want you to stick to Hendrick on our travels tomorrow. Gain as much information as you can about Kendry. We need to find her. Once we have her, we'll have no problem getting General Walbrek."

Sleege nodded and then got up and left. The Prince paced around the room for a while. Kendry watched him intently. Her instincts told her he was not a good man.

159

After a bit, he rang for a servant to come to the large room he was pacing about in and seemed annoyed that it was taking her so long to arrive. Kendry assumed the room was some sort of study or library based on the number of scrolls and books and seats. Not long after, a servant opened the door. "Yes, your highness," a woman said.

"Matel, is my sister already asleep for the night?"

The servant looked hesitant to answer. "I'm sure she probably has retired, your Highness," Matel said humbly.

"I'm not sure she has, Matel. Nor are you. Find her and tell her to get herself in bed and to stay away from that dreaded stable manager or I will make sure he does not continue his employment here or anywhere in Crestavia! Do you understand?"

"Yes, yes, your Highness," Matel said, staring at the ground. She rushed out of the room.

As soon as Matel left, Prince Casper downed the rest of his drink and then threw his glass across the room in anger. It hit a bookshelf and shattered. Another servant hurried to the door and knocked. He opened it and told the servant to clean up the mess and then left.

The servant ran off to get a broom and another servant joined her. One of them asked the other, "What was that all about this time?"

"I think Princess Gendella and Orfe have been caught together again."

"Oh, goodness," the other responded. "Won't she learn! She has to be a lot sneakier if she doesn't want Casper to find things out."

They finished cleaning up the glass and then Kendry watched the two servants leave. Kendry took her time and finally made it back to the hall where Hendrick's room was located. She knew he would be sound asleep, but wanted him to be up to date on all the information she had gotten before the morning.

She quietly turned the doorknob. Surprised it was unlocked, she was glad to see his lamp burning and him sitting up on the bed. She bolted in and closed the door behind her while beginning to spill all she needed to share with him.

"Hendrick, Malark's here! He's working with Prince Casper to get my dad. They think he's in Bulenduria! Casper wants me, too! And, King Gadden is dead! And…"

Before she could say another word, Hendrick stood up and the look on his face terrified her. He turned his eyes to the other side of the room and Kendry realized they were not alone.

CHAPTER TWENTY-THREE

W ell, hey there, Sweetheart! You're a girl!" Graeme stood up straight from the desk he had been lounging against.

Kendry almost choked. She looked back at Hendrick. What was Graeme doing here? How could she have been so stupid to start talking without scoping out the room first? Why didn't she knock before bolting inside?

"I'm...I'm his sister," Kendry began.

"Sounds like a lot of family business going on. Who's your dad? What's he doing in Bulenduria? That's not a nice place to visit, ya know? Lots of savages intent on killing those who don't belong there."

Kendry was shaking. She looked back to Hendrick. "Can we talk...alone?"

"Aw, now why do you want to go and exclude me?" Graeme asked. "This is the most interesting thing that's happened since we've gotten here. I want to hear all the details!"

Hendrick was silent. He was unsure what to do. Kendry ignored Graeme and looked right at Hendrick, holding his glare awaiting him to respond.

"King Gadden's dead?" Hendrick finally asked.

"Yes, King Gadden is dead," she began. Not wanting to say more, she analyzed the situation before her. She'd already spilled the beans. There was not much she could say to hide the facts. This guy sitting in Hendrick's room could use this information in many ways. He could blackmail them or turn them in for the things she had said. But then she decided she didn't care. She knew where her father was at and that he was alive and that was all that mattered.

"Look, Sleege is going to use the ride out of town tomorrow to try to get information about me. You are going to need to come up with something good to mislead him. Something that he will think he got out of you or manipulated you into sharing. When we get to the Great Divide, I'm taking off to Bulenduria. You can come or stay."

"Kendry..." Hendrick began with a sound of warning in his voice. But Graeme interrupted.

"This is hilarious! So, you are a girl, dressed like a boy... and Sleege, the king's right-hand man, is trying to find you? And you are going to ride with us all to the Great Divide and then take off to Bulenduria, alone or with him," he pointed at Hendrick. "...to a place with savages that will chop you up and have you for breakfast. All because you think your dad is there? Did I get this right, Sweetheart?"

Hendrick was shaking his head in frustration. Kendry was getting angry at the condescending tone in Graeme's voice.

She snapped back, "Yes, that is correct! The palace is looking for me because a man named Malark framed me. He says that I am the traitor who got the residents of Tavern's End taken by slave traders. But I did not. And Hendrick knows that because he was with me when we just barely escaped from getting taken ourselves! King Gadden is dead and his awful son, Prince Casper, is trying to find me and kill my father, who Malark tried to convince me was dead! But I just overheard Prince Casper, Sleege, and Malark saying that he is Bulenduria! There, you know everything, now! You happy?" she yelled.

He was shocked at her outburst. But he smiled and laughed a little. "I'm very happy," he said. "Very happy, indeed."

Kendry was fuming. "You disgusting, horrible, human being!

Graeme just laughed a little. "You are cute when you're angry, aren't you?"

Hendrick looked at Graeme. "Knock it off. Was anything you told me before Kendry bolted in here, true? Are you really looking to run away from Crestavia and have no interest in the tournament in the fall after you get your money?"

Graeme was taken back by the change in topic. He nodded. "The princess is not going to choose me to court her. She's going to choose a nobleman, obviously. And, I don't have any strategic battle talent that would qualify me to become the Regency Advisor. Therefore, I just want the award money and then I want to get out of this place. Head somewhere west and start anew. But..." he paused and looked and Kendry. "It's not safe to travel alone. I've tried it. Didn't go well. I'd become a sitting duck for any bandit traveling by. So, if I was to travel with you two, between Hendrick and me, we could..."

Kendry stopped him. "No! No way!"

Graeme walked two steps closer to Kendry and gave her a wink. "Don't think you really have a say in the matter, Sweetheart. You made the mistake of telling me that Sleege and Prince Casper want your head on a silver platter and I happen to know right where you are and what your plans are. If you didn't want a new travel partner, well, you should've thought about that before you blabbed everything to me."

Kendry made a groaning noise. Graeme ignored her. He turned to Hendrick.

"I get that your first priority is taking care of your...uh, sister. I'm on board for traveling with you guys to the outskirts of Bulenduria. But I won't enter that land. It's suicide to go there. I'll wait in one of the villages in the valley for a few days. If you make it back, we can continue on together west. If not, we can part ways. I'm not asking for anything except someone to watch my back. And, in return, I'll keep your little secret and watch your backs. What do ya say? We get along well enough, don't we?"

"Just until the outskirts of Bulenduria," Hendrick replied. "Taking off from the Great Divide without arousing suspicion isn't going to be easy. Especially if two out of the three victors from the competition disappear. We're going to need to plan carefully."

Graeme nodded. "We might want to think of a better way to hide your servant, too? As of tomorrow, Sleege is going to be trailing you like a shadow, and anyone who looks at her too long will see that she's way too pretty to be a boy."

Kendry's blood pressure rose. She wanted to slap Graeme for even looking at her. Instead, she turned her back to him, took a deep breath, and ran her fingers through her hair. He was right. She wasn't going to be able to hide in plain sight for the whole journey to the Great Divide.

"I've got a plan," she said.

CHAPTER TWENTY-FOUR

This plan was probably Kendry's dumbest idea yet. Stealing a sword from Director Druble or sneaking around the palace paled in comparison. But she felt she didn't have any other choice. She was careful not to tell Hendrick or Graeme anything about it. She just told them to wait for news.

She spent the next hour crawling along rafters until she got lucky. There was Matel, down below, quietly leaving a room with a huge fancy door. If Kendry had to bet her life on it, she would guess that behind that door was Princess Gendella's room.

Sneaking in the room without going through the door was the difficult part. None of the rooms nearby had a way for her to get up into the air ducts. She had to circle back quite a bit until she found an entrance. Once inside the dark duct, she got her bearings mixed up and had a hard time finding the princess' room. Eventually, she came to a duct inside a closet that connected to the room where Gendella slept. Kendry quietly lowered her body down from the duct. She hung there for a moment wondering if her fall to the ground would be loud. She took a deep breath and dropped.

She landed on a hard brick floor, which seemed strange for a closet. Her fall had been louder than she had hoped so she stayed frozen for a few minutes to erase any suspicion that someone might be in the closet. She then snuck toward the door.

Gently, she pushed on it to get a feel for how heavy it was and realized it would push open quite easily. She pushed it just enough to peek her face through. She could see an elaborate four post bed with a velvet canopy in the middle of the room. She stepped out slowly and felt something sharp poke against her neck.

Hiding behind the door that Kendry had just slid open was Princess Gendella with a sword in hand. She had it pressed against Kendry's throat. Kendry's hands immediately rose to show they were empty.

The princess squinted at her. "Are you a girl?" she asked, taken back by Kendry's disguise. "A spy from Shadenberg?" she asked.

Kendry was afraid that talking might make the sword slice into her throat, but she whispered, "No, I'm not your enemy. I need your help. Please..."

Princess Gendella's face scrunched with curiosity. She stared at Kendry for a long time. Finally, removing the sword barely an inch away from Kendry, she asked, "You snuck into my bedroom in the middle of the night, dressed like a boy, because you need MY help? I'm really curious to hear you out before I call for my father's guards to execute you."

Kendry knew this was her only chance. She wasn't sure how to spit out everything she needed to say without upsetting the princess and getting decapitated.

"This is all going to sound crazy," Kendry began. "But I know a lot of things I probably shouldn't know. I don't want you to overreact with that sword, though. Would it be possible for you to hear me out before you do any damage to my throat?" The princess frowned and stepped a foot away, lowering the sword a little.

"Go on. I'm extremely curious to hear your explanation."

"I know your father's dead," she began. She saw the princess' surprise and tried to evaluate if it was safe to continue on.

"How do you know that?"

"I also know that you are in love with the stable manager named Orfe."
Again, Kendry held her breath hoping the princess wouldn't react in rage.

Gendella's face got white. "Who are you? How do you know these things?"

"I know that your brother will never allow you to be with Orfe and wants you to marry the nobleman that wins the tournament in the fall," Kendry was guessing on this point, but could tell by the princess' expression that it must be correct.

"I am the daughter of General Walbrek who was a close friend of your father's, from what I've heard."

"You're Walbrek's daughter!" The princess blinked a few times and analyzed Kendry's face. "Yes, you are! But you look so different! Oh, if my brother knew you were here..."

"Please don't tell him! Please hear me out!"

The princess wandered over to a large comfy chair near her bed and sat down. She lowered the sword to the ground, but kept it in her hand.

"I did not do what your father accused me of. I never worked with Shadenberg or helped any slave traders. I was attacked along with the others in Tavern's End and when I survived and was able to escape, I was shocked to hear I was getting accused of treason."

"That was my father's idea," the princess said. "Walbrek came here and told my father he was heading straight toward the Outpost and needed to keep you safe. He communicated to my father that you were stubborn and there was no way you'd leave Tavern's End or the Academy to come to the Capital. So, my father thought if he put a pretend warrant out for you, his soldiers could bring you in without you being able to decline the trip. He told the soldiers to invent a crime and bring you here. They must've heard about the slave traders and decided to name you as a traitor. Once you got here, my father planned to explain everything to you."

"Explain what?" Kendry asked, hoping for answers.

"I really don't know," Gendella responded. "I was present for part of their conversation but they were talking in code. Casper was there, too. He ordered your father not to go and they got in an argument. It upset my father. After Walbrek left, Casper and my dad started yelling at each other. I was dismissed." She took a deep breath and then continued, "I just know that your father wanted you safe and my father was willing to do anything to help your father. But…"

"What?" Kendry asked, eager for information.

"That was the night…the worse night…"

Gendella's eyes filled with tears. "My father got sick. Fast. It came on like food poisoning. That's what they are saying. I believe he was poisoned, but I'm not so sure it was accidental."

Kendry was shocked to hear this.

"Casper took over immediately. He wanted your dad brought back and sent soldiers after him. He wanted to be informed of your status and was livid when he found out that the guards my dad had sent were not able to find you. Casper decided that since we were on the brink of war with Shadenberg, it would endanger us to let news get out of my dad's death. Imagine if Shadenberg knew King Gadden was dead! They would attack for sure! So…Casper is getting used to running things and we keep telling people that my dad is under the weather or busy. But it has been killing me that we have not had the chance to mourn him, individually, or as a nation. My dad was a good man."

"My father always spoke highly about King Gadden," Kendry said and then offered condolences. She was very sorry that Gendella was mourning, but she needed to get back to why she was there.

"Gendella, I'm here in the palace because I am pretending to be the servant of Hendrick, one of the three men that won the competition. Unfortunately, Hendrick let your brother know that he is from Tavern's End and now Sleege is stuck to Hendrick like feathers on a bird."

"Sleege will find you! He will! You have to get out of here!"

"That's the plan," Kendry said. "Tomorrow morning, when everyone leaves for the Great Divide, will you be going?"

Princess Gendella shrugged. "Casper wants me to, but I told him I refuse. He's insisting. Making me go! He won't leave me here alone with Orfe. He has already planned to remove Orfe from his position beginning tomorrow. I found out about it, but can't do anything to stop it."

"Would Orfe be willing to help us out?" Kendry asked, resulting in a confused look by Gendella.

Kendry shared her idea that Orfe pretend to be Hendrick's servant. And, Kendry could come along, dressed back as a girl, as Gendella's servant. She figured she'd be safest behind the princess as Sleege would not think to look for her there.

Gendella actually loved the idea. She believed it would be easiest to sneak away with Orfe when they were on travel since she got ignored on journeys, riding in the back away from the business up front. She also knew that no one would bother Kendry. She would suggest they travel by carriage and she and Kendry could be inside.

Kendry was so relieved. Malark and Sleege wouldn't see her inside a carriage with the princess!

Gendella said she'd call for Matel, her personal servant, who would communicate to Orfe that he should report as Hendrick's servant in the morning. She'd also get servant's clothes for Kendry and told her to meet back there in the morning, which was only a few hours away now.

Kendry made her way back to Hendrick's room and was relieved to find that Graeme was gone. Now, they could plan on how they would ditch him when they took off. But Hendrick suggested they actually have him travel with them.

"Why would we want him to come with us?" Kendry asked. "No way!"

Hendrick answered, "He's fluent in Regarian, Kendry. Completely fluent."

"So," she responded quickly. But she knew what he was implying. If they made it to Regaria and wanted to bribe people to find out about their friends, knowing more than a couple of words here and there would be helpful. Kendry might be able to communicate some, and most people there were multi-lingual and would understand them, since it was a border town, but if they could hear what was being said behind their backs, it could be helpful. Yet, she did not feel that was enough to warrant having that arrogant prig with them. Plus, she had hoped they'd have a better translator.

"If we get my dad back from Bulenduria, he can translate for us. He's fluent in Regarian."

"About that," Hendrick began. "Graeme filled me in a little about the Bulendurians. I don't know that we are going to be able to find your dad there. It's a tribal land with savages, Kendry. If your dad is there, he is doing a really good job disguising himself to fit in. Otherwise, he's probably dead by now."

"Agh," Kendry let out her frustration with a noise that sounded almost like a growl. "My dad is NOT dead! Malark and Sleege even said so. If they think he is in Bulenduria, then we need to at least go there and see what we can find out. Maybe we can talk to locals in villages outside of Bulenduria? But I am not giving up, now. I will go alone if I have to!"

"You are not going alone," Hendrick said in a calming voice. He smiled at her to let her know they were in this together.

"Yeah, and apparently WE'RE not going alone, either, since you invited your new best friend," she said sarcastically, angry about Graeme. "I still say we ditch him."

"He's right that there is safety in numbers. He'll stay away from Bulenduria and we can decide if we want to meet back up with him or not. But I like the idea of having him travel with us. It's a good plan, Kendry."

"Speaking of plans..." she paused, realizing she needed to explain her plan to him. "...you'll be meeting your new servant in the morning. His name's Orfe. But you better come up with a code name for him."

Hendrick's face showed just how confused he was.

CHAPTER TWENTY-FIVE

Traveling to the Great Divide, Kendry rode in the bumpy carriage with Princess Gendella. What could have seemed like a torturous long ride, went by fast as they got to know a lot about each other, sharing their upbringings. Gendella was so impressed to hear that Kendry was allowed at the Academy. She asked many questions and was intrigued by the small-town life of Tavern's End. Her own life had been very lonely in the palace. She missed her father greatly and talked about her memories of her mother from when she was young. She also shared how things had changed drastically once Casper took over.

Kendry could tell Gendella's brother was very controlling. Most all the staff answered immediately to Prince Casper if Gendella did anything she wasn't supposed to do. Her one loyal servant, Matel, was the only person the princess trusted. She explained how her passion was riding horses and she had spent most of her time doing so in their pastures behind the palace gate.

"At the stables was where I met Orfe," she shared with Kendry, quietly, as they bounced along in the carriage. "He only started at the palace about a year ago. We quickly became friends. I began really looking forward to going down to the stables each day so I could see him." She smiled a lovesick smile that made Kendry grin back.

"Casper had no idea until a servant saw Orfe and me too close together, recently. I was ordered to stay away from him. And, I just found out that

Casper is firing him from his position." Her face looked downcast. "I can't imagine never getting to see Orfe again."

Kendry listened as Gendella shared about Orfe's personality and stories about how they started to become more than friends and eventually fell in love. "I just want to be with him, Kendry. I don't care if I never return to the palace or Crestavia. As long as I get to be with Orfe."

Kendry thought about this declaration. It almost made her want to share her plans to take off with Hendrick and Graeme and include Gendella and Orfe, but that was a complication they did not need.

Gendella explained how she dreamed of what it would be like to live in a small town with no one knowing she was royalty. How amazing it would be to get to go down to a river to swim or shop at a market without guards. The more Gendella daydreamed about freedom, the more Kendry found herself encouraging Gendella to run away with Orfe.

"You only live once," Kendry declared. "You've tried palace life. Maybe it's time you get to try life outside the palace."

"If I stay at the palace, I will be married to the winner of the tournament in the fall. I have no say in it. Casper is using me as a trophy to try to find a new general to replace your father. He wants to discover who the best fighters are in the kingdom and thinks this tournament is a perfect way to see everyone compete at once. He'll be forming his new special forces team and will use me to lure the men to come out and compete."

"Have you told Casper how you feel?" Kendry asked, not even able to imagine how Gendella must feel being used as bait by her brother.

"Are you kidding? All we did was fight after my father died. That's when he started taking away all my privileges. Did you know this is the first time I have left the palace since my father's passing? And I have not been able to have a single visitor! He is afraid that I might tell someone that their king isn't alive. He's basically kept me under lock and key! I was actually okay with it because it gave me time to spend with Orfe and Casper seemed to ignore me. But, now that he knows about Orfe, he is going to take him away from me, too! Kendry, you have to help me!"

176

"What can I do?" Kendry asked, sincerely wanting to help.

"I don't know," the princess resigned to saying. "I'm so glad you got Orfe to come with Hendrick. As long as Casper doesn't know he's here, we should be able to sneak off at some point. I'm hoping I can suggest to him that we run away together. But I don't know how he will feel about that."

Kendry placed a hand on the princess' shoulder, "I am so sorry."

"Oh goodness, listen to me," Gendella said apologetically. "I'm complaining about myself and you are the one with a bounty on your head! You are the one who needs to escape!"

Kendry nodded. She did need to escape. And without Malark ever knowing she was there.

"How will you escape? Where will you go?" Gendella asked her.

"I don't know exactly. I've heard that my father is in Bulenduria." Gendella flinched at hearing this news.

"Oh Kendry, if he's there...well, he's probably been killed already. Everyone stays away from Bulenduria. Even Shadenberg won't go near those savages. They keep to themselves and are harmless if you leave them alone, but if you barge into town uninvited, you're a goner."

"That's what I keep hearing," Kendry said disappointed. "But, Sleege and Malark seemed to think that they could find my father there. So, they must think he is doing an excellent job hiding out or is working with them somehow."

"If Sleege wanted to look for your father there, he'd send an envoy to the Tribal Chief's Elders' Gate. It's a place where outside nations can congregate to negotiate or discuss matters with the elite elders who work for the chief. My father sent men there with gifts or questions many times. As long as you don't enter their land, they can be civil."

Kendry processed the new information. She didn't have any better ideas, but was a little nervous at the thought of approaching the Bulendurian Elders. Discussing with Gendella what she knew about maps and geography and how to get from the Great Divide to Bulenduria, Kendry realized there was a lot to learn. The Great Divide was a vast area that separated many nations. If she headed east long enough, she should arrive at a creek which she could follow through the otherwise deserted area to the Midlands. The Midlands consisted of a section on the outskirts known as the Outpost which would be a good rest stop. Kendry should be able to get information there on how to continue on to Bulenduria.

Relief and thankfulness flooded Kendry as she thought about what a help Gendella's information would be for her trip. Unfortunately, Gendella didn't know anything about the men in dark clothes who had come to Tavern's End and kidnapped her friends. She had heard the rumors of the slave traders like everyone else. Casper assumed it was a threat from Shadenberg and they were getting bolder and bolder as a way to push war to begin. But hearing that they spoke Regarian, made Gendella wonder if there was more to it.

"They could be bounty hunters who were looking for someone specific. Maybe your father? They could've been hoping to sell him to Shadenberg to get very wealthy."

Kendry nodded. She had thought something similar. She remembered hearing them say something about a warrior.

Travel continued for a few days. Gendella and Kendry's friendship strengthened with each night they camped together, off away from the men, and each day they stayed hidden in the carriage as it was pulled by horses. Finally, they reached a military base on the border of the Great Divide.

Hendrick, Ruttin, and Graeme were given a tour of the expansive base by Prince Casper and Sleege. The edge of the base backed up to a steep mountain. The prince showed them how there were over fifty tunnels dug from the back of the mountain through to the front, but were camouflaged on the other side with rocks and brush. He explained how if Shadenberg were to come from the east and approached this mountain, they would have no idea that they could be ambushed by hundreds of Crestavian soldiers who would be signaled from those watching above and could slide secretly into position in the side of the mountain.

He also divulged another tunnel that connected to an old abandoned mine on the other side. Crestavia could rush through reinforcements without Shadenberg knowing what hit them.

Guided only with torch light, the men's tour led them to truck through the tunnel that connected to the mine. Eventually, they came out on the other side. Once their eyes adjusted to the bright outside light, Hendrick observed that this side of the mountain looked bare and empty. There was a vast desert space to the east and forest to the southwest. The prince explained how Shadenberg would come from the east. Getting to this point, if they crossed in front of the mountain or tried to explore the mine, they would be ambushed. There was no way they would have any clue that one of Crestavia's largest military bases lay behind this mountain. Sleege pointed to the top of the steep mountain above them and pointed out where they had guards always hidden who could signal for an ambush if anyone was seen approaching.

If any of the Shadenberg's troops did manage to get past the mountain and through the ambush, they would head toward the forest or have to go back the way they came. Sleege and Prince Casper, along with a few soldiers, led Ruttin, Graeme, and Hendrick from the area in front of the mine toward the forest.

"Stop," Sleege said in a demanding voice. Hendrick shuddered. He had already endured hours of questions by Sleege about Kendry, her upbringings, her personality, and so forth. He had done his best to try to throw Sleege off her track mentioning made up details and fictional acquaintances from other towns. But he didn't like the way Sleege stared at him all day. The man didn't trust him and it was obvious.

"This," Prince Casper began, "was a military genius creation by General Walbek, himself." He pointed toward the forest. "What do you see?

Ruttin answered. "Mostly oak and brandy trees. Thick, but not impossible to infiltrate. If Shadenberg was being chased by the remnants of an ambush, they would probably seek refuge in that forest."

"You can't see the forest for the trees," Prince Casper snapped. Ruttin looked confused.

"Yes, the forest would be prepped with our men so that as Shadenberg troops rushed in, we could ambush them, yet again. We'd have men already stationed up high in trees. They would take off to their positions as soon as signaled by our lookouts atop the mountain that an enemy was approaching. But…" he looked at Graeme and Hendrick. "What else do you see?

Hendrick looked around. The mountain with the abandoned mine was now behind them. Yards of dirt, leaves, and brush lay between it and the forest. It was an open space where men could be shot at from soldiers both in the forest and up on the mountain. But, before he could speak, Graeme answered.

"Too much open space."

Prince Casper smiled. "What you don't see is a very deep crevice dug from an already existent steep crack. From the tip of the base of the mountain until the first tree in the forest, imagine an invisible line." The men's eyes followed the direction his finger was pointing. "It's about four yards across this wide hole in the ground. Our experts have created thick, hardened 'fake' land to cover the canyon drop. We laid them out like a blanket across the holes in the ground. They are covered with dirt, brush, leaves, plants, and completely camouflaged to look like the ground. Yet, if you or your horse stepped on it, you would fall to your death, or at least to an injured existence trapped in a crack in the ground."

Hendrick's mouth dropped open. He couldn't believe it. The ground looked normal. Sleege took them slowly closer and pointed out exactly where the fake ground began. They started to get a sense for the difference between the real ground and fake cover and were all impressed by the trap that lay invisible before them. It was very clever.

"There's no way for your own troops to get across it, either," said Graeme. "That could be a problem if your troops get stuck on the wrong side of this thing."

"Actually," Casper countered, "there are natural paths without holes in four different places throughout the trap. The ground isn't thick and you have to be careful where to walk, but we will show you."

He led them to an area and pointed out a formation of small rocks that was formed in a symbol that almost looked like an arrow. He walked over a couple of feet to the left and showed another spot with similar rocks. No one would notice them on their own, but if looking for them, they could be easily located.

Prince Casper then carefully walked between the two rock symbols across to the other side where the forest boldly stood. Hendrick and the others hesitantly followed on the land bridge marked by the rocks.

They were impressed. Due to the tunnels through the mountain leading to the military base on the other side, with the openings hidden, the larger opening in the abandoned mine, the guards hidden atop the mountain to shoot arrows down below and be on lookout, and the hidden crevice covered by fake ground, Shadenberg would have a very rough time getting to the forest. Once there, they would be on enemy's turf in a sea of trees already stacked against them with soldiers and ambushes.

"General Walbrek was brilliant," Ruttin quietly exclaimed in awe.

"Yes," Prince Casper stated. "He had many more ideas that he wanted to share with my father, so we have all been disappointed by his death." He paused for a moment, whether out to feign respect to Walbrek for his apparent death or out of self-pity for never learning more strategies from Walbrek, Hendrick did not know.

Casper led the men back the way they came, carefully crossing the land bridge to the other side. "I would love to hear any of your ideas regarding strategy and defense." He looked at Ruttin, Graeme, and Hendrick expectantly.

Ruttin pounced at the invitation to share his ideas. He rambled on as the men walked back toward the old mine. Hendrick, on the other hand, was distracted trying to figure out how they could possibly escape to Bulenduria from where they were currently located. His directionality was a little thrown off after tunneling through a mountain.

Later, when Hendrick and Graeme talked, they decided it was best to just leave the Military Base the way they had arrived from Crestavia and go the long way around to the Great Divide toward the Midlands. Avoiding any of General Walbrek's ambushes would be smartest.

CHAPTER TWENTY-SIX

After supper was served at the Military Base's dining hall, the three men were all left to themselves. Prince Casper had awarded Ruttin, Hendrick, and Graeme their prize money and a special medal for winning the competition. He advised how any discussion with outsiders of what they had seen or learned on their excursion would be considered treason and came with the penalty of death, as it was all top secret. If they talked about anything with anyone, they could be executed. They were told that Prince Casper and Sleege would be staying at the base, but they would be led home the next morning by soldiers. Once back in Crestavia-Capitalia, they were to go back to their normal lives, but be available in case they were called to the palace at any time. In the fall, they would be invited to the tournament with the nobles for a chance to court the princess and be named the palace's Regency Advisor. With that, they said their goodbyes to the prince and princess and took off to their tents.

While the men were at dinner, Kendry had slipped into Hendrick's tent and introduced herself to Orfe. She was able to help Orfe sneak into Princess Gendella's empty tent without being seen. It took some distracting of servants and guards, but now Orfe and Gendella could finally be together and discuss their plans for the future, while Kendry could meet with Hendrick and start planning their escape to Bulenduria.

Awhile later, Hendrick and Graeme both arrived back at Hendrick's tent. They couldn't get over the knapsack full of money they had each received. Kendry was shocked. It was more than she had expected. But it worried her too, because they would definitely be targets traveling through the Great Divide with huge stashes of money.

The boys left Kendry alone, hidden in the tent, while they went to scope out the scene outside. They scanned to see if they would be tracked as they wandered about in the early evening.

Alone in the tent, Kendry felt nervous for what lie ahead. Would they be able to find her dad? It didn't sound like Bulenduria was going to be practical to search. Would they have found out more information about her dad if she had stayed in Crestavia and snuck around eavesdropping on the king's officials? Maybe their current plan wasn't the best idea. Her stomach turned as she started doubting the success and safety of moving forward.

Hendrick was gone for a long time as he decided to walk the whole perimeter of the base and scan for the easiest access points to leave it. Graeme came back earlier. He was avoiding his own servant back at his tent, so he joined Kendry.

"You okay, Sweetheart?" he asked, genuinely looking concerned.

"You call me 'Sweetheart' one more time and you will not be okay," she said emphatically.

"Sorry," he said rudely. "What's got you in such a lovely mood? We've got money. We're leaving tonight. You should be walking on clouds."

She wanted to ignore him, but reluctantly answered. "I just hope we're doing the right thing. I don't know how we're going to find my father."

Graeme sat there quietly for a moment. "Ya miss him a lot, huh? Sounds like he must've been a good father." He brushed his long brown hair out of his eyes and leaned back on his hands to make himself more comfortable.

"He was the best," Kendry said. "Strong, brave, loving, fun, loyal, and...just the best dad ever."

"So, what's the story with why he's in Bulenduria? I've heard that you were framed for the slave trader thing back at Tavern's End, but how did your dad end up in savage land?"

184

Kendry rocked in place as she thought about his question.

"He was on a mission...or so I thought...I've been given so much false information I'm not even sure what is true anymore. Malark, who was like an uncle to me...my dad's best friend...told me that he and my dad were weeding out a traitor named Lieutenant Trent and then said that my dad went on a mission for the king. He was suspected of being dead. But, I'm not sure what's true."

"Your dad was in the military?" Graeme asked, nonchalantly.

Kendry was taken back. Didn't he know who her dad was? "My dad is General Walbrek," she stated, watching his reaction. He definitely didn't know.

"What! THE General Walbrek? You're his daughter?" He put his hand to his forehead and shook his head. "Wow, I feel like I'm in the presence of royalty. Wait, I thought General Walbrek was dead?"

"Exactly," said Kendry. "We all thought so. But I overheard Malark, Sleege, and Prince Casper say that they needed to hunt him down and that it was believed he was in Bulenduria."

"But, why would they need to hunt him down? Isn't he on their side?"

"I'm assuming it has something to do with Malark." Even saying Malark's name hurt. The betrayal she felt when she thought of him would exasperate a deep wound for a long time. "Like I said, he was my dad's best friend, and he had tried to have me arrested by framing me for a crime I didn't commit. Princess Gendella told me that initially King Gadden made up the warrant for my arrest to get me to the palace for my safety, but something changed after his death. Prince Casper and Malark seem to want me and my dad out of the way."

"Why did you need to be kept safe?" Graeme asked.

"I don't know," Kendry said. "I mean, when I do the timing in my head it seems like my dad would've gone to King Gadden to ask him to help keep me safe before they even knew about the slave traders attacking us in Tavern's End. Maybe they knew it was coming? It's all so strange."

"Wow, I'm really sorry," Graeme said, empathetically. "You've really had a lot of bad stuff happen to you. No wonder you're eager to find your dad and get some of your life back."

Kendry nodded. It was silent for a minute and the awkwardness of being alone with a guy in a tent hit her. Especially since Graeme was extremely handsome. It made her think about her own appearance, which she normally didn't care about. How odd she must look with her darkened, shortened hair and sweaty servants' clothes. She resituated herself and tried fixing her hair a little.

"And you don't know what Malark's play in all this is, huh? How frustrating." He looked genuinely sad for her.

Thinking about Malark made her angry, but then a wave of sadness hit her. She had to fight back a tear.

"You, okay?" he asked, scooting closer. He put his hand on the palm of her back. This made her nervous and her heart started racing. He took it off and his eyes asked again if she was alright.

"I'm fine," she said unconvincingly.

"Yeah, you look ready to throw a party," he said sarcastically. "You know it's okay to be upset. No one is around. You can cry or scream...as long as it's a quiet scream," he added jokingly. "You've been through a lot and you're obviously a strong woman to handle it as you have."

She blushed a little. It had been hard these past weeks. She had barely given herself time to process it all. Strangely, she felt more comfortable talking to this guy she barely knew than anyone at the Refuge or even Hendrick.

"It's just that Malark and my dad were my world, ya know? And, Tarah. She was my best friend. Her parents were like family to me. I watched her dad murdered by those awful slave traders," she choked up a bit when she thought about Mister Lansing. Graeme put his hand back on her back where it had been a moment earlier and rubbed it slowly, trying to calm her. "Tarah got taken. Everyone got taken or killed. Right in front of me and I did nothing to help." Tears started pouring down her cheeks as she continued. "I lost my friends, my family, my home...all at once. And before I could even process it, I had the king's men after me." She wiped the tears away, and took a deep breath trying to control her emotions.

Graeme put his arm around her and pulled her in. She leaned on his shoulder and started crying uncontrollably. He patted her back and whispered, "It's gonna be okay."

It felt good to finally let go. All the emotions that had been tied up and contained so she could survive, finally surfaced and spilled out. After a minute she pulled herself together. She was embarrassed that she had lost her composure like that and wiped her face again and apologized. He shook it off, telling her there was nothing to be sorry about.

Scooting away from her, Graeme casually commented, "Well, at least you'd win a contest against anyone claiming to have had a bad month." She laughed, awkwardly.

"What about you?" Kendry asked. "What's your story?"

He shifted a little and then confidently began, "I was born..." he paused. "Do you want the real story or the one I tell everyone?"

She smiled. "Why would I want a fake story?"

"It's a lot better than the real one."

She half-laughed. "I always prefer the truth."

"Even if the truth isn't pretty?"

Her smile faded. He noticed and tried to act like it wasn't a big deal. "I'm just teasing you. The real story just involves a mom that had one too many kids with one too many different fathers. She didn't care about any of us because we were mouths to feed and she was busy trying to find herself another bread winner. My father wasn't a winner, either, but I loved him. He was a good guy, deep down."

"Was?" Kendry asked.

"Yeah, he was killed. His so-called friends said it was a wild animal, but I have reason to believe they ended his life over a gambling debt."

Kendry shuddered.

"It was a long time ago," he said, ready to change the subject. "You should feel special that I told you the truth. I've never told anyone any of that before."

Kendry's heart started racing a bit, again.

"Why did you tell me?" she asked, curious. "What makes me so special?"

"I'm not sure but I hope I get to find out," he said staring into her eyes. She could feel her face getting hot. She looked away. He was one of those guys who was confident and knew they were good-looking. He probably flirted with every girl he met. Yet, she had felt that they had connected on a level that broke through some of that surface arrogance.

Just then, Hendrick opened the tent and ducked his head to enter, oblivious to the fact that he was interrupting an awkward but rare moment. For some reason, Kendry immediately felt guilty and scooted a little further away from Graeme. Hendrick paused for a second. "Everything okay?" he asked.

They both nodded.

Hendrick then gave an account of the perimeter of the base he had scoped. He discussed how the stables were far enough away that if they got their horses, they definitely would be seen crossing to an area with weaker security.

"I think we should go without horses," Hendrick suggested. "It's the only way we'll get out of here without being noticed.

Graeme groaned. "Do you know how long it will take to get across the Great Divide if we don't have horses? We'll die of hunger or get caught wandering for sure."

"Well, what do you suggest?" Hendrick asked, frustrated.

Graeme thought about it for a second. He glanced at Kendry and she spotted a half-smile. "What if we could create some sort of distraction? Maybe something that caused the guards to lose interest in watching the back border of the base for a bit."

Kendry liked the way he thought. But, what sort of distraction? And, what would do the job enough for the three of them to escape without being noticed on horseback?

Kendry and Graeme went back and forth with ideas they knew were ridiculous and Hendrick tried to convince them to just go without horses. They were all getting a bit frustrated and Kendry was starting to feel like it was a little hopeless, when they heard a commotion outside.

Graeme perked up. "Did someone order a distraction?" Kendry smiled big.

CHAPTER TWENTY-SEVEN

Hendrick and Graeme went outside to see what was going on. The camp was in an uproar. People were riding by on horses and Hendrick saw Ruttin galloping toward them.

"What's going on?" he asked. Ruttin, looking bothered that he had to stop to acknowledge Hendrick and Graeme, quickly told them that the princess was missing.

"Prince Casper is offering a reward for anyone who finds her," he said before riding off.

Graeme looked at Hendrick. "Let's get horses and get out of here!"

Kendry overheard Ruttin and secretly hoped that Gendella and Orfe had gotten far away. She was thankful for the distraction, but worried about her new friend. Casper would not be happy if he found her with Orfe and would probably never let her leave the palace again.

It hit Kendry that Casper and his men would be unaware of Orfe's presence at the base. While looking for the princess, they would notice Gendella's servant was gone. Since there were only a couple of female servants anywhere on the base, Kendry realized she needed to change clothes and disguise herself as a male before leaving. She quickly sorted through Hendrick's bag and pulled out some clothes. She knew they wouldn't fit well, but did her best to speedily dress. She put a hat over her hair and wandered out of the tent.

It didn't take long for Hendrick and Graeme to come back with horses. Kendry climbed up onto the back of Hendrick's horse. Taking advantage of the opportunity to join the search party, they rode to the large group gathering outside the gates. They listened as some man gave orders informing groups of them which different areas to search. They were all to report back by the next evening. They waited until their group was dismissed and shot off into the night.

Kendry held tight to Hendrick. She was impressed at how fast he could ride. Graeme was lagging behind, but there was no wasting this opportunity. They needed to get as far away from the base as they could, as fast as they could. They rode all night long. Exhaustion started to hit a couple of hours before dawn. Deciding it was probably safer to sleep in the dark, they turned deeper into the forest they were in and looked for a place to rest. Their horses needed water. They would need to find a creek or water source soon. But, for now, they would sleep.

It was cold and they didn't have tents or sleeping sacks. They put their knapsacks in a line as a barrier from the wind and lay low behind high tree roots. They all piled up together, with Kendry between the two boys. They discussed a schedule for one of them to stay awake and guard, but were all equally tired. Hendrick stayed up first and a couple of hours later woke Kendry. As dawn came, she woke Graeme and then went back to sleep for a few more hours. While she slept, the boys took the horses and found dew puddles. Then they woke Kendry and began their first full day of travel.

They rode for hours and hours. They knew they would have to leave the safety of the forest to go through the Great Divide. It would be extremely dangerous. Bandits out in the Great Divide were known for being lethal. They came from all different nations and border towns and would prey on anyone who dared travel through the vast space. There could also be soldiers from Shadenberg, Breckenride, or even Crestavia, touring and surveying. Most travelers would choose to go by boat to their destination, even though travel could take months longer, just to avoid this area.

Kendry, Graeme, and Hendrick had no weapons. They did have money which they could use to bribe soldiers to let them pass, but any soldier or bandit could easily demand their money when they realized they had no way to protect themselves. Their plan of attack would simply be to cross the vast expanse as fast as they could. So, they decided to settle down in the forest and allow their horses time to rest. They found a place near a creek so they could hydrate their horses and collected berries and roots to eat. They were all famished.

"Do we still think this running away toward Bulenduria is a good idea?" Graeme asked as he forced himself to swallow a root that's taste immediately made him want to throw it back up.

"I don't know," Kendry said, exhausted. "We're tired, we're hungry...and the goal is to arrive at the home of savages. Maybe we didn't think this through."

Hendrick wasn't enjoying his bitter berries, but responded, "I think if we can get to the Outpost in the Midlands, we'll be able to find out something. I've heard the Outpost is like an information post. They'll have news of everyone who has passed through there and what's going on with all the neighboring nations. Word that General Walbrek came through may have spread. We might finally be able to get some real answers."

Hendrick's response gave Kendry hope. It was worth practically starving, losing sleep, and risking their lives to bandits if she could actually get answers.

When their horses were fully rested and they knew they couldn't wait any longer, the three of them mounted their mares and took off. They rode fast and didn't stop. Only once did they see riders in the far distance, but they were heading in their own direction and didn't pay them attention. Otherwise, it was desert. Hot and windy, desolate and dry. As evening approached, they finally started seeing trees and hills in the distance. By night time they came across the edge of a dead meadow, sparse with trees. They passed a couple of broken-down shacks and some rotten tents as they got closer to a forest.

Being beyond tired, they decided to try to find a spot to settle down for the night. They rode up to an old broken down one-room shack. Kendry suggested they camp behind it, if not inside, to keep them warm from the wind. They tied the horses up and went over to check out the shack. Graeme warned that there could be someone inside. Kendry walked around it, scoping out the area for tracks. She pointed out the cobwebs around the door and lack of windows. "If anyone is inside, they are probably dead," she stated. Hendrick's disgusted look on his face showed how he felt about that comment.

"What about wild animals?" Graeme asked, impressed with Kendry's observation skills.

"There's a few holes in the roof and one in the wall up there, so I'm sure we'll find critters."

"Great," Hendrick said sarcastically.

Graeme took a deep breath. "Let's do this." He put his hand on the door and pulled. It wouldn't budge. He tried again and then used both hands. He shook it a little and pulled really hard. It peeled open. As he pulled it back far enough to see inside, they all leaned forward in suspense. The boys jumped. Kendry ducked and screamed.

CHAPTER TWENTY-EIGHT

A large barn owl screeched across the shack and flew out right over Kendry's head. It took a moment for their hearts to stop racing and then Kendry started laughing. Graeme started cracking up and finally Hendrick joined in. It felt good to let off some steam and laugh.

Inside the shack was unremarkable. Just an old wooden box shaped room with no windows for light, but plenty of splintered wood allowing moonlight to leak in. Lots of insects and webs everywhere. Kendry liked the idea of sleeping in it, but Hendrick preferred sleeping outside. They were discussing their reasons for why one was more preferred than the other when Graeme interrupted.

"Do ya hear that?"

They all froze and listened. Horses. It was definitely the sound of horses heading right toward them. Graeme instinctively closed the shack's door. He had to pull it tight again to get the expanded wood to fit. Kendry didn't like the feeling of being trapped. And, their horses were outside!

The riders were getting closer. Graeme instinctively wanted to stand in front of Kendry to help her feel protected, but she was already using Hendrick's knee as a springboard to pull herself up onto a rafter. It wasn't the firmest beam and there was so much rot throughout the old shack that Kendry prayed it would hold her. She balanced her body on the beam, lowering her head not to hit it.

Graeme was freaking out a bit seeing Kendry up on the beam. He motioned silently for her to get down. Hendrick shook his head at him. There was no way to explain to Graeme that Kendry was in her element when she was up high on something dangerous.

Kendry could barely see out a hole along the wall and was pretty sure there were two soldiers approaching the shack. One motioned at the horses. Kendry wondered if they thought the princess was inside. These looked like they could be soldiers that were a part of Prince Casper's search party.

"Princess Genedlla," one of the men yelled in a deep voice. "If you are in there, we need you to come out." The man waited a moment and then reached for the door. As soon as it was opened, Hendrick socked the soldier right in the face. Having the advantage of their eyes already adjusted to the dark, Graeme and Hendrick took turns fighting the soldier and were able to get his sword off him.

The other soldier ran in right after. Kendry fell from above and landed squarely on the man, knocking him to the ground with a groan of pain. She was alert and ready to fight by the time he managed to stand back up. Looking dazed, he tried reaching for his sword, but Kendry was too fast. Graeme's mouth dropped as he watched Kendry's martial arts expertise come into play. The guard ended up on the ground, unconscious.

Dissatisfied with the condition of the soldier Graeme and Hendrick were holding, she went over to him and took off his belt. She then used it, with the help of the boys, to tie his hands and feet all together. She then removed one of the man's dirty boots and peeled his sock off his foot. She wadded up the sweaty sock and shoved it in his mouth. Then she asked Hendrick for help to do the same with the other guard who was already starting to wake up.

Graeme just stood there shocked as they finished gagging the second soldier. He stared at Kendry trying to figure out what he had just witnessed. She noticed his expression.

"I've been taught to fight until you render them unconscious or can tie them up," she said innocently. Graeme just nodded. Hendrick was a little amused. Kendry was like a secret weapon and it never seemed to fail that she would surprise someone with her skills.

196

"Now what do we do with them?" Hendrick asked, looking at the soldiers, gagged and bound. "Do we just leave them here?"

"If we leave their horses out front, someone will come by soon and check on them," Kendry said, hoping that was true. She didn't want the men to starve to death or get eaten by wild animals.

"We need to find somewhere else to stay the night, then," Graeme suggested. "We don't want to be associated with them.

"Bummer, I really wanted to sleep in here tonight. It would be so much warmer," Kendry stated. She was getting to the point where the cold at night was unbearable. She needed a good night's sleep and she wasn't going to be able to have one with this weather. "What if we hide them and their horses in the woods until we leave in the morning? We could drag them in a ways, tie their horses with them, and then when we get up in the morning, we can do our best to feed them something. And then we'll drag them back into the shack and leave their horses out to be seen before we take off."

The boys were not thrilled with the idea, but reluctantly agreed. They pulled and dragged the men, who wiggled and writhed and fought against their mission, into the woods. They took all four of the horses and tied them near the men. Kendry was pleased to find coils of rope on the soldier's horses that could be used to tie the men up more securely and put them in a better position.

Completely exhausted, the three of them made their way back to the little shack to sleep for the night. As soon as they were inside with the door closed, they heard it again. More horses.

CHAPTER TWENTY-NINE

Kendry was back up on the beam looking out the hole. Three more men on horses were riding their way. When they got near the shack, they slowed down. One of the men got off his horse and was looking down at the ground. Kendry knew he'd see fresh footprints and hoof prints in the bright moonlight. She mentally prepared herself for what was coming.

But before approaching the shack's door, the man instead walked a way into the forest. The other two men stayed right outside the shack with their swords drawn. Kendry felt sick. They were trapped. The man in the forest would follow the tracks right to the two men tied up. They'd be released and back with a vengeance. There had to be some way out of this shack from the back end. She searched every corner and Hendrick and Graeme joined her when they realized what she was doing. They could try to kick down the weaker parts of the wood, but the soldiers outside would hear and just come to the back of the shack.

Kendry leaned against the front wall and stared through a crack in the wood. The first man was indeed coming back with two very angry soldiers.

The man spoke loudly, "We are prepared to siege this little shack and leave you in there until you starve." His voice terrified Kendry. Not just because it sounded evil or the words that were spoken, but because she recognized it. Malark was here.

Malark continued, "But, I really don't feel like wasting that much time." He took a piece of flint rock and steel out of his pocket and started striking them. "So instead, I think we'll just smoke you out."

Kendry turned and looked at the boys. She could feel the hair on her arms sticking straight up. They needed a plan and quick. If they stayed inside, he'd burn them down. But if they left the shack, there were five men outside waiting for them. Still, their odds were probably better to try to fight the five men.

By the time Kendry looked out the crack, again, Malark had started a tiny campfire of sorts. He was taking a stick and lighting the end on fire. She began to panic. He didn't know who was in the shack, just that it was three people who assaulted the king's soldiers. What if they locked them in as the shack burned?

It didn't take long for Kendry to see that Malark wasn't bluffing. He had lit the shack on fire. The dry, rotted wood went up in flames quickly. Smoke started to fill the little cabin. All three of them instinctively put their shirts up over their noses, and tried moving back. Kendry knew this shack was coming down fast. They started coughing. The smoke got thicker. The situation was becoming more dire with each second that passed.

They all three got down on their bellies, trying to stay under the smoke that was rising. But it was of no use. They couldn't breathe. Kendry was coughing the worse. She had to open the door and get out, but what if it was locked?

She moved forward and Hendrick beat her there, pushing the door open. It was hot. And, it was stuck. Kendry felt herself getting light-headed. She was coughing so hard she could barely see. Graeme was at the door, too. He started kicking it. Hendrick kicked, too. It was pulled open by a man on the other side. They each scooted out as fast as they could. It took all Kendry's energy to make it outside. She fell face down into the dirt, coughing and struggling to breathe.

Hendrick and Graeme were also bent over trying to breathe. The soldiers hovered over them, waiting impatiently for them to regain composure. As soon as Hendrick calmed down enough to take a couple normal breaths, one of the soldiers whacked him across the face. The same thing happened to

Graeme. Kendry still lie face down. She didn't even have enough energy to pull herself up.

One of the soldiers who they had attacked and bound earlier yelled at one of the soldiers who had just arrived with Malark, "That one's actually a girl. But, don't take it easy on her...she's more deadly than these two!"

At that, she braced herself for a kick in the face, but instead heard Malark's order for them to freeze.

Slowly, he walked over to Kendry and stood above her. He told the soldier to pull her up from the ground. She did not have energy to fight. The soldier easily lifted her and she strained to raise her chin, while still coughing sporadically and wheezing. Malark just stared at her and mumbled slowly, "What am I going to do with you?"

The soldier yanked her hair back to force her chin up further, so she would look straight at Malark. Seeing him pierced her heart with pain, but she was so overcome with exhaustion from coughing she just sat there frozen.

But then, anger rose within her. How could Malark have betrayed her father?

She wrestled a bit, trying to free her arms. She didn't say a word. Malark asked, calmly, "What are you doing here?"

Kendry struggled. One of her arms got out of the soldier's grip, but before she could do anything with it, Malark grabbed it and held her wrist steady. Just then the sound of horses was heard from afar.

Malark leaned down, his forehead inches from her's. He looked as though he was going to say something stern, but she beat him to it.

"I will find him," she whispered. "I won't stop until I find him."

With that, Malark jerked her up by the forearm and dragged her over to the campfire he had started earlier in order to light the shack on fire. Hendrick and Graeme both tried to help Kendry, but each one had a soldier holding them back. She wrestled, but didn't have much energy due to the smoke inhalation.

Malark yelled at a soldier to hold Kendry still. She was grabbed from behind by one of the men she had beat up earlier. He looked thrilled to assist. Malark was still holding her forearm, tight, and it was starting to really hurt her. He yelled, loud enough for all to hear, "Where is she? Where is the princess?"

Kendry was taken back. The princess? Why was Gendella so important to him? Wasn't he out this way trying to hunt down her father or find her for Prince Casper?

"Tell me now or I will torture it out of you," he looked dead serious. "I know you know where she is! Tell me NOW!"

Before Kendry could even think of a clever way to tell him she wouldn't help him even if she had known where Gendella was, he grabbed a stick and put it in the fire until it sparked. Kendry's eyes got big. He wasn't really going to torture her?

As he pulled the flaming stick toward her, she looked into his eyes. Those big grey eyes that used to equate love and protection. This man had kissed her scrapes and bruises to make them heal. He had tucked her in bed when her father was busy. He had sung her lullabies and rocked her to sleep when she was scared of the thunder. He had created many games to play with her and allowed her to win when they wrestled. He had always promised her he'd love and take care of her. And now, here they were what felt like a million years later.

He had deceived her. Betrayed her. Lied to her. Framed her. Almost killed her in the fire. And now was threatening to burn her.

She watched in horror as he took the flaming stick and brought it toward her forearm, just above her wrist. The stick flew toward her crescent shaped birthmark as if a magnet pulled it. The flame struck her forearm and he pressed the stick into it. Her arm singed. She screamed in intense pain! Hendrick and Graeme both received punches as they tried to escape the soldiers holding them.

Kendry's pain was so intense, she started to get dizzy. She fell to the ground, screaming. Malark had turned away. He was instructing his men with orders, but Kendry couldn't think straight. The horses they had heard in the distance, approached. Malark bolted ahead to meet up with them. Sleege was there with a group of other soldiers.

"What's going on here, Malark?" Sleege asked.

"Not much. It's just the two guys who won that competition. They were looking for Gendella and attacked some of my men, thinking they were bandits. We had a little fun with them, but they will be back on their way to base in a minute."

"What about that fellow on the ground?" he asked pointing to Kendry. She was writhing in pain, slithering around, face-down, in the ground by the campfire.

"A servant. I tortured him, just in case he knew anything. He doesn't."

"I see," Sleege said, not looking like he completely believed Malark. "Well, clean up this mess, and head to the Outpost."

Sleege and his men took off past Malark and the others, riding into the distance. Malark looked back at his men. "No need to upset Prince Casper with all that went on here," he said to cover any fibs they may have heard. "I want these two men tied up on horses with you and I want that one," he said pointing over toward Kendry, "tied up and on my horse with me."

The soldiers started retrieving rope and discussing who would tie up which of them.

Without warning, an arrow flew through the air and hit a soldier in the neck. Looking up, Hendrick could tell it came from the forest. Then another, shot right at the soldier that was holding Hendrick. The pain caused the man to release his grip on him. Free, Hendrick dropped to the ground and scurried on his knees to the side of the shack for cover. Commotion broke out. Malark was yelling orders. Hendrick was screaming at Kendry. Graeme had gotten the upper hand on the guard that was holding him and after a good slug to the face, was running toward Hendrick. An arrow struck the guard as he headed after Graeme.

Malark ran toward the arrows firing at him, straight to Kendry. He grabbed her and started dragging her away from the forest, toward the shack. A couple of the soldiers started shooting back toward the forest. Malark had Kendry over his shoulder and was running as fast as he could toward his horse. He threw her on the back and mounted. An arrow flew right by his head.

Kicking his horse, he started riding away. He did not get far when he pulled to brake his horse. Kendry held on tight so she wouldn't fall off. Then she noticed it. An arrow in the side of Malark's chest. He stopped the horse and sort of rolled off onto the ground.

Kendry was in shock. She knew she should just take off with the horse, but she instinctively hopped off and got on her knees studying Malark, who lay on the ground shuddering. Blood was everywhere.

Kendry's hands shook. Her arm still felt like it was on fire. She wrapped her vibrating fingers around the arrow, trying to figure out how to pull it out. Malark put his hand on her hand, steadying it, and shook his head. He stared into her eyes and smiled a little.

"I was just trying to protect you," he forced the words out. "You...you...have to get away from here...far away." He started shaking. Kendry automatically started rubbing his shoulder, trying to calm him down.

"Shh," she repeated over and over. Tears started streaming from her eyes.

"Don't trust him, Kendry," Malark began again. His eyes were looking upward and rolling about like he was trying to find something to focus on. "He...he knows who you are...he's tricked you..."

Kendry tried to get Malark to focus on her again. "Who? Who?" she asked.

"Don't let them find you..." Then, he used all the strength he could muster and took her hand again and looked at her wrist where he had just burned it. "I'm so..so...sorry." Tears began pouring from the corners of his eyes. Blood was soaking through his whole shirt and onto Kendry's leg. "I was trying to....protect..."

He paused and started shaking again. Then he made a horrible gurgling noise and within seconds froze. Dead. Kendry was horrified. "No!" she yelled. "No! Malark! Wake up!" She began bawling.

After a few minutes of crying over his blood-stained body, she looked behind her to see what was going on. It looked like the king's soldiers that hadn't been hit with arrows had managed to capture some bandits from the forest. They were busy tying them up and collecting the bodies of the other soldiers. Hendrick and Graeme were nowhere to be found. Kendry didn't know what to do. She stood up, slowly. Then, taking a deep breath and shaking her head to snap herself out of her shock, climbed up onto Malark's horse. That's when she saw Hendrick and Graeme racing toward her on their horses. They must've gone into the woods to get them from where they had tied them up earlier.

As soon as she saw them galloping toward her, she kicked Malark's horse and off they went. Riding as fast as they could for as long as they could, they headed into the Midlands. They finally stopped briefly to give the horses some water a couple of hours later. It was the middle of the night and they all needed sleep. They tied the horses to a tree, set up a schedule for guarding, and took turns sleeping. Kendry sat up as guard first. She cried silently while the boys slept.

Malark was dead. What did he mean by he was trying to protect her? Who was she not supposed to trust? Why didn't he want her to know that her dad might be alive or where he might be? So much time had passed since the awful day she had received the note saying her father and his men were dead and she had more questions now than she did back then. Her burnt wrist was hot and flaring with pain.

Kendry looked at Graeme and Hendrick sleeping. She looked up at the three horses they had tied to the tree. She thanked God above that she was not alone and she prayed that their plans to find her father would come to fruition. But for now, she would count down the minutes until she could sleep. Her heavy eyelids wouldn't stay open much longer.

CHAPTER THIRTY

Kendry, Hendrick, and Graeme had been riding all day. The Midlands had much more brush and greenery than the Great Divide. They were able to locate creeks to water their horses and berries and edible plants to eat. Thankfully, Kendry found Keroton leaves, known for their healing benefits, that she wet and plastered over her small burn. She bandaged up her wrist and forearm and tried to ignore the intense pain. But the pain of knowing it was caused by Malark, who was now dead and had left her with more questions, hurt worse than the pain from the burn.

Being in the Midlands was very different than the last few days through the desert terrain of the Great Divide because they sporadically saw other travelers. A couple of times they were able to ask directions to the Outpost, knowing it was the sole place of industry one could arrive at after leaving the Great Divide.

Their goal, once at the Outpost, would be to load up on food, purchase weapons and supplies, and try to get information about Kendry's father. After that, they really had no idea what they were going to do. Initially, the plan had been to leave Graeme behind and go on to Bulenduria, the tribal lands rumored to be where Kendry's dad was, but now that plan seemed foolish. The more information Kendry received about the Bulendurians, the more she realized they'd probably be killed before they even got to search for her father. And Graeme was now committed to their little group. The night prior, while Hendrick was sleeping and Kendry woke Graeme to tell him it was his turn to stay guard, they had a private conversation.

"I felt like I was going to die when I saw that man burning your arm," Graeme confessed to Kendry, referring to when Malark had burned her purposely as a form of torture.

Malark had claimed he wanted information about the missing princess, Gendella, but Kendry was starting to wonder if that had all been lip service for the soldiers present. She had no idea what to think of Malark now. When bandits had attacked, he grabbed Kendry and took off, seemingly to protect her from them. And, as he lay dying from a bandit's arrow, he had claimed that everything he did was to protect her. This confused Kendry more than anything. How was it protecting her to try to get her caught by guards when Prince Casper wanted to find her? How was it protecting her to burn her arm after lighting the shack on fire where she and the boys were hiding inside? How was it protecting her to lie to her about her father being dead only for her to overhear his discussion with Prince Casper and his official, Sleege, saying that they knew General Walbrek was alive in Bulenduria?

Nothing made sense. Malark had also issued her some warnings moments before taking his last breath. He had told her not to trust 'him' and that 'he' knew who she was…but who was this mysterious man? Was Malark referring to Prince Casper? Or Graeme? Or Sleege, Prince Casper's top official? Or someone she had not met yet? He had also warned her to run far away and not to let 'them' find her. She was assuming he meant the prince's men, but his warnings left her with so many questions.

Graeme continued, "I wanted to kill him for doing that to you." Kendry couldn't even respond. Graeme had no idea the confusing feelings swarming inside of her regarding Malark. He didn't understand that he hadn't just been her dad's best friend, but had been like an uncle to her. She loved him and had spent much of her childhood being loved by him. Then, she had experienced the heartbreak of thinking he was dead only to be betrayed by him when she discovered he was alive.

"I'm not going to let anything happen to you again," he said, seriously. "Even if I have to follow you into Bulenduria." Kendry didn't know how to respond. She was barely awake and so overwhelmed, emotionally. She just reached her hand out to him and he grabbed it, interlocking his fingers with her's. They both stared forward as their hands squeezed each other's for encouragement. Finally, Kendry released her grip and lay down to fall asleep. It helped knowing Graeme was watching over her.

The next morning, they gathered plants and berries for breakfast. Graeme was teasing Kendry about being capable of slaughtering the king's soldiers if she had wanted to and yet not being able to choose ripe berries. He complained at how sour the ones she had collected were. Kendry giggled at the silly face he made in response to their tartness.

Hendrick, annoyed, processed how something had definitely changed in the last few days. At the palace, Kendry had begged him not to let Graeme come with them. In fact, he had been quite sure she would've talked him into ditching Graeme by now. He had gone from watching them insult and annoy each other to tease and smile at each other. And, he didn't like it.

It was true that he felt protective of Kendry. They had been through so much together. He thought back to how he had been so frustrated with her in Tavern's End. But lots had changed since then. They had learned to depend on each other. And even learned to really care about one another.

As they were eating breakfast, Hendrick began to really feel like he was being left out. Kendry and Graeme were conversing about hunting techniques and joking about things without even acknowledging his presence. It was strange and infuriating. To remind them of his existence, he suggested they get moving. He was afraid if they sat there much longer he may say or do something he'd later regret. Kendry and Graeme agreed it was time to go, and they mounted their horses.

Hours later, they could see the Outpost in the distance. The Outpost was the one main center of life in the intersection between roads leading in different directions to Drilian, Durstein, Wolgon, Skvorton, Regaria, Lumera, and Breckendride. It was the hub of information, trading of currencies, and shopping.

It felt strange to be heading back toward civilization. Riding in, Hendrick took in the smells and sounds of the place bubbling with activity. Their growling stomachs immediately led them to a stand where men were grilling meat. They purchased supper and found an area on the outskirts to sit and eat. It helped them all greatly to finally have full bellies. Then, they asked around for news and found that rumors of Shadenberg's attack on Crestavia were still circulating. They purposely questioned the men who grilled their meat about Bulenduria. The most information they got was that the Festival of the Hidden Moon was coming up in a week and that the tribal people of Bulenduria were preparing for a huge sacrifice to their moon gods.

Since asking and spreading information was the norm at the Outpost, they easily found lots of people to talk to while shopping to replenish their supplies. Kendry had Hendrick ask some of them if they'd heard anything about General Walbrek from Crestavia. A few had heard that he had died and that Crestavia had a monument in his honor. But there was no word of him alive or active in the Midlands.

Hendrick took the horses to some stable boys to pick at their hooves, adjust their horseshoes, and give them some fodder. He asked them for information, as well, and was surprised that they knew about the slave traders who had kidnapped the people from the tavern in the outskirts of Crestavia. He was hoping someone would have information about who those slave traders were, but he found that they didn't.

After purchasing dried food, three bows and quivers of arrows, and three small daggers, they entered a trading post to see if they could find rope and medicine. Kendry's burnt arm hadn't gotten infected and actually appeared to be less severe than she had expected from the pain, but she hoped to find a calming salve to help with the tinge of pain that lingered.

They entered the old trading post and were greeted by a gruff, older looking man. He looked sun kissed and wrinkled, but once Kendry got closer she guessed he probably wasn't much older than her father.

"What can I do for ya, there, darling?" he asked, looking a little confused because she was wearing such boyish clothes. But, Kendry figured the Outpost was used to seeing all sorts of people in all sorts of disguises.

She held her arm up to the counter and carefully and painfully peeled away the bandage she had created from leaves and shredded clothing. He took a look at it and then glanced up at her.

"What happened there?"

"Got too close to a stick we were using for the fire's poker," she said without hesitation. "Do you have any salves for burns?"

"Sure do," he said and walked back through a door into a back room. He came back a minute later and looked at her wound again. "We should wash that out, first." He motioned for her to follow him into the back. There was a pail of water and he told her she could dip her wrist right in it. She did. The water was cooler than she expected.

Plunging the burned arm in felt both wonderful and painful at the same time. After, he helped blot it dry and applied the salve. Then, he retrieved some clean bandages and even took the time to help her wrap it. Kendry was impressed with his attention to her. He made little small talk, but did ask where she was from and where she was heading.

"Came from Crestavia-Capitalia and heading to..." she paused a moment too long and he gave her a questioning look.

"..Durstein," she added quickly, thinking of a place not too far away that travelers might go to do trade without creating suspicion. "Been traveling for a while," she added. "Curious for news of the surrounding areas?"

He filled her in on the looming war of Crestavia and Shadenberg, which he admitted she probably knew about. He talked about bandits popping up in the Great Divide and famine hitting Durstein.

"Heard anything about General Walbrek?" she asked. "They tell us in the Capital that he died, but many think he's s just on a mission." She looked at him carefully to try to analyze his response.

"He's alive," the man said as if he was bored.

"What?" Kendry perked up. "Have you seen him? What have you heard?"

"How old are you?" The man asked, ignoring her question.

She wanted answers, but submitted to his question. "Sixteen," she said.

He nodded.

"Those your friends you came in with?" he asked, referring to Hendrick and Graeme.

She nodded. "I'd really love to hear more about General Walbek," she said trying to get him back on track, without being suspicious. "I've been a huge fan of him and his military career."

Just then, she could hear Graeme saying her name. She wanted to ignore him, but then heard Hendrick call it with urgency. She walked over to the doorway and saw them. "Soldiers coming," they whispered.

The old man stood up joined them at the doorway. He motioned for them to follow him and led them to the back. He calmly walked to the far side of the room and pulled up the rug, revealing a trap door. He pointed at it. They looked back and forth at each other and decided it was worth the gamble.

Graeme threw open the door and began descending down a rope ladder into the room below. Kendry and Hendrick followed. The old man closed the door, replaced the rug and went back out to the front of the trading post to welcome the customers coming in.

"What did we just do?" Graeme asked in a whisper.

The hidden room was strangely lit. It turned out there was a lantern toward the back wall. The three of them explored the expansive room hidden under the shop. There were chairs and a table at one end of the room and two cots at the other. It reminded Kendry a little of the hidden room under her father's living quarters at the Academy. There were remnants of food on the table. Crumbs and bones, not rotted or stale. Someone had been there recently.

"Is this where the old man lives?" Hendrick asked, whispering.

"I think I saw a small bedroom in the back when he was bandaging my arm," Kendry answered hardly loud enough to hear. "So, I don't think so. But someone must live here."

She then told the boys what he had said about her dad being alive. Graeme was stoked that they had a lead. Hendrick looked nervous.

"You don't think the old man was just leading us down here so he could keep us cornered for the soldiers?" he asked.

"No," Kendry replied. "They'd have us out by now."

Just then, they heard the creak as the trap door was being lifted open. The brighter light from above blinded them. Kendry squinted, ready to defend herself if needed. The old man spoke, "You're welcome to stay down there until closing time. Another hour or so. Then, we can talk," he said. "Or, you're free to leave."

Kendry looked at the boys and they nodded in unspoken agreement. "Thank you," she said. "We'll be here waiting."

CHAPTER THIRTY-ONE

As it got dark, the man who had bandaged Kendry's arm closed up the trading post. Kendry, Graeme, and Hendrick were now waiting for him in the back room, after he had opened the trap door and let them climb up. Kendry was impatient. She really wanted information about her father and hoped that this man actually knew something.

After what seemed like an eternity to Kendry, the man slowly sauntered into the back room, dragging a stool from the front counter with him. He finally sat down and looked at the three who were staring at him, expectantly. He didn't say a word.

Finally, Hendrick decided to break the ice. "Uh, I'm Hendrick. And this is Graeme and...Kelly." He decided using a fake name was probably safer in case her real name had been tied to the traitor from Tavern's End. Unfortunately, he had forgotten that he and Graeme had both called her by her real name to get her attention when they saw soldiers approaching, earlier.

"If you're going to lie to me, boy," the man started gruffly, "then there's no point in doing this."

Kendry got nervous. This man had hidden them from the soldiers knowing nothing about them. Would he be willing to turn her in for a bounty if he knew who she was? At the same time, this may be her only chance to get information about her father and she wasn't willing to risk not getting that intel. She was willing to gamble her safety for it.

"My name is Kendry. General Walbrek is my father," she said boldly. Hendrick looked unsure of whether that was the best idea, but sat back in his chair ready to witness the outcome.

"There's a story," the man began, "about a prophesy." He got up and poured himself a pitcher of something to drink. The silence was unbearable for Kendry. This man was in absolutely no rush to help them. Finally, he sat back down with his drink, took a sip, and then continued. "The tribal people of Bulenduria have held the prophesy for hundreds of years. Passing it down from generation to generation." He just stopped talking after that as if he was done. Kendry glanced at Graeme and Hendrick who looked as confused as she was. The man just sipped his drink.

Frustrated, but trying to remain polite, Kendry asked, "What did the prophesy say?"

"It said," he began slowly, "The year the sun hides at noon, a daughter will be born. She will be red as fire and white as snow. And she will be known by the sign of the moon. She must be sacrificed when the moon hides at night or all terror will fill the land until it be so."

"Oh, I was afraid it wouldn't be a clear prophesy," Graeme said sarcastically. The man looked at him and a slight smile formed on his face.

"The Bulendurians understood it to mean that at their Lunar Eclipse they'd need to make a human sacrifice. A girl. Or catastrophe would encroach on their land."

"Huh?" Graeme said in response.

"So, they searched for this girl. And...they found her."

Kendry's eyebrows scrunched. The man noticed her confusion. He pointed at her dyed hair. "Red as fire," he said, even though her hair was almost black. He pointed at her face. "White as snow." She was dirty but it was obvious she had a pale skin tone. "Known by the sign of the moon." His eyes directed down to the burn on her forearm. The burn that hid her crescent moon birthmark.

Kendry froze. Heart racing, her breath refused to release. Hendrick stared at the ground, stunned, as he started to catch on to what the man meant.

But Graeme, unimpressed, wanted to change the subject. "So," he interrupted, "we were actually hoping you could give us some information about the great General Walbrek. Not that this fairy tale from the savages isn't interesting or anything."

The man ignored Graeme and continued on. "The girl they found was born the year there was a solar eclipse. Sixteen years ago."

Kendry closed her eyes. She took a deep breath to slow her racing heart. Her whole world was starting to unravel. What did this mean?

"General Walbrek was a good friend of mine," the man said. Then his pace picked up a little and he started sharing more information. "He and Malark and I trained together at the army a million years ago. We'd done at least twenty missions together. This trading post became my last mission. I was to make this my permanent residency. Play that I was neutral to every nation and gain intel for King Gadden. Walbrek and Malark would come through here and personally stay as my guests in the room below. We'd discuss business and share in some great times reliving memories," he smiled as he said this.

Kendry was trying not to interrupt because she didn't want him to stop talking, but her mind was reeling. This man was a friend of her father's? And Malark's? He had said her father was alive. It must be true. She tried to encourage him to continue with the eager look in her eyes.

"I'd been here a couple of years. Got used to the locals. Married a woman from a nearby tribe. At this time, the Bulendurians weren't quite so lethal to everyone around. They would still come to the Midlands, now and then. Trade at the Outpost. Word spread that they were searching for a baby born that year with certain characteristics. They would pay good money for information if anyone discovered her. My wife..." he paused for a moment and took a slow breath, "...she was a midwife. Was told to keep her eyes out."

217

The man refused to make eye contact with any of them as he continued talking. "She delivered a baby to a young peasant girl traveling through town. The woman's husband had just died in war and she was a refugee trying to make it to Crestavia. She went into labor early. Her daughter was born right here." He pointed to the room they were in. Kendry looked around, feeling sick to her stomach.

"As soon as the woman fell asleep, my wife grabbed that red-headed, pale baby, with a small crescent moon birthmark on her forearm, and rode straight to Bulenduria. She didn't even tell me. I was down the road at a pub. Came back to the poor peasant girl asking where her baby was...she was weak and scared."

Hendrick moved uncomfortably in his seat. He wasn't enjoying this story and was worried about Kendry.

"The Bulendurians had a huge festival. Festival of the Hidden Moon. Everyone was present in their square to witness the baby to be sacrificed to their moon gods. They believed if it didn't happen that night, they would be doomed with disasters, plagues, famines, droughts and more. But, your father..."

Kendry now sat taller in her chair. She was eager not to miss a word of this next part of his story.

"...your father and Malark had been coming back from a mission and decided to venture through Bulenduria, hoping to pick up any intel. They had to be very careful to dress the part. They looked like savages, really. Nothing but loin cloths on and hair and beards grown long, strung with beads. They wouldn't have chanced it except the huge masses due to the festival allowed them to blend into the crowds. They had hoped to just journey through the crowd and come out toward the Outpost. But, as they got to the center of the main village, they saw the baby girl being held up before the masses at the festival.

"As Walbrek tells it, something snapped inside him and all his training and restraint went out the window. He knew he had to save that baby. Malark tells it that Walbrek turned into some savage super hero and leapt through the crowd to the elevated pavilion. He grabbed that baby and fought off the

218

surprised tribal priest that was about to sacrifice her. The chief and other officials had not expected anyone to interfere with their ceremony and were not prepared at all. They tried to fight him, but he was no match for them. They were weaponless, except for the knife the priest was going to use to sacrifice the baby and Walbrek took that with him."

Graeme's mouth was open a little, stunned. Hendrick was staring at Kendry. Kendry could not believe what she was hearing. They all three knew that she was indeed that baby girl.

The man, who they later discovered was called Gipp, explained how Walbrek hid out with the baby and even Malark was unable to find him. For Malark's own protection, he had tried to blend in with the furious crowd in Bulenduria until he could safely slip away.

"Walbrek ended up here. I hid him in the room you all hid in earlier today. He and the baby stayed there for quite some time with your mother," as he said the last word, he looked at Kendry.

Her mother?

Emotions flooded through Kendry's body as she tried to accept the fact that the mother she had grown up believing died giving birth to her, probably never existed. And, now she desired to know as much as she could about this woman. Her real mother.

"After a few weeks, your father planned to take you and your mother back to the Capital and ask King Gadden for protection for you. I warned him that King Gadden wouldn't care about a peasant woman nor want to put himself and his kingdom in danger by hiding the Sacrifice. But, Walbrek insisted that King Gadden was a good man and would help them. Walbrek assumed you could be hidden in plain sight in the Capital and he could head back out on the next mission the king assigned him. So, Malark and I helped him sneak you and your mother of town in the middle of the night."

Kendry nodded, trying to keep Gipp talking. *Where was her mother now?*

"Traveling alone through the Great Divide with an exhausted peasant woman and a newborn baby was not easy for your father. He got attacked by

Bulendurians right away. It's a miracle he was able to get away alive with you."

It was quiet for a moment while Kendry processed his words. "What about my mother?" she blurted out. "Did she get away?"

Gipp looked into her eyes and slowly shook his head. "She died saving your life," he said quietly. "Walbrek later told me she made him promise he'd save you and then she took off with a bundled blanket, pretending she had you, allowing Walbrek enough space and time to escape. The Bulendurians, though wanting revenge on your father, made getting the baby their top priority. They chased her and her horse and eventually caught up with them. The rest is history."

"No," Kendry whispered. Tears streamed down her face. She had just gotten her mother back and now she lost her again.

"What about your wife?" Graeme asked, trying to break up the tension after the revelation of Kendry's mother's death.

"By the time Walbrek brought the baby here, my wife had already hung herself." They all were shocked at his blunt answer. "Guilt," he said. "She couldn't forgive herself. Had lied to your mother that you had died. Your mother had fallen apart. We sent her to the inn down the road and paid for a couple of nights for her to rest. After my wife's death, Walbrek brought the very hungry baby here, and so I went out and found your mother so she could feed you.

"I've never seen a woman so happy before in my life. You were brought back from the dead. She swore she'd never let anything happen to you again."

Kendry cried harder. Hendrick put an arm around her, but she shoved him off, wanting to be left alone.

"Eventually, the Bulendurians showed up at the Outpost searching for Walbrek," Gipp continued. "They called him 'the Warrior,' a name that has stuck with him in lots of circles. Thankfully, they never seemed to put together that the Warrior that took their Sacrifice was the same Warrior that is called General Walbrek in Crestavia.

"The Bulendurians had searched for you and Walbrek here immediately after you had been taken, but at that point in time Walbrek had not yet showed up here. They recognized my wife as the one they paid a load of money to for the baby and didn't suspect her, but still searched well. They came back a second time when your mother and Walbrek were here. You all hid down below as they tore this place apart."

Kendry looked around. She'd been born here. She'd been hidden here. She knew her mother here. It was all so surreal. She couldn't take any more of the story. Wiping the tears from her cheeks, she looked straight into Gipp's eyes. She needed to know where her dad was now.

"Where is my dad? You said he's alive."

Gipp stared off into space. He took a deep breath and sighed. Then, he got up, ignoring her question, and filled three mugs with liquid from his pitcher. Kendry was getting angry. She didn't want a drink. She wanted answers.

"Malark's been staying here. Down below. Off and on for awhile, when he isn't in Crestavia. Trying to figure out how to help your father."

"Malark's dead," Kendry interrupted. She didn't care about Malark right now. Gipp was changing the subject again. She needed to know about her dad.

"I know he's dead," Gipp responded without emotion. I have my own surveillance teams and information network reporting back to me. The way I hear it, he died trying to rescue you from bandits. Was prob'ly going to bring you here."

Kendry was a little surprised to hear that, as it had just happened and she didn't see how anyone would have had time to report to Gipp.

"He burned your birthmark off, too, I see. Didn't want anyone to put it together who you were and report it to the Bulendurians. Smart guy, that Malark."

"Huh," Graeme said aloud as he was putting two and two together and it was making sense.

221

It stabbed Kendry in the heart a little to realize that Malark really was trying to protect her.

"Malark and a couple of others have been here for a few days," Gipp continued. "I've received many updates. I can fill you in."

Hendrick spoke for the first time in a while. "Kendry and I were in Tavern's End when we were all told that General Walbrek, Malark, and all their men had died. Then slave traders showed up and attacked our town. Everyone was either killed or kidnapped. Kendry and I were the only two to survive and then the King's men showed up to arrest Kendry. Can you fill us in on any of that?"

Gipp grunted a little and nodded. He stretched and yawned. Then he began to explain in his blunt way what he knew. "Those weren't slave traders. They were bounty hunters. They were looking for the Sacrifice so they could trade her in to the Bulendurians for a lot of money. The way my wife did," he stopped talking after he mentioned his wife.

Kendry began shaking. The men at Tavern's End had been searching for her? Her friends were dead because those men had come in search of her. Tears began filling the corners of her eyes.

Graeme was getting restless. He got up and paced around. "Let's get back to Kendry's father? Where is he?"

As if Graeme hadn't spoken, Gipp continued on where he left off. "Rumor has it a man recognized Kendry's birthmark and red hair when she was working at the tavern. Malark said he caught the guy staring at it on your forearm and even rubbing it."

Kendry thought back to the time a man had grabbed her wrist while she was serving him a drink at the tavern. Malark had exploded with anger, dragging the man out of the tavern.

Gipp continued, "From that point on, Malark and Walbrek were on alert. We all knew another Lunar Eclipse was coming up. The Bulendurians have blamed every bad occurrence over the past sixteen years on not sacrificing

Kendry. They were spreading lots of decrees to bounty hunters, especially in Regaria, to keep an eye out for her."

Graeme looked like he was going to be sick. Gipp suggested he sit back down and gave him a mug of water.

Hendrick was annoyed with Graeme's overreaction to the news. He and Kendry had lived and experienced this nightmare, not Graeme. If there was anyone who should have been green in the face and needed to sit down, it should've been them, not him.

Gipp continued on at his casual, slow pace. "Word got back to Regaria and the bounty hunters were ready, but Walbrek had other problems. King Gadden had received intel that Lieutenant Trent was actually a spy from Shadenberg. Trent knew way too much about everything, including the Academy. They staged a training event, leaving Trent behind, and led him to think they had all been killed. Then, a group of them staked out and followed Trent as he left the Academy. Your father and Malark were part of that group. Followed Trent through the forest. At one point, Trent stumbled upon an injured man…"

"Enough!" Graeme yelled as he stood. Kendry was shocked at Graeme's outburst. Hendrick looked at him quizzically. "I can't take another minute of listening to you ramble on about things in the past when we're trying to find her father now."

Gipp looked at Graeme with a glare that made him shut his mouth and tremble. He stared at him until it was no longer comfortable and Graeme apologized for his outburst and sat back down. Gipp continued.

"The injured guy that was talking to Trent needed a horse into town. He was trying to bribe Trent, but Trent had no interest in anything he had to offer. The man promised Trent he could tell him information that would make him very rich. He then said that he knew the location of the lost Sacrifice the Bulendurians wanted. Obviously, this got the interest of your father and Malark who were spying on them."

Kendry was glued to Gipp's every word. Each new bit of information was a piece in the puzzle of what had really been going on. She kept nodding, hoping that would help stir Gipp on to continue talking, possibly at a faster pace.

"Trent didn't care and took off," Gipp continued. "Most the search party took off after him, but your father and Malark wanted to question the guy with the hurt ankle. Didn't take long until they figured out that the injured guy had been travelling with a group of bounty hunters from Regaria who had left him behind when he rolled his ankle." Gipp paused again to take another long drink out of his cup. "Realizing bounty hunters were on their way to Tavern's End, your dad and Malark rushed back to the tavern to check on you. All seemed okay, but your father knew that if word got back to Bulenduria that you were living in Tavern's End, they would never give up until they had you. They needed you for their next sacrifice at the Lunar Eclipse."

Kendry's head was spinning. These savages wanted her for their next sacrifice. That sacrifice was in a couple of weeks. No wonder Malark, with his dying words, had told her to run far away.

"That's when your father decided the only way to protect you was to try to convince the Bulendurians that you were dead and ask them to sacrifice him in your place."

Kendry gasped. Hendrick's mouth dropped open. Graeme had his head between his two hands, leaning over in disbelief.

Gipp continued, "He believed that he could convince them their gods would accept him since he was the one that stole you. He thought they'd never give up looking for you if he didn't get them to believe you had died."

"No!" Kendry yelled. She jumped up out of her chair and began pacing.

Gipp, unmoved by her emotions, continued on in his calm manner. "Malark said Walbrek gave him the medallion around his neck and told him to give it to you. Convince you he was dead so you wouldn't search for him, ya see?"

Kendry reached for the necklace. She was wearing it under Hendrick's shirt. But Mister Lansing had found the medallion in the pocket of one of the bounty hunters on the boat the night her friends were kidnapped from

Tavern's End. That made no sense. Kendry shook her head slowly, trying to figure out how a bounty hunter got the medallion from Malark.

"Poor Malark," Gipp said. "He didn't know what hit 'im. After your dad left, to go turn himself in to the Bulendurians, Malark was supposed to bring you to the palace for safe keepin'. But instead, he got knocked unconscious. Said he woke up on a boat, bound."

Kendry looked at Hendrick. The bounty hunters had attacked Malark, too? They had put him on the boat? That explained how they took her dad's medallion.

"Said he was lucky, though. Able to get away with minimum damage to himself. Swam far across the bay, but could barely walk. Worse part for him was watching from a distance as the townspeople got rounded up on the boat. Said he tried to make his way back, but injury won out. Then, he saw as you rescued those people. Ya should've heard him tell me that part. He was so proud of you."

Kendry felt a large tear forming in her eye. Just talking about Malark was killing her. She had just watched him die and now she knew he was protecting her all along.

"Anyhow, Malark said that night after the bounty hunters, who obviously couldn't find the Sacrifice and decided instead to kidnap the townfolk as slaves...after they left, he slowly and painfully made his way back to the tavern. Said he saw you and Hendrick sleeping, but decided not to disturb you until he was ready to take you away. So, he made his way to the Academy on a horse from the stables, instead."

Kendry thought back to the footprint she had seen outside the tavern that night. She knew someone had been watching them.

"Malark found the Academy ransacked by Lieutenant Trent. He buried the guards that Trent killed. He said Trent had thrown every weapon from the armory into the well."

Kendry nodded. It made sense now. Malark had buried those bodies. And, she hadn't thought to look down the well. She figured that was probably when Malark, knowing Hendrick was safe with Kendry, searched Mister Carter's house and took the portrait of her, too. The portrait, drawn by Hendrick, had ended up in the hands of guards at the palace when they were searching for Kendry at the Refuge. Hendrick had it rolled up in his knapsack, now, but they hadn't been able to figure out how it disappeared from Mister Carter's house in Tavern's End, until Gipp's revelation explained it.

"Unfortunately, though…" Gipp said, yawning again as if this whole thing was sort of boring. "…Malark said when he got back to the tavern, there were soldiers from King Gadden there looking for Kendry. He told them how ridiculous their charge was and that he had seen the bounty hunters with his own eyes, but they insisted that they had orders to take you in."

Kendry nodded, following his explanation. Malark had told her about seeing the soldiers and how he had gone with them to the Academy and seen the note she had pretended to leave saying she was going to her imagined aunt's house. Gendella, King Gadden's daughter, had told Kendry that her father, the king, had created the fake charge against Kendry to bring her to the palace, safely, as a favor to Walbrek.

"King Gadden's dead, though," Hendrick piped in.

"Yep," Gipp responded. "Died after Walbrek told him he was leaving to sacrifice himself to the Bulendurians. His bratty son, Casper, didn't like that Walbrek was choosing Kendry's life over leading the troops in the upcoming war against Shadenberg. Casper has been trying to find Kendry ever since, so he can trade her to the Bulendurians for Walbrek. He wants Walbrek back at any cost and doesn't care about Kendry, at all."

That made sense to Kendry. She had heard Prince Casper, Sleege, and Malark fighting about Walbrek. Malark wanted them to get him. He must've meant to save him from the savages. But Casper was stalling, wanting Kendry found.

"So…my father?" Kendry asked, yet again, hoping for a response.

"He came here weeks ago to say goodbye to me. Made me promise I'd spread any intel I could that you were dead so people would stop searching for you. Then he marched himself into Bulenduria and let them have at him."

Kendry gasped. "You said he's alive, though?" She held onto hope.

"Yes, that's the word I've heard. They are saving him until the Lunar Eclipse. Hopin' they find you before then as they've amped up the bounty. They will kill him, regardless, of course. Bu, they know he knows where you are and they think if they torture him enough, they'll get it out of 'im."

Kendry hid her face in her palms. She didn't want to think about her father getting tortured.

"Since they are not going to find you, they will sacrifice him at the lunar eclipse at their festival instead." Gipp concluded, matter-of-factly.

"No!" Kendry yelled. "No! Please help me stop them! There has to be something we can do...what about Prince Casper...can he help?"

"Prince Casper only wants Walbrek alive and will gladly give you over for him."

"Well, what if I hide and Hendrick and Graeme ask him for help?"

"Nah, Malark has been trying to get him to help get Walbrek out of there for weeks. Casper is too scared of the Bulendurians. He doesn't want to start a war with them. They'll team up with Shadenberg and he knows he's outnumbered."

Kendry paced around the room. There had to be something they could do. They had to rescue her father. They just needed a plan.

Gipp asked if they were hungry and started prepping some food. Kendry could not think about eating. Graeme and Hendrick both tried calming her down and talked through all the new information with her. She couldn't stomach thinking about her father sacrificing himself for her. Why hadn't he just told her? They could have run off together? Her father could've protected her from any bounty hunters looking for her. They could have lived on the run. She just couldn't fathom why he thought sacrificing himself was the only answer.

The night dragged on with lots of talk and frustration. Gipp finally got Kendry to eat by telling her that her father wouldn't want her to starve on his account. Eventually, they all decided it was time to go to bed. Gipp secured them in the hidden room underground.

There were only two cots and Hendrick insisted on sleeping on the ground. His heart hurt so much for Kendry. He knew they had come to the end of this story for her. There was nothing left they could do. Walbrek would be sacrificed in her place. They would need to keep Kendry hidden until after the Lunar Eclipse and then continue to keep her disguised until they could get far from here.

But as he lay there listening to Graeme breathe deeply in his sleep and Kendry toss and turn at her lack of sleep, something occurred to him. Kendry would not be on the same page. She would insist on going after her father. In fact, with how well he knew Kendry, he was positive she was probably planning at that very moment how she could sacrifice herself in her father's place.

He whispered, "You know if you go, they will kill both of you. They'd never let him go free even if you sacrificed yourself."

In response, he listened to her sob loudly.

CHAPTER THIRTY-TWO

The next morning Kendry woke to noise above. The trading post was bursting with activity and therefore Gipp was busy. Kendry, Graeme, and Hendrick brainstormed ideas for how to help her father, but none were realistic.

Kendry couldn't help but let certain thoughts distract her. Malark had warned her not to trust someone. What if that someone was Gipp? He knew who she was, and Malark had said that about the one she wasn't supposed to trust. What if some of the information Gipp was giving them wasn't accurate?

Hendrick and Graeme both took turns getting out of the hideout and spending time around the Outpost at different venues, but they all insisted that Kendry stay hidden. This made her livid as she didn't think anyone would connect her as the 'Lost Sacrifice' with her darkened hair and burned birthmark. Gipp told her that her father would never forgive him if he knew he was letting her strut around when the Festival of the Hidden Moon was only days away. The Bulendurians would be increasing their search for her.

As afternoon neared, Kendry's edginess from sitting and doing nothing caused her to get grumpy. She made some rude remarks to Hendrick and so he decided to go look for Graeme who was supposed to be bringing lunch back to them.

Alone in the hideout, emotions rose and she wanted to scream. Of course, she didn't scream, because she knew that would not help her stay hidden.

She did, though, kick the cot she had been sleeping in. Kicking something felt good. She needed to let out frustration. The cot wiggled on two legs and eventually fell over. Annoyed that she had to pick it back up, she grabbed it gruffly and the blanket fell off. Under the blanket was a thin magenta scarf. She picked it up and rubbed the silky material between her fingers. Kendry had seen that scarf before somewhere. Just then, noise from above became louder. She hid the scarf back under the blanket as the trap door was being opened.

Gipp handed down some bread and dried meat through the hole.

"Where are the boys?" she asked annoyed that they were probably feasting on some freshly grilled meat while she was down there locked away like a wild animal.

"They'll be back soon. Got busy with something." Gipp closed the trap door again and she was back to being isolated. Hours went by. Frustration filled every ounce of her. Finally, after it had been quiet upstairs for some time, Gipp came and opened the trap door.

"What is going on?" Kendry demanded.

Gipp, never quick to answer, pulled his stool over close to the trap door and looked down at her. She stared up at him, desiring an answer.

"Closed up shop for the night," he began slowly.

"Where's Hendrick and Graeme?" she asked, starting to get a little concerned.

"Those two boys? They decided to go and get themselves killed."

"What!" Kendry yelled. "What do you mean?"

"Well, not yet, I'm guessing. But soon."

"What do you mean?" Kendry asked with urgency. "Are they okay?"

Gipp sighed. "Guessing they are okay at the moment. But they won't be."

"Agh," Kendry grunted at the man's slow pace and way of deflecting from real information. "Where are they?" she demanded.

"They went to try to figure out the situation with your dad," he said. "I thought it was pretty stupid, myself. But I sent them with sandwiches and wished them well. If someone's willing to die for a cause, there's not much you can do to stop them."

Die? Kendry felt sick. She wanted out. The rope ladder to leave the hidden room was up with Gipp, connected to the trapdoor. They had purposely wound it up earlier that morning so she wouldn't be tempted to leave her hiding spot. At the time, she had let them. Now, she wanted out of there.

"You let them go to Bulenduria?" she yelled. "Get me out of here! I've got to stop them!"

"I can't let you leave until after the lunar eclipse. I promised the boys and I've made a promise to your father to keep you safe if I ever saw you. You're stuck here, girly."

She didn't know whether to threaten him or kiss up in order to get him to let her out. She was so angry and scared for Hendrick and Graeme. If Gipp didn't let her out, they would die.

"Gipp, don't you understand? They are going to be killed! Let me out! I can save them!" she begged, as tears started running out of the corners of her eyes. "Please!"

"Kendry," he said slowly, looking into her damp eyes. "Your father loves you so much he was willing to give his life for you. There's no greater love than that. If you were to rush off there, they'd kill both of you. Those boys must care for you, too, because they got it in their heads that they can try to mislead the savages on their search for you. They'll probably be killed. But they knew the risk when they took off from here earlier today. If you go and get yourself killed, then they will all have died in vain. I'm sorry, Sweetie, but you are staying put." And with that, he closed the trapdoor.

Kendry cried and screamed and kicked and threw things until she ended up bawling herself to sleep, hours later, out of hopelessness and exhaustion.

231

CHAPTER THIRTY-THREE

H endrick knew what they were doing was stupid. Actually, it was probably suicidal. Trying to meet with the Bulendurians to discuss their Lost Sacrifice was like stoking a fire, dancing in it, and trying not to get burned.

He still didn't know why Graeme agreed to go with him. He actually didn't want him to come, but the thought of leaving him behind with Kendry wasn't appealing either. And Graeme had insisted. He said he understood the risk and that he knew they probably wouldn't return. Hendrick figured Graeme was allowed to make his own life choices and so he let him come.

"So, what exactly is your plan, again?" Graeme asked, as they sat down to eat the sandwiches Gipp had packed them. They'd been traveling for over four hours and they were both hungry.

"I figure the best we can do is try to lead them away from Kendry's trail," he said between bites. "We're going to pretend to be Regarian bounty hunters and say that we want to be paid for information. Then, we'll tell them that we had followed her and a group of undercover soldiers to Breckenride. That she's harvesting grapes in the lower vineyards there. If we can get them hooked on that trail, they will be going far away from the Outpost and will be distracted long enough for us to keep her alive through the lunar eclipse."

"But what if they figure out that we're not really from Regaria? I mean, I speak Regarian, but you don't."

"Gipp said they'd bring out one of the tribal leaders to translate and that the translator knows most languages. We can start with Crestavian because that's what most people speak at the Outpost, but you'll have to include some Regarian to make us sound legit."

"So, we're risking our lives...probably giving up our lives...just to send them on the wrong trail? I just don't think it's enough."

"I'm up for any other ideas?" Hendrick stopped eating and stared at him. Graeme just shrugged.

Hendrick continued, "Maybe while we're there we can get some more information on Walbrek. Figure out where they have him. If Prince Casper wants him bad enough and we can find out any information about his whereabouts, we could spread it around the Outpost. It would get back to Casper and maybe he could send his soldiers in to free Walbrek."

Graeme shrugged again. "I think if Casper could have gotten Walbrek out, he'd have done it by now."

The boys finished up eating and went on their way. They arrived in the valley of the Bulendure Mountains that led to Bulenduria a couple of hours later. "Last chance to change your mind," Hendrick said, taking a deep breath and stepping forward.

Graeme nodded. "Let's do this."

The boys spent the next hour heading in toward the outer gates of Bulenduria. Gipp had explained to them how they were not to pass the line of pine trees outside the gate or they would be killed on the spot. Instead, they were to show their respect by bowing down and waiting. They did as Gipp told them and after what seemed like forever, got fidgety.

Face to the ground, Graeme whispered, "I don't think anyone's here. Think maybe Gipp was pulling one over on us?"

"I don't know," answered Hendrick. His feet and legs were falling asleep.

Just then, they heard the sound of footsteps. A lot of footsteps. It sounded like they were being surrounded. They waited until they were tapped before they stood up. Gipp had warned them that the Bulendurians found it threatening to be approached without their welcoming tap. They were very careful not to appear threatening.

As they slowly stood up, they took in the view. Before them stood huge men dressed only in loincloths. They were all tanned dark by the sun, very muscular, and holding spears. With their long wild hair, they stared straight at Hendrick and Graeme and their faces showed anger.

A tribal translator stepped forward. They only figured out who he was because he began speaking in many different languages. When he got to Crestavian, Hendrick clearly understood him asking, 'Who are you and what do you want?"

Graeme answered first, "We come here humbly to ask to meet with your leaders regarding the whereabouts of your Lost Sacrifice."

Hendrick shook a little as he noticed the look on the faces of the men as the translator relayed Graeme's words to the other Bulendurians.

One of the men stormed over close to them and aimed his spear inches from Hendrick's forehead. He yelled something. Hendrick trembled. Sweat was dripping down his face. The translator then spoke, "Tell us where she is NOW or you die."

Hendrick froze. He tried to spit out the words to ask for money, but it didn't seem wise to do that with his life being threatened. Instead, he figured he'd try telling them that he was from Regaria and had followed her to Breckenride, but Graeme spoke first.

"If you kill or even hurt either of us, you will never find her."

The translator communicated Graeme's message back. The man then moved his spear from Hendrick's forehead over to Graeme. He stared Graeme in the eyes. He rambled off something that was translated, "Then, tell us where she is and live."

Graeme continued, boldly speaking, even with a spear toward his face. "She's not far from here. You can have her in time for your festival. We can take you there. I will lead you myself. But, I do demand something in return."

Hendrick was confused. This wasn't the story they had agreed on. What was Graeme up to?

After the translator told Graeme that he was in no position to be making demands, Graeme took off his knapsack and laid it on the floor. The man with the spear reached in and looked through it. He pulled out a scroll. As he unrolled the scroll, Hendrick's eyes widened with disbelief. It was the portrait he had drawn of Kendry! The one that Malark must've taken and given to the king's guards when they were searching for her at the Refuge. Thron had kept the portrait when the guards left and given it to Hendrick. He'd had it in his knapsack ever since. How did Graeme get it? And why was he showing it to the men that wanted to find her?

"That's what she looks like today," Graeme said.

Hendrick's blood boiled. What was Graeme doing? The last thing they want is for them to know what Kendry looks like!

The man with the spear showed the portrait to the other others.

"I know exactly where she is hiding. She believes I am helping to keep her safe. But I am willing to give you her location for something I want," Graeme stated loudly.

At that moment, something in Hendrick snapped. He looked at Graeme, jaw clenched with anger. Graeme wouldn't look back at him, instead staring at the ground.

Hendrick felt sick. Graeme was betraying them. He was going to tell these savages Kendry was hiding at the trading post. Hendrick couldn't hold in his fury and he shouted at him, "Stop it!"

The savages noticed the anger on Hendrick's face and the guilt on Graeme's. They watched closely as Hendrick tried to attack Graeme to get him to stop talking as he began to tell them more. Graeme pushed Hendrick's initial attack off and then they stood opposite each other, staring each other down. The man with the spear stepped between them, amused at their conflict, but guarding Graeme from Hendrick.

"How could you do this?" Hendrick asked. "Think about what you're doing!"

Graeme ignored him and looked back at the translator. "Tell them I will ONLY give you the location of the Lost Sacrifice IF I get to take the Warrior back with me.

The translator laughed a little and relayed the message. The rest of the tribal men grumbled and even chuckled. It was obvious that they saw Graeme's demand as ridiculous.

Hendrick tried to hold out hope that maybe Graeme thought getting Walbrek released would then help them to fight these men and save Kendry, but they weren't going to release Walbrek unless they had Kendry, and Graeme had to know that.

More discussion took place with the Bulendurians telling Graeme that they would not release the Warrior until they had sacrificed the girl at their festival.

"The Warrior is worth a lot to me," Graeme said. "I can get more money than you can imagine for him. He's practically priceless. The girl," he continued, "is only worth something to you and your tribe. Therefore, you need to decide what the price tag is for her. Is she worth giving up the Warrior or not?"

More grumbling and discussion after the translator relayed Graeme's message. They told him that if he brought them the girl, they would release the Warrior, but Graeme told them he did not trust them. He countered with that they follow him with the Warrior in tow, and when they had the girl, they could take her and leave him be with the Warrior. The men would not agree to that.

Listening to their bargaining, was more than Hendrick could handle. He yelled at Graeme, "You traitor! How could you? I will kill you!"

Graeme, ignoring him, began speaking in another language. Hendrick, unable to understand their continued discussion, was overcome with hopelessness. He jumped toward Graeme, ready to pound him, but the man with the spear socked him in the face. He fell to the ground, his nose swelling with pain and feeling like it was a foot long. His head was dizzy, but he started to pull himself up, when another tribal man walked over and forcefully covered his mouth with a cloth. The cloth tasted and smelled weird. Within seconds, the world was spinning, sound slowed down, everything got blurry, and Hendrick fell unconscious to the ground.

CHAPTER THIRTY-FOUR

When Hendrick awoke, he couldn't see anything. His hands were tied together. He was riding on a horse, connected to another person who he assumed had the reins to lead the trotting animal. His body was arched forward onto the man's bare back. A sack of some sort was over his head. It was dark and smelled like sweat. He had no idea how long he had been unconscious. He had some flashes of memories or dreams making him think that he may have awoken and knocked out again, many times over the past hours or days. He was extremely dizzy and tried using his bound hands to hold on so he wouldn't fall off the horse as he lifted his covered head.

Occasionally he'd hear a voice, but it was in a dialect he didn't recognize. Obviously the Bulendurians were taking him somewhere. At one point, when they stopped for a bit, he heard Graeme's voice, too.

Anger and exhaustion flooded Hendrick as he helplessly bobbed along on the horse for many hours. He knew he had to get his hands free. He had to do something to help Kendry or warn her. She would trust Graeme if he told her to come out of the hidden room. Or, maybe Graeme would just lead the savage Bulendurians to the front door and let them raid the place, letting them know she was down below under the rug in the back. Either way, Hendrick knew he and Gipp were Kendry's only hope.

After a bit, the riders slowed down and gathered near one another. Hendrick could feel the presence of the other horses and hear the Bulendurians voices close to him. The man leading his horse got too close to a tree and the bag on

Hendrick's head caught on a small branch. It pulled the sack up, just a bit, but enough to allow one eye to see out a ripped hole. Hendrick's eyes struggled to adjust after they'd been in the dark so long, so he closed them and squinted.

Surveying his surroundings, he could tell they were traveling in a group. From what Hendrick could hear, the Bulendurians appeared to be following Graeme's leading. There must have been fifty or sixty of the tribal men, all on horseback with weapons. They were staring in the direction Hendrick had heard Graeme's voice coming from, though he couldn't see Graeme over the crowd with his one exposed eye.

Off to the side, a few horses over, was another man with a bag on his head. He was bound up really well. Hendrick could tell by his physique that it was General Walbrek, the Warrior that had stolen the Bulendurians' Sacrifice sixteen years prior.

Graeme instructed the translator, in the Crestavian language, that he would go in first and bring the girl out to them. The translator repeated it. The men obviously did not like this plan. There was an immediate uproar followed by many men cornering Graeme with spears. It was as they spread out to surround Graeme that Hendrick's one eye peeking from behind the bag saw the mountain before them.

They were not at the trading post. They were not even near the Outpost, at all. They were approaching the mountain used as a decoy to hide Crestavia's military base on the other side.

Off to the right, in the side of the mountain was the old mine that Hendrick knew had a tunnel through to the soldiers on the other side.

 Up above on the mountain were soldiers at lookout points that no one down below would suspect to be there because they were hidden so well.

The mountain before them had many tunnels cut into it leading to the military base, but each of their openings was camouflaged and hidden behind rocks and brush.

And off to the left was the deep ditch hidden with blankets of dirt and covered with brush, which would lure enemies to their death as they'd attempt to cross, only to fall in the hidden large crevice.

Hendrick could hear Graeme trying to tell the threatening tribal men that he should enter the mine first and bring the girl out, but the Bulendurians, at this point, were getting restless and threw his idea to the side as they threatened him and ordered their own men to enter the mine.

The Bulendurians looked hesitant as they approached the large mountain, ready for any ambush or trick. A group of seven of them had their weapons out and in military formation crept carefully toward the mine.

Graeme yelled, loudly, "What about the Warrior? I want the Warrior released!"

As the Bulendurian closest to Walbrek laughed at Graeme's suggestion, Hendrick purposely, and painfully, fell off his horse. This caught the man he was connected to off guard and the savage was pulled halfway off his horse, holding on as best he could. Hendrick's weight was tugging on the man. Angry, he took a knife and cut Hendrick apart from him, kicking him to the ground.

Hendrick used his bound hands to pull the rest of the sack of his face. It still sat on his head like a hat, but he could now see. He looked over at Walbrek and, without hesitation, yelled loudly, "Walbrek! We need a battle cry, now!"

Whether General Walbrek recognized Hendrick's voice or was just surprised by another Crestavian voice, it was obvious he took notice. Hendrick wasn't even sure if the Bulendurians had any clue that he was actually the great general from Crestavia. But, Walbrek knew that someone there recognized who he was since Hendrick had just yelled his name. "Walbrek, now!" Hendrick yelled again. This outburst got a sword drawn at him from one man and a kick in the face by the other.

Hendrick held his mouth, which was bleeding. His forehead hit the dirt on the ground. He was kicked again, in the stomach, but then he heard it.

"Men of Valor...AAAATACK!!!!" The deep battle cry of a general that many of Crestavia's soldiers had either fought for or trained with rang out across the mountain, echoing.

Immediately, arrows flew through the air from the tops of the mountain and from the hidden tunnels throughout the side of the mountain, hitting the tribal men. Hundreds of soldiers poured from the mine, itself, overriding the seven men that were attempting to enter. Fighting broke out. Swords clanging. Screams of victory and anguish. The Bulendurians were extremely outnumbered.

Hendrick quickly crawled over to Walbrek who was still tied up on a horse, though the man who had been guarding him lay dead on the ground with an arrow in his heart. Hendrick stepped over the puddle of blood and took the sack off Walbrek's head.

It took the general a few moments to gain composure and assess what was before him. He was surprised to see Hendrick and eager to join the fighting. He yelled at Hendrick to cut his ties. Hendrick grabbed a dagger off the dead man and began cutting apart Walbrek's rope. Walbrek looked at Hendrick and asked, "Kendry?"

"She's safe," he replied as he nervously tried faster to cut the ropes. "Gipp's got her hidden."

Walbrek grunted his approval as Hendrick cut him free. In a flash, the general was gone. He rode into the crowd on horseback, taking charge of the attack.

A few unharmed Bulendurians raced after him on their horses. He smiled big as he took off as fast as he could toward the forest. Hendrick knew that though it looked like he was running for his life, he was instead very careful to pass through a specific, cleverly marked section over the hidden ditch. The Bulendurians chasing him were not careful to ride in his exact tracks, and each one of them plunged deep into the earth's crevice as the blankets of fake ground gave way.

Hendrick's heart hurt watching the horses fall to their deaths, but he could see the satisfaction on Walbrek's face as he got to witness one of his planned traps succeed. It had all happened fast and the battle was over as quick as it had begun. Every Bulendurian was dead.

The soldiers' professionalism was lost as they rushed to greet the general who they had believed to be dead. Some of the soldiers had known he was being kept hostage in Bulenduria and were apologizing that they hadn't received orders to try to free him. Avoiding Walbrek and the soldiers' comradery, Hendrick searched for Graeme, who had pretty much hidden through the whole battle.

Hendrick warred within himself as to whether he should punch Graeme for making him think he was betraying them, or hug him for the successful ploy. He chose the latter.

"That was a much better plan than I had thought of," Hendrick admitted. "Would have been nice to be in on it!" he added, angrily. Graeme just gave him a big smile.

"I needed to convince the Bulendurians that I was betraying you so that they would actually believe me. Best way to do that was to make you believe it, too," he explained.

Hendrick shook his head. He gave half a smile. "I would've killed you if I had the chance," Hendrick admitted. "I would do anything to keep Kendry safe." He said it with a little bit of threat in his voice.

Graeme nodded, acknowledging he had caught the threat.

Their conversation was disrupted when they noticed the soldiers going back to their positions and getting serious. Walbrek yelled from across the way, ordering Hendrick and his friend to hide. Then they heard it, the subtle sound in the distance of horses.

Quickly, soldiers escorted the boys into the mine. From a distance, they could hear Walbrek yelling commands at the soldiers. They were taken to the back of the mine and then filed through the long tunnel. They hurried until they came out the other side. Soldiers in the base were lined up, waiting for orders. Hendrick and Graeme were told to get out of the way.

Catching pieces of conversation regarding intel, they inferred that Shadenberg was attacking.

Hendrick looked at Graeme. "We have to get Kendry back here."

CHAPTER THIRTY-FIVE

Kendry had been trapped in the room under the trading post for days. Gipp had communicated with her very little. Hoping to manipulate him into letting her leave, she had tried to figure out something that would work. She faked an injury and asked him to help her. Once he came down, she was planning on showing him some of her best martial arts moves and then racing to Bulenduria to try to save her friends and locate her father.

But, Gipp was on to her. He wouldn't enter the room she was hiding in. He wouldn't even listen to her cries when she begged through tears for him to let her go. They were real tears, too. The anguish of recognizing everyone left that she loved was about to die or could already be dead was too much for her to endure. Especially when she knew their lives would be lost because of their connection to her.

After a torturous day of being trapped and feeling helpless, Gipp opened the trap door to drop her some food and shared some shocking information. He told her that the whole Outpost had been invaded with Bulendurians who were searching for a group of their leaders who had never returned from an outing to find the Lost Sacrifice, who they believed may have been located by bounty hunters. They bullied everyone throughout the Outpost, looting and breaking things. Eventually they left with no answers.

Kendry and Gipp brainstormed what that could mean. Had Hendrick and Graeme been a part of the reason why their men took off looking for her? Were they able to convince the tribe that Kendry was far off somewhere?

Sleep escaped Kendry that night. She struggled to even rest. If Hendrick and Graeme had sent the men off looking for her in the wrong direction, then whey weren't they back? Did the men kill them? Her heart sunk. Deep down she feared they were gone. It was her fault. Everything was her fault. Everyone was trying to save her. She hadn't wanted anyone to save her! She didn't want the people she was closest to risking their lives for her.

The next morning, Gipp shared that news around the Outpost was spreading that some of the Crestavian army had been attacked by a small entourage from Shadenberg, near the Great Divide. He said that both sides lost some men, but that Crestavia dominated because they had more forces and defenses ready. Kendry wondered about Prince Casper and Sleege and how they were handling their first battle without King Gadden or her father.

With each day passing and Hendrick and Graeme unaccounted for, Kendry started to fear the worse really had come true. But then she was awoken one morning before dawn, by Gipp saying she had visitors. Super relieved, she ran over to the trap door to welcome them back safely and then to yell at them for leaving in the first place. But instead of the boys, she looked up to see her father gazing back down at her.

Shock and tears took over. He quickly lowered the ladder and climbed down to her. Picking her up, he hugged her tight. "Kendry!" he exclaimed with emotion dripping from his voice.

She couldn't believe it was him. She was so thrilled and overcome with joy that she couldn't stop weeping. He hugged her and hugged her again. Finally, he started stroking her hair to get her to calm down enough to talk.

"How...how...?" was all she could spit out.

"Hendrick told me Gipp was hiding you," he said gently. "I came as soon as our little battle with Shadenberg subsided. Haven't even seen Prince Casper, yet," he added with a chuckle. "Can't believe King Gadden's gone. His son is going to run our nation into the ground if he doesn't listen to some good advisors."

Kendry didn't want to talk politics. She was surprised to hear that her father knew of King Gadden's death, since Princess Gendella had said that Walbrek had left the palace for Bulenduria before he had died. She asked him about it.

"I just found out. On the battlefield of all places," he explained. "Can't tell you how surprised I was to see Hendrick there. Still trying to figure that all out. Haven't talked to the boy since the battle started. Probably should've gone back to base and checked on him before coming here, but I knew if I stepped foot on base, it would be a long time before I could cut away. So, I came straight here."

They tried to piece together what the boys had done to get Walbrek out of there. Kendry was impressed to hear that they had led them to the ambush mountain in front of the Military Base. Walbrek thought it was brilliant.

"So, who is Graeme then?" Walbrek asked.

"A friend of ours. We met him in Crestavia-Capitalia. Actually, Hendrick and he won a competition and got to be guests at the palace."

"Hendrick won a competition? What kind? He doesn't seem the type."

"A fighting and skills competition. I trained him," Kendry said proudly.

"Of course, you did," he smiled. "Well, congratulations to Hendrick. He will always have my appreciation and respect for rescuing me and keeping you safe. What brought him out of Tavern's End in the first place?"

Kendry's stomach sank. Her father didn't even know that Tavern's End was no more. For the next hour they spent sitting on the floor catching each other up on what had happened since the last time they had seen each other. There were many shocks and surprises.

Kendry was able to piece most things together now. Her father and Malark had found out about Lieutenant Trent being a traitor and decided to seize upon their exit from the Academy to convince him to think they were all dead. They planned on following him to discover his contacts with Shadenberg, expecting he'd head straight there with the supposed death of General Walbrek and his men.

Trent fulfilled their suspicions and they tracked him through the woods. Not even a day from Tavern's End, they watched Trent stop for water and he met an injured man. The horseless man had wanted a ride to a village or town. Trent had no interest in helping the man and so the man tried to bargain with him by offering information that could be worth money. He offered to tell him where the Lost Sacrifice from Bulenduria could be found. Trent, believing the Lost Sacrifice to just be a fairy tale, ignored the man and took off. Malark and Walbrek's men continued to track Trent, but once Walbrek heard the words 'Lost Sacrifice', he and Malark changed their plans.

They got the injured man to talk after persuading him through threats on his life. He admitted, finally, to being a bounty hunter from Regaria. He had been traveling with a group of bounty hunters, but when he fell and injured his ankle, the men thought it would be funny to take his horse and leave him behind. It was more profitable for them to have less people to split the bounty with if they were able to get Kendry back to Bulenduria.

Afraid for Kendry's life, Malark and Walbrek left the injured man in the woods and took off as fast as they could ride back to Tavern's End. They approached the tavern as the sun set and spied on everyone inside. Kendry was upstairs on her bed, alive, though crying. It was seeing her cry that caused Walbrek to make his decision.

He told Kendry that, at that point, he had taken off his medallion and given it to Malark. He instructed Malark to make his first priority to take Kendry safely back to the palace and then to share with her that her father was, indeed dead, and to gift her the medallion. Walbrek then took off ahead, planning to sacrifice himself so they would stop searching for Kendry.

He explained how he quickly met with King Gadden to let him know that he was giving himself over to the Bulendurians. He only told King Gadden his plans out of respect for their friendship. He also felt the king should know that he would not be available to lead during the pending war with Shadenberg that was on the horizon. As his last request, Walbrek had begged King Gadden to make sure Kendry was brought in safely. Only after Kendry's prying, did Walbrek admit that he had an argument with Prince Casper before leaving, as Princess Gendella had told her.

Next, it was Kendry's turn to help fill in the blanks. She shared with her dad how Gipp had explained that Malark was jumped and knocked unconscious, after Walbrek took off. Malark had awoken on a boat, with is hands bound. Somehow, he escaped and swam to the opposite side of the small bay.

Kendry then explained her own story of everything that had happened since she read the note that her father was dead. Walbrek listened intently. Anger rose in his face as he heard that Mister Lansing and others were killed. He vowed that the murderers would pay.

After an hour or so, Gipp brought them down food and added a few more details he had heard from Malark. Kendry ate the moist bread Gipp provided, feeling so relieved to know that her father, Graeme, and Hendrick were all alive.

Gipp and her father reminded her that the danger was not over, yet. She still needed to be very careful because the Bulendurians would be actively searching for her, not to mention their missing tribal leaders and the Warrior.

Walbrek had left soldiers outside Gipp's trading post to keep an eye on things. He went out to check with them and see how things were going at the Outpost.

Kendry, left alone with Gipp in the underground room, went over to the cot where she had been sleeping. Moving back the blanket, she took the magenta scarf out from where it was still hidden. She walked it back to Gipp and handed it to him. She knew where she had seen it before.

He smiled at her. "What can I say? I like to take in troublemakers," he said, smirking.

CHAPTER THIRTY-SIX

Hendrick and Graeme had tried numerous times to 'escape' the Military Base. Word had spread quickly that Walbrek didn't want them to leave. Many soldiers were eager to impress the great General Walbrek who was discovered to be alive, so they found it difficult to sneak out.

Prince Casper was furious that Walbrek had disappeared with a few of his men after the short battle with Shadenberg. Publicly he proclaimed that he wanted to honor the General, but those close to him could tell that he didn't like being kept out of the loop. And he had no idea where General Walbrek went or if he would ever come back.

Hendrick and Graeme desperately wanted to get back to Kendry. They both worried that she wouldn't stay hidden very long. They were afraid she'd figure a way out of the hidden room or trick Gipp into letting her out. If she went anywhere near Bulenduria, she would be a goner.

Casper's guards kept an eye on Hendrick and Graeme as they sat in a tent, frustrated. They didn't want to be sitting ducks at the Military Base when Crestavia was on the verge of a full out war with Shadenberg. The attack by Shadenberg had come quickly after Crestavia's ambush on the Bulendurians. It had definitely surprised Prince Casper. Their intel hadn't revealed that Shadenberg would even know to look for them at that area of the Great Divide, and they seemed to come mission-oriented. Luckily for Crestavia, Shadenberg had only sent a small group as more of a trial battle to see what they were up against.

Though both sides had suffered losses, none of Shadenberg's men would be making it back to King Smolden to give him any updates. They had all either been killed or captured. For this reason, Prince Casper was feeling pretty good about all that had happened and was not looking to execute Hendrick and Graeme for leading tribal savages right to their base, showing Shadenberg their location.

Hendrick had politely reminded Prince Casper that General Walbrek was back because of them. But Prince Casper had snapped back that General Walbrek had not stuck around long enough to be helpful. That, of course, was a lie, since Walbrek had just led Casper's men against the Bulendurians and the soldiers from Shadenberg. But Hendrick figured he'd just keep his mouth closed and be thankful he and Graeme were only being monitored and not hung.

"How long do you think they'll hold us here?" Graeme asked. He was lying on his back in their tent and was tossing a rock up in the air and catching it, over and over again.

"Honestly," Hendrick responded, "I think they plan to hold us here until Walbrek comes back. So, if he doesn't come back...we may live the rest of our lives here." He said it with sarcasm, but sort of meant it, too. Would Walbrek come back?

"Do you think Walbrek went to get Kendry?" Graeme asked.

"Yep," said Hendrick. "Problem is, I think once he got her, he probably took her somewhere very far away and doesn't plan to ever come back."

"Well," Graeme rebutted, "maybe we'll get lucky and Shadenberg will attack again and the war will get so bad that everyone will have to go fight and we can sneak out of here without anyone noticing."

"Could happen," Hendrick responded. "But, then where do we go? Do we go to the Outpost and grab Kendry from Gipp's trading post or do we assume Walbrek has her safe somewhere? I mean obviously we go get her...but, if she's not there...what's our next step?"

"Personally…" Graeme threw the rock up and it hit the top of the tent causing it to land off to his side. He reached for it and continued. "…I don't have any desire to run into any Bulendurians. I'm not sure if everyone who got a good look at us came with us or not. There may still be men from that tribe searching for us. I'm positive they're searching for their lost tribal leaders and for their precious Sacrifice. The lunar eclipse is tomorrow. Can you imagine their urgency to find Kendry?"

Hendrick cringed. The Bulendurians were scary. He would love to stay far away from them, as well. If Kendry stayed put under Gipp's floor, she would most likely stay safe. But, could Kendry be counted on to stay hidden? Every time he thought of her, he got sick to his stomach with worry. He hoped her dad had located her and was keeping her safe.

Just then there was a commotion outside that caused Graeme to sit up and Hendrick to peek out. The noise sounded positive. People were cheering and celebrating.

"What's going on?" Hendrick yelled from out of their tent to the guards posted outside.

"The General's back!" one of them responded.

Answers! Hendrick hoped that Walbrek's return would bring with him some answers. Did he find Kendry? Did he hide her? Were the Bulendurians out searching for her?

It was quite a while before they got any answers. But their first answer did not come from Walbrek. Instead, Kendry herself, was directed over toward them. Hendrick's heart almost burst with relief.

She gave each of them a huge hug. Smiling, ear to ear, she told them how glad she was to see them. Then, she smacked Hendrick in the face. Graeme was shocked, but before he could even process what he witnessed, she smacked him in the face, too.

They both instinctively got angry with her for the slaps, but then they mindfully tried to calm themselves down and see things from her perspective. None of them would've enjoyed being stuck hidden in an underground room while their friends took off to risk their lives for them. And then, to not hear from them for days wouldn't have helped. So, they listened to her lecture about her frustration. Finally, she calmed down and went back to hugging them.

Once they settled down to relax, they filled each other in on all that had happened since they had last seen each other. Kendry told them that her father was meeting with Prince Casper and Sleege and felt obligated to go around and mingle with the troops. He'd probably been catching up with old friends and meeting new ones. But she said that at some point, he wanted to come thank them in person for saving both her and himself.

"Does that mean we're free?" Graeme asked. "I mean, we've kinda been treated like prisoners here since the great General Walbrek told his men not to let us leave base. Now that he's back, can we take off?"

"I'm sure you can," Kendry said a little confused. "But I'm sure you'll want to wait for morning, right? And, where are you planning on going?"

"Actually, I don't mean to sound rude, really," Graeme responded kinda harshly. "But I am ready to leave now. Tell your father I'm glad it all worked out. It's just been a really rough couple of weeks and I've gotten pretty homesick. I'm going to head back to Munker Bay."

Hendrick was super surprised by this. They had just been talking earlier that night about how they had no plans of where to go next. What had possibly happened to make Graeme change his tune? Didn't he know traveling alone was dangerous? Kendry felt a little hurt by Graeme's sudden eagerness to leave them and be on his own again. Since she didn't have any clue what her own plans would be, she didn't have any alternatives to offer Graeme.

"We've all come so far together," she said sort of sadly. "Just doesn't seem right for you to take off tonight."

"I'll keep in touch," he said, winking at her. She opened her mouth to respond but could hear sounds outside implicating her father was approaching.

"Just going to check on my daughter and I'll be right back to the dining hall," Walbrek's deep voice said outside their tent.

Kendry perked up. "At least you'll get to meet my dad before you go," she said to Graeme. Graeme looked strangely uneasy. "He's not that scary," she said jokingly.

Kendry met her father outside the tent and Hendrick came out after her. Graeme stayed inside for a moment. Walbrek shook Hendrick's hand.

"Good job, there, young man! Wait until everyone at Tavern's End hears how Mister Carter's young stable boy saved Crestavia, the Warrior, and Kendry!" Then he realized what he had said and that Tavern's End was vacant and Mister Carter was gone. All three of them paused in sadness.

"We'll figure out a way to find them," Walbrek said with less boldness.

Hendrick nodded.

Wanting to change the subject, Kendry went back in the tent and grabbed Graeme's arm, pulling him out.

"Dad, this is..." but before she could finish her introduction, she saw the look on her father's face.

"Guards," Walbrek said to two men hanging out nearby. "Apprehend this man at once!"

Graeme didn't look surprised. In fact, Kendry realized he looked guilty. Hendrick was confused.

"This is Graeme, Dad," Kendry said trying to figure out what was going on. The two guards had come over and each grabbed one of Graeme's arms. He didn't try to fight them or get away.

"Take this man to a holding cell. He's a Regarian bounty hunter." The men started dragging Graeme, but he cooperated. He looked back at Kendry. His eyes showed his repentance but he lipped the word, "sorry".

Kendry looked to her father for answers.

"That's the man with the rolled ankle that was willing to sell Trent your location for a horse ride!" Walbrek said, angrily. "That man could have been the cause of your death! He deserves to die!"

CHAPTER THIRTY-SEVEN

Kendry's head was spinning. Graeme? The bounty hunter? The one that was injured in the woods? The one that Malark and her father had threatened, or maybe tortured, to get the information that the bounty hunters knew the location of the Lost Sacrifice? This made no sense.

Walbrek saw the confused look on Kendry's and Hendrick's faces. He told them again about how Graeme had been one of the men who were trying to kidnap her from Tavern's End and sell her to the Bulendurians.

"He was willing to have you killed in order to get money for gambling, Kendry!" Walbrek said, harshly. "That's what bounty hunters do!"

Hendrick interjected, "But, I met him in the Capital at the tournament."

"Of course, he competed! Trying to make more money!" Walbrek stated. "I know the type, believe me. Worthless, greedy...I can't believe he manipulated you into trusting him!"

As thoughts stirred around in Kendry's head, she found herself feeling hurt. She couldn't believe Graeme had lied to them. To her. Had he been planning the whole time to take her to Bulenduria? But if he had, he changed his mind somewhere along the way. That had to mean something.

She allowed the moment they held hands while falling asleep to enter her mind. Then, she wished it away.

Without even wanting to defend him, she found herself doing just that. "If Graeme had wanted me traded to the Bulendurians for a lot of money, I would be with them now. He didn't go through with it. He saved me. And, he saved you," she pointed out, to her father.

"Hmph," he said not impressed. His frustration showed as soldiers kept walking by trying to get a minute of his time. But his concerned eyes only stuck on Kendry. He had just gotten her back and the idea that she could have been gone for good was too much for him to accept.

"Well, we'll thank the Lord of the Eternal Kingdom for His mercy in not allowing that piece of Regarian trash to go through with it. But I will not rest until I know he is executed." With that, Walbrek marched away.

Kendry watched him leave too shocked to cry after him. Hendrick could tell she was in pain. Pain from being betrayed, but also pain at the thought of Graeme being killed. He took a few steps over to her and put his arms around her. She fell into them, and cried. For some reason her tears over Graeme's impending execution and discovered betrayal hurt him more than the betrayal itself. He got angry thinking of Graeme's ability to hurt Kendry.

Kendry slept horribly that night. Her dad had put her in a tent with him. They fought about Graeme over and over again. She was so angry and hurt by his lies, but didn't let her father know that. Instead, she spent the whole night trying to convince Walbrek that Graeme was a hero.

The next morning, Kendry awoke to an empty tent. She was surprised that her dad was able to slip out without her hearing. She hadn't felt that she ever really fell sound asleep. Her mixed emotions of anger and heartbreak at Graeme's betrayal and sadness and fear over his impending execution made her feel physically sick.

She found Hendrick outside his tent, and plopped down on the dirt next to him. "How'd you sleep?" he asked.

She never answered, but the glare she gave him let him know it had been a rough night.

"I'm so sorry, Kendry. I'm the one who got him involved with us. I wanted him traveling with us. I can't help but feel responsible."

"The only one responsible for lying is Graeme. He knew the whole time who I was, don't you think?"

"I don't know. I think he probably didn't know until Gipp told all three of us about the Lost Sacrifice." Kendry nodded, thinking he was probably right. "But," he added. "I think Malark knew when he saw us at the shack he lit on fire. Thinking back, he looked at Graeme lethally. I thought it was just because we had all attacked those two guards we tied up in the woods. But, if Malark was trying to protect you, he would've probably killed Graeme that night had he the chance."

Kendry looked up at Hendrick. He was right. "Malark tried to warn me. As he was dying. He told me not to trust him and that he knew who I was. I guess I thought he was referring to Prince Casper or something. But it was definitely Graeme."

Hendrick nodded. That made sense. "Do you think they'll let us talk to Graeme?" Hendrick asked. "I really want to give him a piece of my mind. But I also feel bad if they are going to...ya know...kill him."

Kendry shook her head with exhaustion and dropped her face into her folded knees. She was tired. Tired of worrying. Tired of betrayals. Tired of not knowing what to do next.

"Why don't we try to find my father and see if they'll let us talk to him before executing him?"

The two reluctantly stood up and started wandering around base. They weren't sure where to even look for Walbrek. They asked a few people where the holding cells were located and were told each time that they were not permitted to visit the holding cells.

"Kendry!" She relaxed hearing the sound of her father's voice saying her name. It truly was still unbelievable that they were both safe and together again. Hendrick and Kendry turned toward where Walbrek was calling and made their way to him.

General Walbrek looked like a rooster hovering over chicks. He stood in a small group of men, prominent and demanding respect. As his daughter and her friend approached, he signaled for the men to leave.

"Intel tells us we need to be prepared for more men from Shadenberg. I want you and Hendrick safe and far away from here. I'm sending you with guards back to Tavern's End. I want you to stay at the Academy until I return."

"No, I don't want to be separated again!" Kendry shrieked. It was too much to think that there would be a chance he may not come back. "Can't you come with us? Or let us stay here?"

"Honestly," he said whispering. "I think war isn't just brewing, but it's here. If that's the case, I might not be home for months. I can do a much better job if I am not worrying about you."

Kendry shook her head. Hendrick nodded, agreeing with Walbrek.

"The men from the Academy and the instructors should all be back within a few weeks from their training exercise. Unless..." he paused. "...we need them for battle...which we probably will."

"I forgot that they were even alive," Hendrick said slowly, processing the news. "I can't believe the note that you were all dead was just for Lieutenant Trent's benefit."

Walbrek nodded. "The workers should be back soon, regardless. I'll have guards stay with you. You'll be safe."

Kendry pouted, but submitted.

Walbrek continued, "I have a couple of men prepared to leave this afternoon for the Capital to run some errands for me. You'll go with them. When you arrive, give yourself a few days to rest if you need it, but then I want you prepared for travel. My two men will escort you from the Capital back to Tavern's End. They will stay at the Academy with you until I return."

"We'll be fine," Kendry muttered with Hendrick nodding. "Travel within Crestavia is still fairly safe."

"I'm taking no chances. It's settled then," Walbrek said showing that their conversation was coming to an end, and she had no authority to change the plans he had already made. Looking around and seeing there was no one nearby, he added, "I have much strategizing to do and have to put up with Prince Casper and his idiotic advisor, Sleege. It will help me to know that you are leaving today."

Kendry reached up and touched the medallion that he was once again wearing. It had been so wonderful to give it back to him and see it around his neck where it belonged. She then surprised him with a large bear hug. He hugged her tightly back, not at all ashamed that a great general was getting weepy over his little girl. "I will miss you so much," she said with tears forming. "Promise me you will be safe and come back to Tavern's End soon!"

"I promise." He kissed her forehead. She knew with that, they were dismissed. She and Hendrick started to walk away when he called after her. "Oh Kendry!" She turned back toward him. "I'm letting that rascal out of his cell because he saved your life. But I told him it was only on one condition."

Kendry's face showed her curiosity at what that one condition might be.

"He must go back to Regaria and get any information he can from his friends who attacked Tavern's End about where our townspeople were taken, and then give me that intel. If he does not follow through," his voice raised to become threatening. "I will track him down and kill him myself." With that, he walked away.

CHAPTER THIRTY-EIGHT

While waiting for the guards to tell them it was time to leave, Kendry and Hendrick sat outside the tent where Hendrick had slept. There was definitely a different aura since Walbrek had told them Graeme wasn't going to be executed and that they may get some answers from him regarding their friends' whereabouts. Knowing that Walbrek was alive and was planning on helping find those kidnapped from Tavern's End gave them hope that they hadn't felt since before the whole ordeal began. Hendrick's anticipation on someday receiving news was starting to excite him. Kendry was relieved at the thought of there being some sort of plan. Everything seemed a million times better than it had that morning when they had awakened. Then, Hendrick noticed that Graeme was being escorted across the field in front of them. He stood up, instinctively.

Kendry looked up at him, curious what had caught his attention, and carried his gaze until she saw Graeme. His hands were tied together, but he was walking freely between two guards.

"Wait!" Kendry yelled at the guards who were leading Graeme past them. The guards would've normally ignored her completely, but seeing it was the General's daughter, they hesitated and slowed down.

"I just want to talk to him," she said to the guards. They looked at each other. One shrugged, the other shook his head no.

"Sorry, Ma'am," the guard who shook his head began. "We've got orders to get him out of camp and keep him away from you."

Graeme was staring at the ground. He wouldn't even look up at Kendry or Hendrick.

"Then I'll talk as you walk," Kendry said matter-of-factly, ignoring the guard. He frowned and led Graeme away from her, but she picked up her pace and tagged along. Hendrick stayed planted.

Kendry spoke quickly. "When did you know? When did you know and when did you decide you weren't going to turn me in?" she asked. "I need to know!"

His handsome face looked up at her. Staring into her dark green eyes, shame drenched him. "I figured it out after we saw Malark at the shack and it was confirmed when Gipp told us the legend," he began. Guilt dripping from his voice, he continued, "I knew of the prophesy and the Sacrifice. I probably should've figured it out when we heard your father was in Bulenduria. But, I hadn't." He paused and stared down at the ground.

A guard got frustrated with his brief pause, and literally started to drag him forward, to get him moving again. He continued, speaking over his shoulder as the guard pushed him forward. "I had been part of the group that was going after you in Tavern's End, but never ever considered giving you over to them after I met you. Didn't even cross my mind. I promise."

The guards shoved him forward and Kendry moved aside. She half nodded at his response. She didn't actually think he was ever going to trade her to the Bulendurians, but she could not wrap her brain around the fact that if he hadn't hurt his ankle, he would've been one of the men they had tried to fight off that night. He would've been just one of the men in dark clothing who had killed her townspeople and kidnapped the rest. She definitely couldn't look at him the same way. He was no longer Graeme. He was just a bounty hunter gone rogue.

She stopped walking and watched him led off in the distance. She felt numb inside. Turning around, she walked back toward Hendrick, glad to have him waiting for her. Hendrick had been the one constant in her life through all the

264

horrors that had happened since the day she had received the note that her father was dead. She was glad he'd be with her for the trip back to Tavern's End. But mostly, she hoped they'd both be part of a plan to help get Tarah and their other friends back home where they belonged.

The End

Turn the page for a preview of...

<u>The Last Remnant</u>

Book Two- The Tavern's End Trilogy

CHAPTER ONE

Leaving her father behind at the Military Base was one of the hardest things

Kendry had ever done. She knew he'd be going to war against Shadenberg. After just spending the last few months believing he was dead, she couldn't imagine if she had to lose him all over again.

He had sent Kendry and Hendrick away with guards for their trip back to Tavern's End, the small rest-stop between Galvenland and Glenville, that they called home. They would stay at the Academy, the secret training center for the elite warriors of the Crestavian kingdom. It was at that place where Kendry grew up watching the most gifted soldiers of Crestavia be trained as spies by her father and Malark, who had been like an uncle to her. First, they were to stop in Crestavia-Capitalia and rest for a few days while her father's men ran some errands for him, preparing for the war ahead.

The two men sent by her father to travel with them were more than just guards. Kendry figured out immediately that these were trained, elite warriors. She felt guilty taking them away from the battle where they were probably needed. But there was comfort in their presence. She didn't have to be so on-guard at all times, and could relax a little.

The leader of the two men was a bronze-skinned guy named Roto. He was tall and well-built. Kendry liked him immediately. He was jolly and fun to travel with, always making jokes and challenging Kendry to mini competitions.

"I've always heard about the gifted daughter of the mighty General and wondered how I would fair against her if I raced her across a balance beam thirty feet above the ground," he said teasingly. Apparently, those who had left the Academy had given Kendry quite the reputation. She was amused to hear the stories they told about her as they were almost as exaggerated as the stories people told about her father.

Roto's dark-skinned, stocky friend, was a little less jovial, but definitely demanded awe. He was professional, but classy. Kendry could tell Hendrick idolized him the moment they met. His name was Letriev and he introduced himself in such a suave manner that Kendry felt butterflies in her stomach. He was extremely good looking and knew it. Both men got along well with Kendry and Hendrick.

Their long journey back to Tavern's End was actually enjoyable. Kendry felt a little bit like they were on vacation. She worried about her father but was hopeful that when he returned, they would find their friends who had been kidnapped from Tavern's End.

Roto and Letriev were impressed with Kendry and Hendrick's adventures thus far. They would listen intently as Kendry shared events of their past weeks and laugh aloud or scream out in surprise at any twist that they didn't see coming. Hendrick wished that all those 'twists' had been fun to actually live through, but instead had been terrifying and confusing.

One evening as they set up camp in a forest, Kendry leaned back against a tree and tearfully shared about the night their friends were killed and taken by the Regarian bounty hunters.

"Well, if your father takes too long at battle, we could always go get them ourselves," Roto stated. Kendry sat up tall. Hendrick, who had been whittling a piece of wood, stopped. "Did I say something startling?" Roto asked with a half-laugh. "You both look shocked."

Kendry bit her lip. "We want nothing more than to find our friends, Roto. We just never dared to believe it could be a real possibility. But now, with my father alive and other trained men like you and Letriev, it's beginning to seem possible."

"Of course, it's possible," Letriev interjected. "You'd insult us if you thought we couldn't handle a little recon mission to rescue a few townspeople. Problem is we're short on intel. We don't know where to find them, am I correct?"

Sadly, Kendry nodded. She rehashed how her father had let Graeme go free with the promise of venturing back to Regaria to question his friends, and see if he could find out where the townspeople ended up.

"Well, then we begin there," Letriev responded. "The guards who had Graeme were instructed by your father to take him to the Capital. We go question the young man and see what he knows."

"He doesn't know anything," Hendrick interjected, despondently. "He wasn't with them when they captured our friends. And, I think if he knew where they were, General Walbrek would've gotten it out of him."

"Well, we're almost to the Capital," responded Roto, encouragingly. "Let's spend a few nights there while Letriev and I run some errands for your father. We'll track down where they will be bringing Graeme and do a little questioning, anyway."

The way he said 'questioning' made Kendry worry they were going to torture information out of him. But, Kendry was fairly sure that Hendrick was correct and Graeme sincerely didn't know anything. He had been left behind when he hurt his ankle in the woods and hadn't seen the other men since. Even if they had told him their plans, things may have changed. They were right back where they had started. Full of questions. No answers.

CHAPTER TWO

It was strange being back at the Capital. In some ways nothing had changed, but in other ways it seemed like it had been a lifetime since they'd been there. Roto and Letriev checked them into a hostel to stay for a few nights and then dismissed themselves to stay at the Military Training Center while they were attending to Walbrek's business in town. They made tentative plans to meet up in two days at the hostel to begin the trip back to Tavern's End.

Kendry was looking forward to a few days in the Capital. She wanted to visit the Refuge and see Kina and Molly. She also wanted to go by the library and discover if news of her father's rescue or rise from his reported death was being passed around as common knowledge or whether they were all still supposed to pretend he was dead. She was expecting the latter to be true since the king's death hadn't yet been announced.

It didn't take long to realize that word had spread throughout the Capital about Shadenberg's attack and that war was beginning. Crestavia-Capitalia was buzzing with a rush and urgency Kendry and Hendrick hadn't experienced the last time they'd been there. Everyone was gearing up for the war ahead. They passed metal workers making weapons. Horses were being brought in droves to the Military Training Center, which was busy with men enlisting for the army. Families were crowded outside the center, visiting with their sons who were expected to go to battle shortly. To her surprise, Kendry found that word had also spread that General Walbrek was alive and leading Crestavia into battle. Some didn't believe it and thought King Gadden was spreading rumors to lift the morale of the army. Others were motivated to join the battle by the news. King Gadden's death was still being hidden. Prince Casper probably didn't think a war was a good time to let news that the king was dead be leaked.

"Let's see if Mavo, Kenan, and Thron are still at the Refuge. Wonder if any of them would get permission from Director Druble to enlist," Hendrick said to Kendry as they walked down a cobblestone road toward the center of town. Young men had to be eighteen to enlist in the king's army, but in times of war, they could be given special permission by their legal guardians.

"Good, I was thinking the Refuge should be our first stop, too." Kendry was eager to see her friends.

As they walked and she passed young men, she couldn't help but think of Marvin. Marvin was Hendrick's good friend from Tavern's End and had enlisted in the army before he was kidnapped by the bounty hunters. She thought about how he'd have already been trained and probably sent to battle against Shadenberg if he hadn't been taken away by the Regarians. Now, she wondered if he was even alive.

It was still early morning, but chances were good that their friends had already left the Refuge for the day to report for work. Yet, the two of them walked that direction knowing they'd pass some of their friends' places of occupation on the way there. As they rounded a corner, a small cobbler shop came into view in the distance. Kendry signaled to Hendrick that they should stop by there. Dola, Kendry's annoying bunkmate from the Refuge, worked as an assistant for the cobbler's wife. Dola had ended up becoming valuable due to her strange obsession with beauty treatments and hair styles that had helped them to disguise Kendry from Prince Casper's guards.

As they approached, they could see Dola through the open-air window. Kendry took a deep breath and tried to motivate herself for the upcoming interaction with Dola. The girl could be extremely tiring with her non-stop talking and nosey personality. But, Kendry knew Dola would be hurt if she heard that Kendry and Hendrick were in town and they hadn't at least paused to greet her.

It didn't take long for Dola to take notice of them. They weren't even close to the little worn-down shop when she came bolting out.

"I told Mrs. Macrabee that I see my old bunkmate walking down the road and I just have to go and say hello!" she screamed as she hurried toward them.

Hendrick rolled his eyes in anticipation of this quick conversation turning into one that would be difficult to escape. They listened politely as she rambled on about Kendry's hair and skin and overall health.

Hendrick urged and guided them into the shade closer to the cobbler shop. Dola didn't stop talking the whole time. It was in the midst of her rambling that she said, "...and at least you two have come back from your trip. I was so worried that they had planned something with you and off you all went together. It was terribly rude of them all to leave like that. I was so angry for so long, but I am actually over it now. I have a new bunkmate and she has velvety black hair, not course like a horse's tail..."

"Whoa," Hendrick interrupted. "Who left?

Dola ignored Hendrick and continued talking about her new bunkmate, sharing a strange skin condition the girl seemed to have on the back of her neck. Annoyed, Hendrick repeated himself louder.

Kendry piped in, too. "Dola, we've been gone for a while. Who left? Who were you angry with?"

Dola had to catch her breath. The girl needed to learn to pace herself when talking. She looked confused that her chatter about the new girl's skin was abruptly being halted.

"Oh, you know, all of them. Your friends," she said with definite annoyance.

"Where'd they go?" Kendry asked.

"How would I know? I wasn't included in their plans. They are always so hush-hush, whispering and gathering like chicks under a hen. I knew they weren't happy about Director Brutt taking over for Director Druble, but..."

"Whoa, what?" Hendrick stopped her. "Brutt is now director?"

Dola nodded. "Yes, it has not been a good change. No one likes it there anymore. I'm not too concerned because I age out in a month, but the rest of them were extremely bothered by it. They ended up running away one night with no notice. Haven't seen them since."

"Who exactly?" Kendry asked.

"Kina, Kenan, Mavo, Molly...and I think Thron," she squinted trying to remember. "He may have left earlier. There have been lots of runaways lately. In fact, Director Brutt has been cracking down the past few days by locking us all in earlier and paying men from the alley to watch the windows and doors at night. He's taken away work privileges from many of us. I still have the privilege because I have not been disobeying like so many of the ungrateful youth staying there. It's been hazardous with all the pranks and fights and disobedience going on. You would not even believe it was the same place!"

Hendrick looked at Kendry. He could tell she was upset. He was, too. There was no way they were going to go anywhere near the Refuge if Brutt was running things and the thought of not getting to see their friends was a real disappointment.

"Do you know where they would've gone?" Kendry asked, hopefully. "I mean, did Kina or Molly say anything?"

"Are you kidding? Why would they say anything to goody-two-shoes me? That's what they started calling me, you know? Just because I don't talk bad about every authority or get annoyed at Director Brutt like they do. They refused to let me into any of their discussions about anything. I told Mildra that they were all up to no good. And, I was right. They are all so arrogant. I don't know how you got to be such good friends with them. For a while I thought they were okay, but once I really started spending more time with them..."

"Dola, I'm so sorry to interrupt, but I think Mrs. Macrabee is calling you," Kendry said, lying. Dola turned to look over her shoulder.

"Are you sure?" she asked, not able to see Mrs. Macrabee from where they were standing.

"Yep," Hendrick added. "And she doesn't sound super happy."

"Oh, goodness. I better get back to work. When will I see you again so we can continue our conversation? I want to tell you all about some of the new girls who have come lately to the Refuge and my plans to beautify them!"

"We'll be in town for a while," Kendry lied, again. "I'm sure we'll have plenty of time to catch up."

Leaving Dola was a relief, but the information she gave them was a bummer.

"Guess catching up with friends is out of the question," Kendry said sadly.

Hendrick nodded.

"Where do you think they all went?" Kendry asked, curious if Hendrick had any leads that could help the situation.

"I don't know. But if they stayed in the Capital, I think Brutt would pay some thugs to find and return them. He'll probably take it personally that they ran away."

Kendry agreed.

Hendrick continued, "I wouldn't be surprised if they left town. We'd have to see if any of them are still showing up for work. If they are, they might be camping out in the forest where we trained."

Kendry perked up. That made sense. If they headed toward the forest, they would pass the bakery where Kenan worked as a janitor. If he wasn't there, then they'd check the forest.

A few hours later they trudged back toward the hostel. They had found no evidence of their friends remaining in town or of having stayed in the forest. All their jobs had been vacated. Kendry and Hendrick agreed the group from the Refuge had made the right choice by running away. But, after losing their friends from Tavern's End, the betrayal by Graeme, and now realizing they would never see their friends from the Refuge again, they were both getting a little depressed.

It was beginning to get dark and they still had a few blocks to go before they could settle in at the hostel for the night. They walked in silence. Hendrick moped a bit as he strolled. Kendry knew that this was even more disappointing for him than her. She had found her father. But he had no one left. No one but her. She mentally reminded herself to give him a break if he got a little cranky the next few days. Feeling alone in the world was the worst feeling Kendry could imagine. She remembered when she and Hendrick had quarreled when they camped in the forest and how she felt when she was by herself. It had been horrible being so isolated. She racked her brain to think of something to say or do to cheer Hendrick up, but nothing came to mind. So, she changed the subject to something that might give him some hope.

"Once we meet up with Roto and Letriev, we can start focusing on figuring out how to get our friends back. Maybe they'll have had some luck with Graeme."

"Doubtful." His response didn't surprise her. He continued, "We're not any further along than we were when we first left Tavern's End and…"

Something flew out of nowhere and hit him in the back of the head. The palm of his hand immediately touched the area that had just been struck.

"What the…?" Hendrick mumbled. His eyes searched all around. "Someone just threw a rock at me," he announced as his eyes located one on the ground up ahead.

He peeled his hand from his head and stared at the blood. He knew head injuries tended to overreact in regards to the amount of blood that resulted from them, but there was quite a lot of it. Kendry pivoted, eyes open wide, ready to defend them.

They both stood silent for a moment. Kendry carefully moved away from the center and toward the outer edge of the deserted alley which they had been walking down. She listened intently. Silence. But something definitely wasn't right.

Hendrick hadn't moved. Cradling the wound on his head, his eyes darted around for answers. Kendry took her time covering the exposed areas of the perimeter of the alley. There was nobody there.

276

"Whoever it was, I think they left," she concluded walking back toward Hendrick. But then, without notice, another rock blazed right past her head.

She circled around and saw that it had come from a dark corner. Not one to cower away, she stalked toward the dark corner, hesitantly, and prepared to duck. As she got a few yards away, she yelled, "Hey! Whoever's there...come out!"

There was no response. She picked up a good size rock and chucked it into the darkness. She heard it plop, knowing it had struck the ground. She paused a second more and then eased up, releasing a breath she had been holding in the silence.

Then, without warning, as if they had been signaled by an invisible alarm, people came out of nowhere, encircling them. Kendry had moved back toward Hendrick, out of instinct. There was a large guy about her age coming toward her with a hateful look on his face. She glanced to her side and saw another guy. One she recognized. It was one of Druvan's buddies. In fact, as she took inventory of the group of thugs that were now surrounding them, she realized this was Druvan's gang.

CHAPTER THREE

Druvan, the bully from the Refuge who had fought Hendrick and lost, was looking like he was prepared for revenge. He carried a big thick piece of wood about the size of his arm and held it like a baseball bat. His four friends all had either rocks or clubs in their hands, as well.

"I knew it was you two losers," Druvan said with an evil smile across his face. "I thought to myself, no way, they wouldn't come back through here. But here you are!"

He tapped his club into his open palm and seemed to be salivating at the thought of fighting them. Kendry's heart raced. Hendrick still seemed a bit stunned from being hit in the head, but his arms were up ready to fight, adrenaline taking over.

"Hi Druvan, nice to see you again," Kendry said with sarcasm, positioning herself to see as many of Druvan's buddies as possible. She and Hendrick were now back-to-back.

Druvan nodded back as to greet her as well. "What happened to your head, Hendrick?" Druvan asked with fake sympathy. "Trying to dye your hair red to disguise yourself from us?" He chuckled at his own joke.

Kendry didn't wait for the attack. She struck the second Druvan started chuckling. He didn't see it coming. Her fist jabbed up into his jaw hard enough to jerk his head backward. She ignored the pain in her knuckles and jammed her knee into his groin as she pulled the wooden club out of his now loosened grip. In one movement, she swung around and whacked one of Druvan's friends across the back of his head as he lunged toward Hendrick with his own club. Someone threw a rock, but with how quickly Kendry was moving, it just brushed the side of her arm, scraping her.

Hendrick jumped into battle mode and danced about with another of Druvan's friends, both trying to lunge toward each other without being hit by the other. The guy swung his fist toward Hendrick, who ducked aside, and countered with his own punch just below the guy's eye.

Kendry with a wooden club was a dangerous thing. Druvan was a bit shocked as he pulled himself together. He watched as she fought and bludgeoned his friends to their knees. They backed off, leaving Kendry and Hendrick facing just Druvan and one other guy. Things were going well until the blood on Hendrick's hands caused him to lose his grip on a club he had picked up. His opponent was able to yank it away from him while another guy came up from behind and got a choke-hold on Hendrick. He struggled to breathe, squirming and doing his best to fight off the guy holding him and the other guy aiming a club at him, ready to strike if he broke loose.

Kendry knew she had to help Hendrick and quick, but Druvan wasn't giving her an inch. He had gained the assistance of two other friends. Backing him up and angry that she had beat them to the ground in the first place, these friends weren't messing around. She knew she could take all three of them. Her martial arts skills and experience excelled beyond any of their fighting abilities, but seeing Hendrick struggling for breath distracted her. One of Druvan's friends picked up a rock and threw it hard at her. This one hit her in the shoulder, causing her to yelp and drop her arm in pain. Druvan jumped at the opportunity to grab her. The other two guys helped. She struggled, trying to fight them off.

Looking over at Hendrick, Kendry could tell he was starting to turn blue. The choke-hold on him was not loosening. She began kicking, but one of the guys grabbed her legs and lifted her off the ground. The other smacked her hard across the face with the heel of his hand. Her eyes blurred. The pain and shock of the hit took her breath away.

280

As she wiggled and shoved, trying to escape the strength of the guy's hands holding her, Kendry could see the bully holding Hendrick's neck in the crook of his arm, grab his own face in pain, slide down to his knees, and collapse. Released from his grip, Hendrick fell to the ground, choking and coughing and gasping for air. Blood was everywhere from his head wound and hands. The other guy standing guard over Hendrick, who had been heckling him, looked around confused. A rock flew through the air and struck the guy's chest. He clutched where it hit and yelled out in pain. He looked around, searching for the source of the flying rock.

The bullies holding Kendry caught on that something was happening. They all started barking questions at each other. Pointing at the direction the rock had come from, one of the guys slowly started in that path. Hendrick still lay on the ground wheezing. The guy who had been choking him was bent over, cradling his face in pain. Kendry was being held tight by two of the bullies, one had her top half and the other her bottom half. Druvan joined another friend to investigate which direction the rock had come from.

Then Kendry saw him. Hiding beside a bush and behind a broken-down piece of fence in the shadows ahead, a figure stood. He had managed to throw the rocks without being located, but now they all saw him. He had two large stones in his hands and ran toward Hendrick while pelting one of the rocks at Druvan. Druvan and the guy with him ducked, but it stalled them long enough for Graeme to dart over to Hendrick and drag him out of the way.

"We have no fight with you!" Druvan yelled, popping out his chest trying to show his muscles. "What's your problem?"

Kendry, once again, took advantage of the distraction and utilized the lack of attention from the two guys holding her to squeeze out of their grip and let them have it. She had both guys beat and on the ground within seconds. Both Druvan and Graeme looked shocked. A smile crept across Graeme's face.

Kendry ran over to check on Hendrick who was now sitting up and had regained his color. Once she was satisfied he was okay, she walked over toward Graeme and they both looked straight at Druvan and the couple of his friends that were still on their feet.

Druvan looked Kendry up and down. Then he snuffed an annoyed sound and signaled to his friends to leave. As they helped their other friends up, Kendry and Graeme waited, staring them down. The guys yelled obscenities over their shoulders, but made their way back out the other end of the alley.

Hendrick struggled to get up, but finally joined Graeme and Kendry. He offered a hand to Graeme who high-fived it in appreciation. Graeme looked over at Kendry, smiling, until he saw the look on her face.

"Don't think this means we forgive you," she mumbled and then sternly walked away.

Graeme and Hendrick stood there for a moment, stunned. Finally, Hendrick ran after her, turning back to Graeme to signal he should wait.

"Kendry..." Hendrick began, but was interrupted by her.

"Don't think I am going to forget what he did just because he shows up here to save the day. We would've been fine without him!"

"Kendry," Hendrick began again, racing to keep up with her fast pace. "Uh, we kind of need him, ya know? To question." Kendry abruptly stopped. She had totally forgot about that.

She turned around and looked back at Graeme. "Well? Are you coming?" she yelled, rudely. Graeme allowed a half smile to creep back across his face and took off to catch up with them.

Acknowledgments

Writing a story doesn't happen without help. This story was only written because my son, who was thirteen-years-old at the time, challenged me to create it during the 'two weeks to flatten the curve' of 2020. He was bored and desired a book to read that would be difficult for him to put down. I was bored and wanted him to enjoy reading something good. So, I typed and he read. Thank you, J, for challenging me, encouraging, and supporting me throughout my writing. You've been my biggest fan since day one, asking me to write more so that you could read more. I love you more than you could ever imagine.

I also need to thank my incredible husband who lets me escape away onto my bed with my laptop and dog in the evenings, while he and our son watch basketball and Holey Moley. He has always supported every dream or crazy idea I've had, and this was no different. His enthusiasm and encouragement for my writing blesses me more than he could ever know. Thanks, Eddy, I love you so much. And thanks for all the time you spent helping me improve my writing.

I also want to thank my parents, Kirk and Irene. My mother graciously edited every page of this book as I sent them to her in sections and my dad read the pages alongside her. Their time, effort, love, and encouragement made this book possible. Love you both!

Next, I need to thank my students. If my seventh and eighth graders at school hadn't consisted of teenagers who loved to read, I don't know if I would have been motivated to want to write a book for their age group. My first class of eighth graders at my current school consisted of Amanda, Lacey, Aspen, Natalia, and Katie who loved their books and discussed their stories' characters like they were chatting about friends. I hope this series is one that they will enjoy and many other students like them.

I can't finish without also thanking God and anyone who has purchased this book, shared it with someone, or told friends or family about it. Thanks for allowing Kendry's world to be a part of other's lives, too!

About the Author

Stacie Crenshaw resides in Southern California with her husband, son, and beloved dog. She enjoys teaching her incredible students, playing board games and cards with family and friends, reading, writing, and going for scenic walks. She has a passion for dark chocolate, Jesus, and trips to Disneyland.

The Lost Sacrifice

Book One- The Tavern's End Trilogy

The Last Remnant

Book Two- The Tavern's End Trilogy

The Last Sacrifice

Book Three- The Tavern's End Trilogy

Made in the USA
Las Vegas, NV
22 June 2021

25218547R00173